John Cheever's short stories are notable for the cool precision of their writing. No one has done a more skillful job of capturing certain aspects of contemporary life. Most of his characters are young, married, and urban; as a writer Mr. Cheever is engrossed by their youth, the strains and burdens they feel in adult relationships, and the uneasy quality of their adjustment to the society in which they live.

It is part of John Cheever's artistry that these characters seem so real. For many readers the act of recognition will be nearly overpowering . . .

ple you knew so
they lived in the
hall, they went to
. Cheever recog-
of spirit and their
ecords it with a
my of style which
they weren't so
own compassion.

ories in this collec-
during the postwar
of the *New Yorker*.
ilt up a following
among readers of that magazine, and they will not be surprised to find that his stories stand up superlatively well under rereading and close scrutiny. Impressive as they are separately, they take on new stature when read as a group.

THE ENORMOUS RADIO

AND OTHER STORIES

THE ENORMOUS RADIO

AND OTHER STORIES

JOHN CHEEVER

FUNK & WAGNALLS COMPANY, INC.

2

The Enormous Radio and Other Stories

LIBRARY OF CONGRESS CATALOG CARD NUMBER 53-6976

PRINTED IN THE UNITED STATES OF AMERICA

All the stories in this collection
appeared originally in
The New Yorker.

CONTENTS

GOODBYE, MY BROTHER   3

THE POT OF GOLD   28

O CITY OF BROKEN DREAMS   47

THE CHILDREN   69

TORCH SONG   96

THE CURE   115

THE HARTLEYS   128

THE SUMMER FARMER   138

THE SUPERINTENDENT   152

THE ENORMOUS RADIO   169

THE SEASON OF DIVORCE   182

CHRISTMAS IS A SAD SEASON
       FOR THE POOR   195

THE SUTTON PLACE STORY   206

CLANCY IN THE TOWER OF BABEL   225

THE ENORMOUS RADIO
AND OTHER STORIES

GOODBYE, MY BROTHER

$\mathcal{W}$E ARE a family that has always been very close in spirit. Our father was drowned in a sailing accident when we were young, and our mother has always stressed the fact that our familial relationships have a kind of permanence that we will never meet with again. I don't think about the family much, but when I remember its members and the coast where they lived and the sea salt that I think is in our blood, I am happy to recall that I am a Pommeroy—that I have the nose, the coloring, and the promise of longevity—and that while we are not a distinguished family, we enjoy the illusion, when we are together, that the Pommeroys are unique. I don't say any of this because I'm interested in family history or because this sense of uniqueness is deep or important to me but in order to advance the point that we are loyal to one another in spite of our differences, and that any rupture in this loyalty is a source of confusion and pain.

We are four children; there is my sister Diana and the three men—Chaddy, Lawrence, and myself. Like most families in which the children are out of their twenties, we have been separated by business, marriage, and war. Helen and I live on Long Island now, with our four children. I teach in a secondary school, and I am past the age where I expect to be made headmaster—or principal, as we say—but I respect the work. Chaddy, who has done better than the rest of us, lives in Manhattan, with Odette and their children. Mother lives in Philadelphia, and Diana, since her divorce, has been living in France, but she comes back to the States in the summer to spend a month at Laud's Head. Laud's Head is a summer place on the shore of one of the Massachusetts islands. We used to have a cottage there, and in the twenties our father built the big house. It stands on a cliff above the sea and, excepting St. Tropez and some of the Apennine villages, it is my favorite place in the world. We each have an equity in the place and we contribute some money to help keep it going.

Our youngest brother, Lawrence, who is a lawyer, got a job with a Cleveland firm after the war, and none of us saw him for four years. When he decided to leave Cleveland and go to work for a firm in Albany, he wrote Mother that he would, between jobs, spend ten days at Laud's Head, with his wife and their two children. This was when I had planned to take my vacation —I had been teaching summer school—and Helen and Chaddy and Odette and Diana were all going to be there, so the family would be together. Lawrence is the member of the family with whom the rest of us have least in common. We have never seen a great deal of him, and I suppose that's why we still call him Tifty—a nickname he was given when he was a child, because when he came down the hall toward the dining room for breakfast, his slippers made a noise that sounded like "Tifty, tifty, tifty." That's what Father called him, and so did everyone else. When he grew older, Diana sometimes used to call him Little Jesus, and Mother often called him The Croaker. We had disliked Lawrence, but we looked forward to his return with a mixture of apprehension and loyalty, and with some of the joy and delight of reclaiming a brother.

Lawrence crossed over from the mainland on the four-o'clock boat one afternoon late in the summer, and Chaddy and I went down to meet him. The arrivals and departures of the summer ferry have all the outward signs that suggest a voyage—whistles, bells, hand trucks, reunions, and the smell of brine—but

[4]

it is a voyage of no import, and when I watched the boat come into the blue harbor that afternoon and thought that it was completing a voyage of no import, I realized that I had hit on exactly the kind of observation that Lawrence would have made. We looked for his face behind the windshields as the cars drove off the boat, and we had no trouble in recognizing him. And we ran over and shook his hand and clumsily kissed his wife and the children. "Tifty!" Chaddy shouted. "Tifty!" It is difficult to judge changes in the appearance of a brother, but both Chaddy and I agreed, as we drove back to Laud's Head, that Lawrence still looked very young. He got to the house first, and we took the suitcases out of his car. When I came in, he was standing in the living room, talking with Mother and Diana. They were in their best clothes and all their jewelry, and they were welcoming him extravagantly, but even then, when everyone was endeavoring to seem most affectionate and at a time when these endeavors come easiest, I was aware of a faint tension in the room. Thinking about this as I carried Lawrence's heavy suitcases up the stairs, I realized that our dislikes are as deeply ingrained as our better passions, and I remembered that once, twenty-five years ago, when I had hit Lawrence on the head with a rock, he had picked himself up and gone directly to our father to complain.

I carried the suitcases up to the third floor, where Ruth, Lawrence's wife, had begun to settle her family. She is a thin girl, and she seemed very tired from the journey, but when I asked her if she didn't want me to bring a drink upstairs to her, she said she didn't think she did.

When I got downstairs, Lawrence wasn't around, but the others were all ready for cocktails, and we decided to go ahead. Lawrence is the only member of the family who has never enjoyed drinking. We took our cocktails onto the terrace, so that we could see the bluffs and the sea and the islands in the east, and the return of Lawrence and his wife, their presence in the house, seemed to refresh our responses to the familiar view; it was as if the pleasure they would take in the sweep and the color

[5]

of that coast, after such a long absence, had been imparted to us. While we were there, Lawrence came up the path from the beach.

"Isn't the beach fabulous, Tifty?" Mother asked. "Isn't it fabulous to be back? Will you have a Martini?"

"I don't care," Lawrence said. "Whiskey, gin—I don't care what I drink. Give me a little rum."

"We don't have any *rum*," Mother said. It was the first note of asperity. She has taught us never to be indecisive, never to reply as Lawrence had. Beyond this, she is deeply concerned with the propriety of her house, and anything irregular by her standards, like drinking straight rum or bringing a beer can to the dinner table, excites in her a conflict that she cannot, even with her capacious sense of humor, surmount. She sensed the asperity and worked to repair it. "Would you like some Irish, Tifty dear?" she said. "Isn't Irish what you've always liked? There's some Irish on the sideboard. Why don't you get yourself some Irish?" Lawrence said that he didn't care. He poured himself a Martini, and then Ruth came down and we went in to dinner.

In spite of the fact that we had, through waiting for Lawrence, drunk too much before dinner, we were all anxious to put our best foot forward and to enjoy a peaceful time. Mother is a small woman whose face is still a striking reminder of how pretty she must have been, and whose conversation is unusually light, but she talked that evening about a soil-reclamation project that is going on up-island. Diana is as pretty as Mother must have been; she is an animated and lovely woman who likes to talk about the dissolute friends that she has made in France, but she talked that night about the school in Switzerland where she had left her two children. I could see that the dinner had been planned to please Lawrence. It was not too rich, and there was nothing to make him worry about extravagance.

After supper, when we went back onto the terrace, the clouds held that kind of light that looks like blood, and I was glad that Lawrence had such a lurid sunset for his homecoming. When we had been out there a few minutes, a man named Edward Chester came to get Diana. She had met him in France, or on the boat home, and he was staying for ten days at the inn in the village. He was introduced to Lawrence and Ruth, and then he and Diana left.

"Is that the one she's sleeping with now?" Lawrence asked.

"What a horrid thing to say!" Helen said.

"You ought to apologize for that, Tifty," Chaddy said.

"I don't know," Mother said tiredly. "I don't know, Tifty. Diana is in a position to do whatever she wants, and I don't ask sordid questions. She's my only daughter. I don't see her often."

"Is she going back to France?"

"She's going back the week after next."

Lawrence and Ruth were sitting at the edge of the terrace, not in the chairs, not in the circle of chairs. With his mouth set, my brother looked to me then like a Puritan cleric. Sometimes, when I try to understand his frame of mind, I think of the beginnings of our family in this country, and his disapproval of Diana and her lovers reminded me of this. The branch of the Pommeroys to which we belong was founded by a minister who was eulogized by Cotton Mather for his untiring abjuration of the Devil. The Pommeroys were ministers until the middle of the nineteenth century, and the harshness of their thought— man is full of misery, and all earthly beauty is lustful and corrupt—has been preserved in books and sermons. The temper of our family changed somewhat and became more lighthearted, but when I was of school age, I can remember a cousinage of old men and women who seemed to hark back to the dark days of the ministry and to be animated by perpetual guilt and the deification of the scourge. If you are raised in this atmosphere —and in a sense we were—I think it is a trial of the spirit to reject its habits of guilt, self-denial, taciturnity, and penitence, and it seemed to me to have been a trial of the spirit in which Lawrence had succumbed.

"Is that Cassiopeia?" Odette asked.

"No, dear," Chaddy said. "That isn't Cassiopeia."

"Who was Cassiopeia?" Odette said.

"She was the wife of Cepheus and the mother of Andromeda," I said.

"The cook is a Giants fan," Chaddy said. "She'll give you even money that they win the pennant."

It had grown so dark that we could see the passage of light through the sky from the lighthouse at Cape Herion. In the dark below the cliff, the continual detonations of the surf sounded. And then, as she often does when it is getting dark and she has drunk too much before dinner, Mother began to talk about the improvements and additions that would someday be made on the house, the wings and bathrooms and gardens.

"This house will be in the sea in five years," Lawrence said.

"Tifty the Croaker," Chaddy said.

"Don't call me Tifty," Lawrence said.

"Little Jesus," Chaddy said.

"The sea wall is badly cracked," Lawrence said. "I looked at it this afternoon. You had it repaired four years ago, and it cost eight thousand dollars. You can't do that every four years."

"Please, Tifty," Mother said.

"Facts are facts," Lawrence said, "and it's a damned-fool idea to build a house at the edge of a cliff on a sinking coastline. In my lifetime, half the garden has washed away and there's four feet of water where we used to have a bathhouse."

"Let's have a very *general* conversation," Mother said bitterly. "Let's talk about politics or the boat-club dance."

"As a matter of fact," Lawrence said, "the house is probably in some danger now. If you had an unusually high sea, a hurricane sea, the wall would crumble and the house would go. We could all be drowned."

"I can't *bear* it," Mother said. She went into the pantry and came back with a full glass of gin.

I have grown too old now to think that I can judge the sentiments of others, but I was conscious of the tension between Lawrence and Mother, and I knew some of the history of it. Lawrence couldn't have been more than sixteen years old when he decided that Mother was frivolous, mischievous, destructive, and overly strong. When he had determined this, he decided to separate himself from her. He was at boarding school then, and I remember that he did not come home for Christmas. He spent Christmas with a friend. He came home very seldom after he had made his unfavorable judgment on Mother, and when he did come home, he always tried, in his conversation, to remind her of his estrangement. When he married Ruth, he did not tell Mother. He did not tell her when his children were born. But in spite of these principled and lengthy exertions he seemed, unlike the rest of us, never to have enjoyed any separation, and when they are together, you feel at once a tension, an unclearness.

And it was unfortunate, in a way, that Mother should have picked that night to get drunk. It's her privilege, and she doesn't get drunk often, and fortunately she wasn't bellicose, but we were all conscious of what was happening. As she quietly drank her gin, she seemed sadly to be parting from us; she seemed to be in the throes of travel. Then her mood changed from travel to injury, and the few remarks she made were petulant and irrelevant. When her glass was nearly empty, she stared angrily at the dark air in front of her nose, moving her head a little, like a fighter. I knew that there was not room in her mind then for all the injuries that were crowding into it. Her children were stupid, her husband was drowned, her servants were thieves, and the chair she sat in was uncomfortable. Suddenly she put down her empty glass and interrupted Chaddy, who was talking about baseball. "I know one *thing*," she said hoarsely. "I know that if there is an afterlife, I'm going to have a very different kind of family. I'm going to have nothing but fabulously rich, witty, and enchanting children." She got up and, starting for the door, nearly fell. Chaddy caught her and helped her up the stairs. I could hear their tender good nights, and then Chaddy came back. I thought that Lawrence by now would be tired from his journey and his return, but he remained on the terrace, as if he were waiting to see the final

[9]

malfeasance, and the rest of us left him there and went swimming in the dark.

When I woke the next morning, or half woke, I could hear the sound of someone rolling the tennis court. It is a fainter and a deeper sound than the iron buoy bells off the point—an unrhythmic iron chiming—that belongs in my mind to the beginnings of a summer day, a good portent. When I went downstairs, Lawrence's two kids were in the living room, dressed in ornate cowboy suits. They are frightened and skinny children. They told me their father was rolling the tennis court but that they did not want to go out because they had seen a snake under the doorstep. I explained to them that their cousins—all the other children—ate breakfast in the kitchen and that they'd better run along in there. At this announcement, the boy began to cry. Then his sister joined him. They cried as if to go in the kitchen and eat would destroy their most precious rights. I told them to sit down with me. Lawrence came in, and I asked him if he wanted to play some tennis. He said no, thanks, although he thought he might play some singles with Chaddy. He was in the right here, because both he and Chaddy play better tennis than I, and he did play some singles with Chaddy after breakfast, but later on, when the others came down to play family doubles, Lawrence disappeared. This made me cross—unreasonably so, I suppose—but we play darned interesting family doubles and he could have played in a set for the sake of courtesy.

Late in the morning, when I came up from the court alone, I saw Tifty on the terrace, prying up a shingle from the wall with his jackknife. "What's the matter, Lawrence?" I said. "Termites?" There are termites in the wood and they've given us a lot of trouble.

He pointed out to me, at the base of each row of shingles, a faint blue line of carpenter's chalk. "This house is about twenty-two years old," he said. "These shingles are about two hundred years old. Dad must have bought shingles from all the farms around here when he built the place, to make it look venerable. You can still see the carpenter's chalk put down where these antiques were nailed into place."

It was true about the shingles, although I had forgotten it. When the house was built, our father, or his architect, had ordered it covered with lichened and weather-beaten shingles. I didn't follow Lawrence's reasons for thinking that this was scandalous.

"And look at these doors," Lawrence said. "Look at these doors and window frames." I followed him over to a big Dutch door that opens onto the terrace and looked at it. It was a relatively new door, but someone had worked hard to conceal its newness. The surface had been deeply scored with some metal implement, and white paint had been rubbed into the incisions to imitate brine, lichen, and weather rot. "Imagine spending thousands of dollars to make a sound house look like a wreck," Lawrence said. "Imagine the frame of mind this implies. Imagine wanting to live so much in the past that you'll pay men carpenters' wages to disfigure your front door." Then I remembered Lawrence's sensitivity to time and his sentiments and opinions about our feelings for the past. I had heard him say, years ago, that we and our friends and our part of the nation, finding ourselves unable to cope with the problems of the present, had, like a wretched adult, turned back to what we supposed was a happier and a simpler time, and that our taste for reconstruction and candlelight was a measure of this irremediable failure. The faint blue line of chalk had reminded him of these ideas, the scarified door had reinforced them, and now clue after clue presented itself to him—the stern light at the door, the bulk of the chimney, the width of the floorboards and the pieces set into them to resemble pegs. While Lawrence was lecturing me on these frailties, the others came up from the court. As soon as Mother saw Lawrence, she responded, and I saw that there was little hope of any rapport between the matriarch and the changeling. She took Chaddy's arm. "Let's go swimming and have Martinis on the beach," she said. "Let's have a *fabulous* morning."

The sea that morning was a solid color, like verd stone. Everyone went to the beach but Tifty and Ruth. "I don't mind *him*," Mother said. She was excited, and she tipped her glass and spilled some gin into the sand. "I don't mind *him*. It doesn't matter to me how *rude* and *horrid* and *gloomy* he is, but what I can't bear are the faces of his wretched little children, those fabulously unhappy little children." With the height of the cliff between us, everyone talked wrathfully about Lawrence; about how he had grown worse instead of better, how unlike the rest of us he was, how he endeavored to spoil every pleasure. We drank our gin; the abuse seemed to reach a crescendo, and then, one by one, we went swimming in the solid green water. But when we came out no one mentioned Lawrence unkindly; the line of abusive conversation had been cut, as if swimming had the cleansing force claimed for baptism. We dried our hands and lighted cigarettes, and if Lawrence was mentioned, it was only to suggest, kindly, something that might please him. Wouldn't he like to sail to Barin's cove, or go fishing?

And now I remember that while Lawrence was visiting us, we went swimming oftener than we usually do, and I think there was a reason for this. When the irritability that accumulated as a result of his company began to lessen our patience, not only with Lawrence but with one another, we would all go swimming and shed our animus in the cold water. I can see the family now, smarting from Lawrence's rebukes as they sat on the sand, and I can see them wading and diving and surface-diving and hear in their voices the restoration of patience and the rediscovery of inexhaustible good will. If Lawrence noticed this change—this illusion of purification—I suppose that he would have found in the vocabulary of psychiatry, or the mythology of the Atlantic, some circumspect name for it, but I don't think he noticed the change. He neglected to name the curative powers of the open sea, but it was one of the few chances for diminution that he missed.

The cook we had that year was a Polish woman named Anna
Ostrovick, a summer cook. She was first-rate—a big, fat, hearty,
industrious woman who took her work very seriously. She liked
to cook and to have the food she cooked appreciated and eaten,
and whenever we saw her, she always urged us to eat. She
cooked hot bread—crescents and brioches—for breakfast two or
three times a week, and she would bring these into the dining
room herself and say, "Eat, eat, eat!" When the maid took the
serving dishes back into the pantry, we could sometimes hear
Anna, who was standing there, say, "Good! They eat." She fed
the garbage man, the milkman, and the gardener. "Eat!" she
told them. "Eat, eat!" On Thursday afternoons, she went to the
movies with the maid, but she didn't enjoy the movies, because
the actors were all so thin. She would sit in the dark theatre for
an hour and a half watching the screen anxiously for the appearance of someone who had enjoyed his food. Bette Davis
merely left with Anna the impression of a woman who has not
eaten well. "They are all so skinny," she would say when she
left the movies. In the evenings, after she had gorged all of us,
and washed the pots and pans, she would collect the table scraps
and go out to feed the creation. We had a few chickens that
year, and although they would have roosted by then, she would
dump food into their trough and urge the sleeping fowl to eat.
She fed the songbirds in the orchard and the chipmunks in the
yard. Her appearance at the edge of the garden and her urgent
voice—we could hear her calling "Eat, eat, eat"—had become,
like the sunset gun at the boat club and the passage of light
from Cape Herion, attached to that hour. "Eat, eat, eat," we
could hear Anna say. "Eat, eat . . ." Then it would be dark.

When Lawrence had been there three days, Anna called me
into the kitchen. "You tell your mother," she said, "that *he*
doesn't come into my kitchen. If *he* comes into my kitchen all
the time, I go. *He* is always coming into my kitchen to tell me
what a sad woman I am. He is always telling me that I work
too hard and that I don't get paid enough and that I should

belong to a union with vacations. Ha! He is so skinny but he is always coming into my kitchen when I am busy to pity me, but I am as good as him, I am as good as *anybody*, and I do not have to have people like that getting into my way all the time and feeling sorry for me. I am a famous and a wonderful cook and I have jobs everywhere and the only reason I come here to work this summer is because I was never before on an island, but I can have other jobs tomorrow, and if he is always coming into my kitchen to pity me, you tell your mother I am going. I am as good as *anybody* and I do not have to have that skinny all the time telling how poor I am."

I was pleased to find that the cook was on our side, but I felt that the situation was delicate. If Mother asked Lawrence to stay out of the kitchen, he would make a grievance out of the request. He could make a grievance out of anything, and it sometimes seemed that as he sat darkly at the dinner table, every word of disparagement, wherever it was aimed, came home to him. I didn't mention the cook's complaint to anyone, but somehow there wasn't any more trouble from that quarter.

The next cause for contention that I had from Lawrence came over our backgammon games.

When we are at Laud's Head, we play a lot of backgammon. At eight o'clock, after we have drunk our coffee, we usually get out the board. In a way, it is one of our pleasantest hours. The lamps in the room are still unlighted, Anna can be seen in the dark garden, and in the sky above her head there are continents of shadow and fire. Mother turns on the light and rattles the dice as a signal. We usually play three games apiece, each with the others. We play for money, and you can win or lose a hundred dollars on a game, but the stakes are usually much lower. I think that Lawrence used to play—I can't remember —but he doesn't play any more. He doesn't gamble. This is not because he is poor or because he has any principles about gambling but because he thinks the game is foolish and a waste of time. He was ready enough, however, to waste his time watching the rest of us play. Night after night, when the game began, he pulled a chair up beside the board, and watched the checkers and the dice. His expression was scornful, and yet he watched carefully. I wondered why he watched us night after night, and, through watching his face, I think that I may have found out.

Lawrence doesn't gamble, so he can't understand the excitement of winning and losing money. He has forgotten how to play the game, I think, so that its complex odds can't interest him. His observations were bound to include the facts that backgammon is an idle game and a game of chance, and that the board, marked with points, was a symbol of our worthlessness. And since he doesn't understand gambling or the odds of the game, I thought that what interested him must be the members of his family. One night when I was playing with Odette—I had won thirty-seven dollars from Mother and Chaddy—I think I saw what was going on in his mind.

Odette has black hair and black eyes. She is careful never to expose her white skin to the sun for long, so the striking contrast of blackness and pallor is not changed in the summer. She needs and deserves admiration—it is the element that contents her—and she will flirt, unseriously, with any man. Her shoulders were bare that night, her dress was cut to show the division of her breasts and to show her breasts when she leaned over the board to play. She kept losing and flirting and making her losses seem like a part of the flirtation. Chaddy was in the other room. She lost three games, and when the third game ended, she fell back on the sofa and, looking at me squarely, said something about going out on the dunes to settle the score. Lawrence heard her. I looked at Lawrence. He seemed shocked and gratified at the same time, as if he had suspected all along that we were not playing for anything so insubstantial as money. I may be wrong, of course, but I think that Lawrence felt that in watching our backgammon he was observing the progress of a mordant tragedy in which the money we won and lost served as a symbol for more vital forfeits. It is like Lawrence to try to read significance and finality into every gesture that we make, and it is certain of Lawrence that when he finds the inner logic to our conduct, it will be sordid.

Chaddy came in to play with me. Chaddy and I have never liked to lose to each other. When we were younger, we used to be forbidden to play games together, because they always ended in a fight. We think we know each other's mettle intimately. I think he is prudent; he thinks I am foolish. There is always bad blood when we play anything—tennis or backgammon or softball or bridge—and it does seem at times as if we were playing for the possession of each other's liberties. When I lose to Chaddy, I can't sleep. All this is only half the truth of our competitive relationship, but it was the half-truth that would be discernible to Lawrence, and his presence at the table made me so self-conscious that I lost two games. I tried not to seem angry when I got up from the board. Lawrence was watching me. I went out onto the terrace to suffer there in the dark the anger I always feel when I lose to Chaddy.

When I came back into the room, Chaddy and Mother were playing. Lawrence was still watching. By his lights, Odette had lost her virtue to me, I had lost my self-esteem to Chaddy, and now I wondered what he saw in the present match. He watched raptly, as if the opaque checkers and the marked board served for an exchange of critical power. How dramatic the board, in its ring of light, and the quiet players and the crash of the sea outside must have seemed to him! Here was spiritual cannibalism made visible; here, under his nose, were the symbols of the rapacious use human beings make of one another.

Mother plays a shrewd, an ardent, and an interfering game. She always has her hands in her opponent's board. When she plays with Chaddy, who is her favorite, she plays intently. Lawrence would have noticed this. Mother is a sentimental woman. Her heart is good and easily moved by tears and frailty, a characteristic that, like her handsome nose, has not been changed at all by age. Grief in another provokes her deeply, and she seems at times to be trying to divine in Chaddy some grief, some loss, that she can succor and redress, and so reëstab-

[16]

lish the relationship that she enjoyed with him when he was sickly and young. She loves defending the weak and the child-like, and now that we are old, she misses it. The world of debts and business, men and war, hunting and fishing has on her an exacerbating effect. (When Father drowned, she threw away his fly rods and his guns.) She has lectured us all endlessly on self-reliance, but when we come back to her for comfort and for help—particularly Chaddy—she seems to feel most like herself. I suppose Lawrence thought that the old woman and her son were playing for each other's soul.

She lost. "Oh *dear*," she said. She looked stricken and be-reaved, as she always does when she loses. "Get me my glasses, get me my checkbook, get me something to drink." Lawrence got up at last and stretched his legs. He looked at us all bleakly. The wind and the sea had risen, and I thought that if he heard the waves, he must hear them only as a dark answer to all his dark questions; that he would think that the tide had expunged the embers of our picnic fires. The company of a lie is unbear-able, and he seemed like the embodiment of a lie. I couldn't explain to him the simple and intense pleasures of playing for money, and it seemed to me hideously wrong that he should have sat at the edge of the board and concluded that we were playing for one another's soul. He walked restlessly around the room two or three times and then, as usual, gave us a parting shot. "I should think you'd go crazy," he said, "cooped up with one another like this, night after night. Come on, Ruth. I'm going to bed."

That night, I dreamed about Lawrence. I saw his plain face magnified into ugliness, and when I woke in the morning, I felt sick, as if I had suffered a great spiritual loss while I slept, like the loss of courage and heart. It was foolish to let myself be troubled by my brother. I needed a vacation. I needed to relax. At school, we live in one of the dormitories, we eat at the house table, and we never get away. I not only teach English winter and summer but I work in the principal's office and fire the pistol at track meets. I needed to get away from this and from every other form of anxiety, and I decided to avoid my brother. Early that day, I took Helen and the children sailing, and we stayed out until suppertime. The next day, we went on a picnic. Then I had to go to New York for a day, and when I got back, there was the costume dance at the boat club. Lawrence wasn't going to this, and it's a party where I always have a wonderful time.

The invitations that year said to come as you wish you were. After several conversations, Helen and I had decided what to wear. The thing she most wanted to be again, she said, was a bride, and so she decided to wear her wedding dress. I thought this was a good choice—sincere, lighthearted, and inexpensive. Her choice influenced mine, and I decided to wear an old football uniform. Mother decided to go as Jenny Lind, because there was an old Jenny Lind costume in the attic. The others decided to rent costumes, and when I went to New York, I got the clothes. Lawrence and Ruth didn't enter into any of this.

Helen was on the dance committee, and she spent most of Friday decorating the club. Diana and Chaddy and I went sailing. Most of the sailing that I do these days is in Manhasset, and I am used to setting a homeward course by the gasoline barge and the tin roofs of the boat shed, and it was a pleasure that afternoon, as we returned, to keep the bow on a white church spire in the village and to find even the inshore water green and clear. At the end of our sail, we stopped at the club to get Helen. The committee had been trying to give a submarine appearance to the ballroom, and the fact that they had nearly succeeded in accomplishing this illusion made Helen very happy. We drove back to Laud's Head. It had been a brilliant afternoon, but on the way home we could smell the east wind—the dark wind, as Lawrence would have said—coming in from the sea.

My wife, Helen, is thirty-eight, and her hair would be gray, I guess, if it were not dyed, but it is dyed an unobtrusive yellow —a faded color—and I think it becomes her. I mixed cocktails that night while she was dressing, and when I took a glass up-stairs to her, I saw her for the first time since our marriage in her wedding dress. There would be no point in saying that she looked to me more beautiful than she did on our wedding day, but because I have grown older and have, I think, a greater depth of feeling, and because I could see in her face that night both youth and age, both her devotion to the young woman that she had been and the positions that she had yielded graciously to time, I think I have never been so deeply moved. I had already put on the football uniform, and the weight of it, the heaviness of the pants and the shoulder guards, had worked a change in me, as if in putting on these old clothes I had put off the reasonable anxieties and troubles of my life. It felt as if we had both returned to the years before our marriage, the years before the war.

The Collards had a big dinner party before the dance, and our family—excepting Lawrence and Ruth—went to this. We drove over to the club, through the fog, at about half past nine. The orchestra was playing a waltz. While I was checking my raincoat, someone hit me on the back. It was Chucky Ewing, and the funny thing was that Chucky had on a football uni-form. This seemed comical as hell to both of us. We were laugh-ing when we went down the hall to the dance floor. I stopped at the door to look at the party, and it was beautiful. The com-mittee had hung fish nets all around the sides and over the high ceiling. The nets on the ceiling were filled with colored balloons. The light was soft and uneven, and the people—our friends and neighbors—dancing in the soft light to "Three O'Clock in the Morning" made a pretty picture. Then I noticed the number of women dressed in white, and I realized that they, like Helen, were wearing wedding dresses. Patsy Hewitt and Mrs. Gear and the Lackland girl waltzed by, dressed as brides. Then Pep Talcott came over to where Chucky and I were standing. He was dressed to be Henry VIII, but he told us that the Auerbach twins and Henry Barrett and Dwight MacGregor were all wear-

[19]

ing football uniforms, and that by the last count there were ten
brides on the floor.

This coincidence, this funny coincidence, kept everybody
laughing, and made this one of the most lighthearted parties
we've ever had at the club. At first I thought that the women
had planned with one another to wear wedding dresses, but the
ones that I danced with said it was a coincidence and I'm sure
that Helen had made her decision alone. Everything went
smoothly for me until a little before midnight. I saw Ruth standing at the edge of the floor. She was wearing a long red dress.
It was all wrong. It wasn't in the spirit of the party at all. I
danced with her, but no one cut in, and I was darned if I'd
spend the rest of the night dancing with her and I asked her
where Lawrence was. She said he was out on the dock, and I
took her over to the bar and left her and went out to get Lawrence.

The east fog was thick and wet, and he was alone on the
dock. He was not in costume. He had not even bothered to get
himself up as a fisherman or a sailor. He looked particularly
saturnine. The fog blew around us like a cold smoke. I wished
that it had been a clear night, because the easterly fog seemed
to play into my misanthropic brother's hands. And I knew that
the buoys—the groaners and bells that we could hear then—
would sound to him like half-human, half-drowned cries, although every sailor knows that buoys are necessary and reliable
fixtures, and I knew that the foghorn at the lighthouse would
mean wanderings and losses to him and that he could miscon-
strue the vivacity of the dance music. "Come on in, Tifty," I
said, "and dance with your wife or get her some partners."

"Why should I?" he said. "Why should I?" And he walked
to the window and looked in at the party. "Look at it," he said.
"Look at that . . ."

Chucky Ewing had got hold of a balloon and was trying to
organize a scrimmage line in the middle of the floor. The others
were dancing a samba. And I knew that Lawrence was looking
bleakly at the party as he had looked at the weather-beaten

[20]

shingles on our house, as if he saw here an abuse and a distor-
tion of time; as if in wanting to be brides and football players
we exposed the fact that, the lights of youth having been put
out in us, we had been unable to find other lights to go by and,
destitute of faith and principle, had become foolish and sad.
And that he was thinking this about so many kind and happy
and generous people made me angry, made me feel for him such
an unnatural abhorrence that I was ashamed, for he is my
brother and a Pommeroy. I put my arm around his shoulders
and tried to force him to come in, but he wouldn't.

I got back in time for the Grand March, and after the prizes
had been given out for the best costumes, they let the balloons
down. The room was hot, and someone opened the big doors
onto the dock, and the easterly wind circled the room and went
out, carrying across the dock and out onto the water most of the
balloons. Chucky Ewing went running out after the balloons,
and when he saw them pass the dock and settle on the water,
he took off his football uniform and dove in. Then Eric Auerbach dove in and Lew Phillips dove in and I dove in, and you
know how it is at a party after midnight when people start
jumping into the water. We recovered most of the balloons and
dried off and went on dancing, and we didn't get home until
morning.

The next day was the day of the flower show. Mother and Helen
and Odette all had entries. We had a pickup lunch, and Chaddy
drove the women and children over to the show. I took a nap, and
in the middle of the afternoon I got some trunks and a towel
and, on leaving the house, passed Ruth in the laundry. She was
washing clothes. I don't know why she should seem to have so
much more work to do than anyone else, but she is always
washing or ironing or mending clothes. She may have been
taught, when she was young, to spend her time like this, or she
may be at the mercy of an expiatory passion. She seems to scrub
and iron with a penitential fervor, although I can't imagine
what it is that she thinks she's done wrong. Her children were

with her in the laundry. I offered to take them to the beach, but they didn't want to go.

It was late in August, and the wild grapes that grow profusely all over the island made the land wind smell of wine. There is a little grove of holly at the end of the path, and then you climb the dunes, where nothing grows but that coarse grass. I could hear the sea, and I remember thinking how Chaddy and I used to talk mystically about the sea. When we were young, we had decided that we could never live in the West because we would miss the sea. "It is very nice here," we used to say politely when we visited people in the mountains, "but we miss the Atlantic." We used to look down our noses at people from Iowa and Colorado who had been denied this revelation, and we scorned the Pacific. Now I could hear the waves, whose heaviness sounded like a reverberation, like a tumult, and it pleased me as it had pleased me when I was young, and it seemed to have a purgative force, as if it had cleared my memory of, among other things, the penitential image of Ruth in the laundry.

But Lawrence was on the beach. There he sat. I went in without speaking. The water was cold, and when I came out, I put on a shirt. I told him that I was going to walk up to Tanners Point, and he said that he would come with me. I tried to walk beside him. His legs are no longer than mine, but he always likes to stay a little ahead of his companion. Walking along behind him, looking at his bent head and his shoulders, I wondered what he could make of that landscape.

There were the dunes and cliffs and then, where they declined, there were some fields that had begun to turn from green to brown and yellow. The fields were used for pasturing sheep, and I guess Lawrence would have noticed that the soil was eroded and that the sheep would accelerate this decay. Beyond the fields there are a few coastal farms, with square and pleasant buildings, but Lawrence could have pointed out the hard lot of an island farmer. The sea, at our other side, was the open sea. We always tell guests that there, to the east, lies the coast

of Portugal, and for Lawrence it would be an easy step from
the coast of Portugal to the tyranny in Spain. The waves broke
with a noise like a "hurrah, hurrah, hurrah," but to Lawrence
they would say "*Vale, vale.*" I suppose it would have occurred
to his baleful and incisive mind that the coast was terminal
moraine, the edge of the prehistoric world, and it must have
occurred to him that we walked along the edge of the known
world in spirit as much as in fact. If he should otherwise have
overlooked this, there were some Navy planes bombing an un-
inhabited island to remind him.

That beach is a vast and preternaturally clean and simple
landscape. It is like a piece of the moon. The surf had pounded
the floor solid, so it was easy walking, and everything left on
the sand had been twice changed by the waves. There was the
spine of a shell, a broomstick, part of a bottle and part of a
brick, both of them milled and broken until they were nearly
unrecognizable, and I suppose Lawrence's sad frame of mind—
for he kept his head down—went from one broken thing to another. The company of his pessimism began to infuriate me, and
I caught up with him and put a hand on his shoulder. "It's only
a summer day, Tifty," I said. "It's only a summer day. What's
the matter? Don't you like it here?"

"I don't like it here," he said blandly, without raising his
eyes. "I'm going to sell my equity in the house to Chaddy. I
didn't expect to have a good time. The only reason I came back
was to say goodbye."

I let him get ahead again and I walked behind him, looking
at his shoulders and thinking of all the goodbyes he had made.
When Father drowned, he went to church and said goodbye to
Father. It was only three years later that he concluded that
Mother was frivolous and said goodbye to her. In his freshman
year at college, he had been very good friends with his room-
mate, but the man drank too much, and at the beginning of the
spring term Lawrence changed roommates and said goodbye to
his friend. When he had been in college for two years, he concluded that the atmosphere was too sequestered and he said

[23]

goodbye to Yale. He enrolled at Columbia and got his law degree there, but he found his first employer dishonest, and at the end of six months he said goodbye to a good job. He married Ruth in City Hall and said goodbye to the Protestant Episcopal Church; they went to live on a back street in Tuckahoe and said goodbye to the middle class. In 1938, he went to Washington to work as a government lawyer, saying goodbye to private enterprise, but after eight months in Washington he concluded that the Roosevelt administration was sentimental and he said goodbye to it. They left Washington for a suburb of Chicago, where he said goodbye to his neighbors, one by one, on counts of drunkenness, boorishness, and stupidity. He said goodbye to Chicago and went to Kansas; he said goodbye to Kansas and went to Cleveland. Now he had said goodbye to Cleveland and come East again, stopping at Laud's Head long enough to say goodbye to the sea.

It was elegiac and it was bigoted and narrow, it mistook circumspection for character, and I wanted to help him. "Come out of it," I said. "Come out of it, Tifty."

"Come out of what?"

"Come out of this gloominess. Come out of it. It's only a summer day. You're spoiling your own good time and you're spoiling everyone else's. We need a vacation, Tifty. I need one. I need to rest. We all do. And you've made everything tense and unpleasant. I only have two weeks in the year. Two weeks. I need to have a good time and so do all the others. We need to rest. You think that your pessimism is an advantage, but it's nothing but an unwillingness to grasp realities."

"What are the realities?" he said. "Diana is a foolish and a promiscuous woman. So is Odette. Mother is an alcoholic. If she doesn't discipline herself, she'll be in a hospital in a year or two. Chaddy is dishonest. He always has been. The house is going to fall into the sea." He looked at me and added, as an afterthought, "You're a fool."

"You're a gloomy son of a bitch," I said. "You're a gloomy son of a bitch."

[24]

"Get your fat face out of mine," he said. He walked along.

Then I picked up a root and, coming at his back—although I have never hit a man from the back before—I swung the root, heavy with sea water, behind me, and the momentum sped my arm and I gave him, my brother, a blow on the head that forced him to his knees on the sand, and I saw the blood come out and begin to darken his hair. Then I wished that he was dead, dead and about to be buried, not buried but about to be buried, because I did not want to be denied ceremony and decorum in putting him away, in putting him out of my consciousness, and I saw the rest of us—Chaddy and Mother and Diana and Helen —in mourning in the house on Belvedere Street that was torn down twenty years ago, greeting our guests and our relatives at the door and answering their mannerly condolences with mannerly grief. Nothing decorous was lacking, so that even if he had been murdered on a beach, one would feel before the tiresome ceremony ended that he had come into the winter of his life and that it was a law of nature, and a beautiful one, that Tifty should be buried in the cold, cold ground.

He was still on his knees. I looked up and down. No one had seen us. The naked beach, like a piece of the moon, reached to invisibility. The spill of a wave, in a glancing run, shot up to where he knelt. I would still have liked to end him, but now I had begun to act like two men, the murderer and the Samaritan. With a swift roar, like hollowness made sound, a white wave reached him and encircled him, boiling over his shoulders, and I held him against the undertow. Then I led him to a higher place. The blood has spread all through his hair, so that it looked black. I took off my shirt and tore it to bind up his head. He was conscious, and I didn't think he was badly hurt. He didn't speak. Neither did I. Then I left him there.

I walked a little way down the beach and turned to watch him, and I was thinking of my own skin then. He had got to his feet and he seemed steady. The daylight was still clear, but on the sea wind fumes of brine were blowing in like a light fog, and when I had walked a little way from him, I could hardly

see his dark figure in this obscurity. All down the beach I could
see the heavy salt air blowing in. Then I turned my back on
him, and as I got near to the house, I went swimming again,
as I seem to have done after every encounter with Lawrence
that summer.

When I got back to the house, I lay down on the terrace.
The others came back. I could hear Mother defaming the flower
arrangements that had won prizes. None of ours had won anything. Then the house quieted, as it always does at that hour.
The children went into the kitchen to get supper and the others
went upstairs to bathe. Then I heard Chaddy making cocktails,
and the conversation about the flower-show judges was resumed.
Then Mother cried, "Tifty! Tifty! Oh, Tifty!"

He stood in the door, looking half dead. He had taken off the
bloody bandage and he held it in his hand. "My brother did
this," he said. "My brother did it. He hit me with a stone—
something—on the beach." His voice broke with self-pity. I
thought he was going to cry. No one else spoke. "Where's
Ruth?" he cried. "Where's Ruth? Where in hell is Ruth? I want
her to start packing. I don't have any more time to waste here.
I have important things to do. I have *important* things to do."
And he went up the stairs.

They left for the mainland the next morning, taking the six-
o'clock boat. Mother got up to say goodbye, but she was the only
one, and it is a harsh and an easy scene to imagine—the matriarch and the changeling, looking at each other with a dismay
that would seem like the powers of love reversed. I heard the
children's voices and the car go down the drive, and I got up
and went to the window, and what a morning that was! Jesus,
what a morning! The wind was northerly. The air was clear.
In the early heat, the roses in the garden smelled like straw-
berry jam. While I was dressing, I heard the boat whistle, first
the warning signal and then the double blast, and I could see
the good people on the top deck drinking coffee out of fragile
paper cups, and Lawrence at the bow, saying to the sea, *"Tha-*

lassa, thalassa," while his timid and unhappy children watched
the creation from the encirclement of their mother's arms. The
buoys would toll mournfully for Lawrence, and while the grace
of the light would make it an exertion not to throw out your
arms and swear exultantly, Lawrence's eyes would trace the
black sea as it fell astern; he would think of the bottom, dark
and strange, where full fathom five our father lies.

Oh, what can you do with a man like that? What can you
do? How can you dissuade his eye in a crowd from seeking out
the cheek with acne, the infirm hand; how can you teach him
to respond to the inestimable greatness of the race, the harsh
surface beauty of life; how can you put his finger for him on
the obdurate truths before which fear and horror are powerless?
The sea that morning was iridescent and dark. My wife and
my sister were swimming—Diana and Helen—and I saw their
uncovered heads, black and gold in the dark water. I saw them
come out and I saw that they were naked, unshy, beautiful, and
full of grace, and I watched the naked women walk out of the
sea.

THE POT OF GOLD

*Y*OU could not say fairly of Ralph and Laura Whittemore that they had the failings and the characteristics of incorrigible treasure hunters, but you could say truthfully of them that the shimmer and the smell, the peculiar force of money, the promise of it, had an untoward influence on their lives. They were always at the threshold of fortune; they always seemed to have something on the fire. Ralph was a fair young man with a tireless commercial imagination and an evangelical credence in the romance and sorcery of business success, and although he held an obscure job with a clothing manufacturer, this never seemed to him anything more than a point of departure.

The Whittemores were not importunate or overbearing people, and they had an uncompromising loyalty to the gentle manners of the middle class. Laura was a pleasant girl of no particular beauty who had come to New York from Wisconsin at about the same time that Ralph had reached the city from Illinois, but it had taken two years of comings and goings before they had been brought together, late one afternoon, in the lobby of a lower Fifth Avenue office building. So true was Ralph's heart, so well did it serve him then, that the moment he saw Laura's light hair and her pretty and sullen face he was enraptured. He followed her out of the lobby, pushing his way through the crowd, and since she had dropped nothing, since there was no legitimate excuse to speak to her, he shouted after her, "*Louise! Louise! Louise!*," and the urgency in his voice made her stop. He said he'd made a mistake. He said he was sorry. He said she looked just like a girl named Louise Hatcher. It was a January night and the dark air tasted of smoke, and because she was a sensible and a lonely girl, she let him buy her a drink.

This was in the thirties, and their courtship was hasty. They were married three months later. Laura moved her belongings into a walkup on Madison Avenue, above a pants presser's and a florist's, where Ralph was living. She worked as a secretary, and her salary, added to what he brought home from the clothing business, was little more than enough to keep them going, but they never seemed touched by the monotony of a saving and gainless life. They ate dinners in drugstores. She hung a reproduction of van Gogh's "Sunflowers" above the sofa she had bought with some of the small sum of money her parents had left her. When their aunts and uncles came to town—their parents were dead—they had dinner at the Ritz and went to the theatre. She sewed curtains and shined his shoes, and on Sundays they stayed in bed until noon. They seemed to be standing at the threshold of plenty; and Laura often told people that she was terribly excited because of this wonderful job that Ralph had lined up.

In the first year of their marriage, Ralph worked nights on a plan that promised him a well-paying job in Texas, but through no fault of his own this promise was never realized. There was an opening in Syracuse a year later, but an older man was decided upon. There were many other profitable but elusive openings and projects between these two. In the third year of their marriage, a firm that was almost identical in size and character with the firm Ralph worked for underwent a change of ownership, and Ralph was approached and asked if he would be interested in joining the overhauled firm. His own job promised only meagre security after a series of slow promotions and he was glad of the chance to escape. He met the new

[29]

owners, and their enthusiasm for him seemed intense. They
were prepared to put him in charge of a department and pay him
twice what he was getting then. The arrangement was to remain
tacit for a month or two, until the new owners had secured their
position, but they shook hands warmly and had a drink on the
deal, and that night Ralph took Laura out to dinner at an expensive restaurant.

They decided, across the table, to look for a larger apartment,
to have a child, and to buy a second-hand car. They faced their
good fortune with perfect calm, for it was what they had expected all along. The city seemed to them a generous place,
where people were rewarded either by a sudden and deserved
development like this or by the capricious bounty of lawsuits,
eccentric and peripheral business ventures, unexpected lega-
cies, and other windfalls. After dinner, they walked in Central
Park in the moonlight while Ralph smoked a cigar. Later, when
Laura had fallen asleep, he sat in the open bedroom window
in his pajamas.

The peculiar excitement with which the air of the city seems
charged after midnight, when its life falls into the hands of
watchmen and drunks, had always pleased him. He knew intimately the sounds of the night street: the bus brakes, the remote
sirens, and the sound of water turning high in the air—the
sound of water turning a mill wheel—the sum, he supposed,
of many echoes, although, often as he had heard the sound, he
had never decided on its source. Now he heard all this more
keenly because the night seemed to him portentous.

He was twenty-eight years old; poverty and youth were in-
separable in his experience, and one was ending with the other.
The life they were about to leave had not been hard, and he
thought with sentiment of the soiled tablecloth in the Italian
restaurant where they usually went for their celebrations, and
the high spirits with which Laura on a wet night ran from the
subway to the bus stop. But they were drawing away from all
this. Shirt sales in department-store basements, lines at meat
counters, weak drinks, the roses he brought her up from the

subway in the spring, when roses were cheap—these were all unmistakably the souvenirs of the poor, and while they seemed to him good and gentle, he was glad that they would soon be memories.

Laura resigned from her job when she got pregnant. The reorganization and Ralph's new position hung fire, but the Whittemores talked about it freely when they were with friends. "We're *terribly* pleased with the way things are going," Laura would say. "All we need is patience." There were many delays and postponements, and they waited with the patience of people expecting justice. The time came when they both needed clothes, and one evening Ralph suggested that they spend some of the money they had put aside. Laura refused. When he brought up the subject, she didn't answer him and seemed not to hear him. He raised his voice and lost his temper. He shouted. She cried. He thought of all the other girls he could have married—the dark blonde, the worshipful Cuban, the rich and pretty one with a cast in her right eye. All his desires seemed to lie outside the small apartment Laura had arranged. They were still not speaking in the morning, and in order to strengthen his position he telephoned his potential employers. Their secretary told him they were both out. This made him apprehensive. He called several times from the telephone booth in the lobby of the building he worked in and was told that they were busy, they were out, they were in conference with lawyers, or they were talking long distance. This variety of excuses frightened him. He said nothing to Laura that evening and tried to call them the next day. Late in the afternoon, after many tries, one of them came to the phone. "We gave the job to somebody else, sonny," he said. Like a saddened father, he spoke to Ralph in a hoarse and gentle voice. "Don't try and get us on the telephone any more. We've got other things to do besides answer the telephone. This other fellow seemed better suited, sonny. That's all I can tell you, and don't try to get me on the telephone any more."

Ralph walked the miles from his office to his apartment that night, hoping to free himself in this way from some of the weight of his disappointment. He was so unprepared for the shock that it affected him like vertigo, and he walked with an odd, high step, as if the paving were quicksand. He stood downstairs in front of the building he lived in, trying to decide how to describe the disaster to Laura, but when he went in, he told her bluntly. "Oh, I'm sorry, darling," she said softly and kissed him. "I'm terribly sorry." She wandered away from him and began to straighten the sofa cushions. His frustration was so ardent, he was such a prisoner of his schemes and expectations, that he was astonished at the serenity with which she regarded the failure. There was nothing to worry about, she said. She still had a few hundred dollars in the bank, from the money her parents had left her. There was nothing to worry about.

When the child, a girl, was born, they named her Rachel, and a week after the delivery Laura returned to the Madison Avenue walkup. She took all the care of the baby and continued to do the cooking and the housework.

Ralph's imagination remained resilient and fertile, but he couldn't seem to hit on a scheme that would fit into his lack of time and capital. He and Laura, like the hosts of the poor everywhere, lived a simple life. They still went to the theatre with visiting relatives and occasionally they went to parties, but Laura's only continuous contact with the bright lights that surrounded them was vicarious and came to her through a friend she made in Central Park.

She spent many afternoons on a park bench during the first years of Rachel's life. It was a tyranny and a pleasure. She resented her enchainment but enjoyed the open sky and the air. One winter afternoon, she recognized a woman she had met at a party, and a little before dark, as Laura and the other mothers were gathering their stuffed animals and preparing their children for the cold journey home, the woman came across the playground and spoke to her. She was Alice Holinshed, she said. They had met at the Galvins'. She was pretty and friendly, and walked with Laura to the edge of the Park. She had a boy of about Rachel's age. The two women met again the following day. They became friends.

Mrs. Holinshed was older than Laura, but she had a more youthful and precise beauty. Her hair and her eyes were black, her pale and perfectly oval face was delicately colored, and her voice was pure. She lighted her cigarettes with Stork Club matches and spoke of the inconvenience of living with a child in a hotel. If Laura had any regrets about her life, they were expressed in her friendship for this pretty woman, who moved so freely through expensive stores and restaurants.

It was a friendship circumscribed, with the exception of the Galvins', by the sorry and touching countryside of Central Park. The women talked principally about their husbands, and this was a game that Laura could play with an empty purse. Vaguely, boastfully, the two women discussed the irons their men had in the fire. They sat together with their children through the sooty twilights, when the city to the south burns like a Bessemer furnace, and the air smells of coal, and the wet boulders shine like slag, and the Park itself seems like a strip of woods on the edge of a coal town. Then Mrs. Holinshed would remember that she was late—she was always late for something mysterious and splendid—and the two women would walk together to the edge of the woods. This vicarious contact with comfort pleased Laura, and the pleasure would stay with her as she pushed the baby carriage over to Madison Avenue and then began to cook supper, hearing the thump of the steam iron and smelling the cleaning fluid from the pants presser's below.

One night, when Rachel was about two years old, the frustration of Ralph's search for the goat track that would let him lead his family to a realm of reasonable contentment kept him awake. He needed sleep urgently, and when this blessing eluded him, he got out of bed and sat in the dark. The charm and excitement of the street after midnight escaped him. The explosive brakes of a Madison Avenue bus made him jump. He shut the window, but the noise of traffic continued to pass through it.

THE POT OF GOLD

It seemed to him that the penetrating voice of the city had a mortal effect on the precious lives of the city's inhabitants and that it should be muffled.

He thought of a Venetian blind whose outer surfaces would be treated with a substance that would deflect or absorb sound waves. With such a blind, friends paying a call on a spring evening would not have to shout to be heard above the noise of trucks in the street below. Bedrooms could be silenced that way —bedrooms, above all, for it seemed to him then that sleep was what everyone in the city sought and only half captured. All the harried faces on the streets at dusk, when even the pretty girls talk to themselves, were looking for sleep. Night-club singers and their amiable customers, the people waiting for taxis in front of the Waldorf on a wet night, policemen, cashiers, window washers—sleep eluded them all.

He talked over this Venetian blind with Laura the following night, and the idea seemed sensible to her. He bought a blind that would fit their bedroom window, and experimented with various paint mixtures. At last he stumbled on one that dried to the consistency of felt and was porous. The paint had a sickening smell, which filled their apartment during the four days it took him to coat and recoat the outer surface of the slats. When the paint had dried, he hung the blind, and they opened the window for a test. Silence—a relative silence— charmed their ears. He wrote down his formula, and took it during his lunch hour to a patent attorney. It took the lawyer several weeks to discover that a similar formula had been patented some years earlier. The patent owner—a man named Fellows—had a New York address, and the lawyer suggested that Ralph get in touch with him and try to reach some agreement.

The search for Mr. Fellows began one evening when Ralph had finished work, and took him first to the attic of a Hudson Street rooming house, where the landlady showed Ralph a pair of socks that Mr. Fellows had left behind when he moved out. Ralph went south from there to another rooming house and

then west to the neighborhood of ship chandlers and marine
boarding houses. The nocturnal search went on for a week. He
followed the thread of Mr. Fellows' goings south to the Bowery
and then to the upper West Side. He climbed stairs past the
open doors of rooms where lessons in Spanish dancing were
going on, past whores, past women practicing the "Emperor"
Concerto, and one evening he found Mr. Fellows sitting on the
edge of his bed in an attic room, rubbing the spots out of his
necktie with a rag soaked in gasoline.

Mr. Fellows was greedy. He wanted a hundred dollars in
cash and fifty per cent of the royalties. Ralph got him to agree
to twenty per cent of the royalties, but he could not get him to
reduce the initial payment. The lawyer drew up a paper defin-
ing's Ralph's and Mr. Fellows' interests, and a few nights later
Ralph went over to Brooklyn and got to a Venetian-blind factory after its doors had closed but while the lights of the office
were still burning. The manager agreed to manufacture some
blinds to Ralph's specifications, but he would not take an order
of less than a hundred dollars. Ralph agreed to this and to
furnish the compound for the outer surface of the slats. These
expenditures had taken more than three-fourths of the Whittemores' capital, and now the problem of money was joined by
the element of time. They put a small advertisement in the
paper for a housewares salesman, and for a week Ralph inter-
viewed candidates in the living room after supper. He chose a
young man who was leaving at the end of the week for the
Midwest. He wanted a fifty-dollar advance, and pointed out to
them that Pittsburgh and Chicago were just as noisy as New
York. A department-store collection agency was threatening to
bring them into the small-claims court at this time, and they
had come to a place where any illness, any fall, any damage
to themselves or to the few clothes they owned would be critical. Their salesman promised to write them from Chicago at
the end of the week, and they counted on good news, but there
was no news from Chicago at all. Ralph wired the salesman
twice, and the wires must have been forwarded, for he replied

[35]

to them from Pittsburgh: "Can't merchandise blinds. Returning samples express." They put another advertisement for a salesman in the paper and took the first one who rang their bell, an old gentleman with a cornflower in his buttonhole. He had a number of other lines—mirror wastebaskets, orange-juicers—and he said that he knew all the Manhattan housewares buyers intimately. He was garrulous, and when he was unable to sell the blinds, he came to the Whittemores' apartment and discussed their product at length, and with a blend of criticism and charity that we usually reserve for human beings.

Ralph tried to borrow money, but neither his salary nor his patent was considered adequate collateral for a loan at anything but ruinous rates, and one day, at his office, he was served a summons by the department-store collection agency. He went out to Brooklyn and offered to sell the Venetian blinds back to the manufacturer. The man gave him sixty dollars for what had cost a hundred, and Ralph was able to pay the collection agency. They hung the samples in their windows and tried to put the venture out of their minds.

Now they were poorer than ever, and they ate lentils for dinner every Monday and sometimes again on Tuesday. Laura washed the dishes after dinner while Ralph read to Rachel. When the girl had fallen asleep, he would go to his desk in the living room and work on one of his projects. There was always something coming. There was a job in Dallas and a job in Peru. There were the plastic arch preserver, the automatic closing device for ice-box doors, and the scheme to pirate marine specifications and undersell Jane's. For a month, he was going to buy some fallow acreage in upstate New York and plant Christmas trees on it, and then, with one of his friends, he projected a luxury mail-order business, for which they could never get backing. When the Whittemores met Uncle George and Aunt Helen at the Ritz, they seemed delighted with the way things were going. They were terribly excited, Laura said, about a sales agency in Paris that had been offered to Ralph but that they had decided against, because of the threat of war.

The Whittemores were apart for two years during the war. Laura took a job. She walked Rachel to school in the morning and met her at the end of the day. Working and saving, Laura was able to buy herself and Rachel some clothes. When Ralph returned at the end of the war, their affairs were in good order. The experience seemed to have refreshed him, and while he took up his old job as an anchor to windward, as an ace in the hole, there had never been more talk about jobs—jobs in Venezuela and jobs in Iran. They resumed all their old habits and economies. They remained poor.

Laura gave up her job and returned to the afternoons with Rachel in Central Park. Alice Holinshed was there. The talk was the same. The Holinsheds were living in a hotel. Mr. Holinshed was vice-president of a new firm manufacturing a soft drink, but the dress that Mrs. Holinshed wore day after day was one that Laura recognized from before the war. Her son was thin and bad-tempered. He was dressed in serge, like an English schoolboy, but his serge, like his mother's dress, looked worn and outgrown. One afternoon when Mrs. Holinshed and her son came into the Park, the boy was crying. "I've done a dreadful thing," Mrs. Holinshed told Laura. "We've been to the doctor's and I forgot to bring any money, and I wonder if you could lend me a few dollars, so I can take a taxi back to the hotel." Laura said she would be glad to. She had only a five-dollar bill with her, and she gave Mrs. Holinshed this. The boy continued to cry, and his mother dragged him off toward Fifth Avenue. Laura never saw them in the Park again.

Ralph's life was, as it had always been, dominated by anticipation. In the years directly after the war, the city appeared to be immensely rich. There seemed to be money everywhere, and the Whittemores, who slept under their worn overcoats in the winter to keep themselves warm, seemed separated from their enjoyment of this prosperity by only a little patience, resourcefulness, and luck. On Sunday, when the weather was fine, they walked with the prosperous crowds on upper Fifth

THE POT OF GOLD

Avenue. It seemed to Ralph that it might only be another month, at the most another year, before he found the key to the prosperity they deserved. They would walk on Fifth Avenue until the afternoon was ended and then go home and eat a can of beans for dinner and, in order to balance the meal, an apple for dessert.

They were returning from such a walk one Sunday when, as they climbed the stairs to their apartment, the telephone began to ring. Ralph went on ahead and answered it.

He heard the voice of his Uncle George, a man of the generation that remains conscious of distance, who spoke into the telephone as if he were calling from shore to a passing boat. "This is Uncle George, Ralphie!" he shouted, and Ralph supposed that he and Aunt Helen were paying a surprise visit to the city, until he realized that his uncle was calling from Illinois. "Can you hear me?" Uncle George shouted. "Can you hear me, Ralphie? . . . I'm calling you about a job, Ralphie. Just in case you're looking for a job. Paul Hadaam came through—can you hear me, Ralphie?—Paul Hadaam came through here on his way East last week and he stopped off to pay me a visit. He's got a lot of money, Ralphie—he's rich—and he's starting this business out in the West to manufacture synthetic wool. Can you hear me, Ralphie? . . . I told him about you, and he's staying at the Waldorf, so you go and see him. I saved his life once. I pulled him out of Lake Erie. You go and see him tomorrow at the Waldorf, Ralphie. You know where that is? The Waldorf Hotel. . . . Wait a minute, here's Aunt Helen. She wants to talk with you."

Now the voice was a woman's, and it came to him faintly. All his cousins had been there for dinner, she told him. They had had a turkey for dinner. All the grandchildren were there and they behaved very well. George took them all for a walk after dinner. It was hot, but they sat on the porch, so they didn't feel the heat. She was interrupted in her account of Sunday by her husband, who must have seized the instrument from her to continue his refrain about going to see Mr. Hadaam at

[38]

the Waldorf. "You go see him tomorrow, Ralphie—the nine-teenth—at the Waldorf. He's expecting you. Can you hear me? . . . The Waldorf Hotel. He's a millionaire. I'll say goodbye now."

Mr. Hadaam had a parlor and a bedroom in the Waldorf Towers, and when Ralph went to see him, late the next after-noon, on his way home from work, Mr. Hadaam was alone. He seemed to Ralph a very old man, but an obdurate one, and in the way he shook hands, pulled at his ear lobes, stretched him-self, and padded around the parlor on his bandy legs Ralph recognized a spirit that was unimpaired, independent, and ca-nine. He poured Ralph a strong drink and himself a weak one. He was undertaking the manufacture of synthetic wool on the West Coast, he explained, and had come East to find men who were experienced in merchandising wool. George had given him Ralph's name, and he wanted a man with Ralph's experi-ence. He would find the Whittemores a suitable house, arrange for their transportation, and begin Ralph at a salary of fifteen thousand. It was the size of the salary that made Ralph realize that the proposition was an oblique attempt to repay his uncle for having saved Mr. Hadaam's life, and the old man seemed to sense what he was feeling. "This hasn't got anything to do with your uncle's saving my life," he said roughly. "I'm grate-ful to him—who wouldn't be?—but this hasn't got anything to do with your uncle, if that's what you're thinking. When you get to be as old and as rich as I am, it's hard to meet people. All my old friends are dead—all of them but George. I'm sur-rounded by a cordon of associates and relatives that's damned near impenetrable, and if it wasn't for George giving me a name now and then, I'd never get to see a new face. Last year, I got into an automobile accident. It was my fault. I'm a ter-rible driver. I hit this young fellow's car and I got right out and went over to him and introduced myself. We had to wait about twenty minutes for the wreckers and we got to talking. Well, he's working for me today and he's one of the best friends

I've got, and if I hadn't run into him, I'd never have met him. When you get to be as old as me, that's the only way you can meet people—automobile accidents, fires, things like that."

He straightened up against the back of his chair and tasted his drink. His rooms were well above the noise of traffic and it was quiet there. Mr. Hadaam's breath was loud and steady, and it sounded, in a pause, like the heavy breath of someone sleeping. "Well, I don't want to rush you into this," he said. "I'm going back to the Coast the day after tomorrow. You think it over and I'll telephone you." He took out an engagement book and wrote down Ralph's name and telephone number. "I'll call you on Tuesday evening, the twenty-seventh, about nine o'clock —nine o'clock your time. George tells me you've got a nice wife, but I haven't got time to meet her now. I'll see her on the Coast." He started talking about baseball and then brought the conversation back to Uncle George. "He saved my life. My damned boat capsized and then righted herself and sunk right from underneath me. I can still feel her going down under my feet. I couldn't swim. Can't swim today. Well, goodbye." They shook hands, and as soon as the door closed, Ralph heard Mr. Hadaam begin to cough. It was the profane, hammering cough of an old man, full of bitter complaints and distempers, and it hit him pitilessly for all the time that Ralph was waiting in the hallway for the elevator to take him down.

On the walk home, Ralph felt that this might be it, that this preposterous chain of contingencies that had begun with his uncle's pulling a friend out of Lake Erie might be the one that would save them. Nothing in his experience made it seem unlikely. He recognized that the proposition was the vagary of an old man and that it originated in the indebtedness Mr. Hadaam felt to his uncle—an indebtedness that age seemed to have deepened. He gave Laura the details of the interview when he came in, and his own views on Mr. Hadaam's conduct, and, to his mild surprise, Laura said that it looked to her like the bonanza. They were both remarkably calm, considering the change that confronted them. There was no talk of celebrating,

and he helped her wash the dishes. He looked up the site of
Mr. Hadaam's factory in an atlas, and the Spanish place name
on the coast north of San Francisco gave them a glimpse of a
life of reasonable contentment.

Eight days lay between Ralph's interview and the telephone
call, and he realized that nothing would be definite until Tuesday, and that there was a possibility that old Mr. Hadaam,
while crossing the country, might, under the subtle influence
of travel, suffer a change of heart. He might be poisoned by a
fish sandwich and be taken off the train in Chicago, to die in
a nursing home there. Among the people meeting him in San
Francisco might be his lawyer, with the news that he was
ruined or that his wife had run away. But eventually Ralph
was unable to invent any new disasters or to believe in the
ones he had invented.

This inability to persevere in doubting his luck showed some
weakening of character. There had hardly been a day when he
had not been made to feel the power of money, but he found
that the force of money was most irresistible when it took the
guise of a promise, and that years of resolute self-denial, instead
of rewarding him with reserves of fortitude, had left him more
than ordinarily susceptible to temptation. Since the change in
their lives still depended upon a telephone call, he refrained
from talking—from thinking, so far as possible—about the life
they might have in California. He would go so far as to say
that he would like some white shirts, but he would not go beyond this deliberately contrite wish, and here, where he thought
he was exercising restraint and intelligence, he was, instead,
beginning to respect the bulk of superstition that is supposed to
attend good fortune, and when he wished for white shirts, it
was not a genuinely modest wish so much as it was a memory
—he could not have put it into words himself—that the gods
of fortune are jealous and easily deceived by false modesty. He
had never been a superstitious man, but on Tuesday he scooped
the money off his coffee and was elated when he saw a ladybug
on the bathroom window sill. He could not remember when he

[41]

had heard money and this insect associated, but neither could he have explained any of the other portents that he had begun to let govern his movements.

Laura watched this subtle change that anticipation worked on her husband, but there was nothing she could say. He did not mention Mr. Hadaam or California. He was quiet; he was gentle with Rachel; he actually grew pale. He had his hair cut on Wednesday. He wore his best suit. On Saturday, he had his hair cut again and his nails manicured. He took two baths a day, put on a fresh shirt for dinner, and frequently went into the bathroom to wash his hands, brush his teeth, and wet down his cowlick. The preternatural care he gave his body and his appearance reminded her of an adolescent surprised by early love.

The Whittemores were invited to a party for Monday night and Laura insisted that they go. The guests at the party were the survivors of a group that had coalesced ten years before, and if anyone had called the roll of the earliest parties in the same room, like the retreat ceremony of a breeched and decimated regiment, "Missing. . . . Missing. . . . Missing" would have been answered for the squad that had gone into Westchester; "Missing. . . . Missing. . . . Missing" would have been spoken for the platoon that divorce, drink, nervous disorders, and adversity had slain or wounded. Because Laura had gone to the party in indifferent spirits, she was conscious of the missing.

She had been at the party less than an hour when she heard some people coming in, and, looking over her shoulder, saw Alice Holinshed and her husband. The room was crowded and she put off speaking to Alice until later. Much later in the evening, Laura went into the toilet, and when she came out of it into the bedroom, she found Alice sitting on the bed. She seemed to be waiting for Laura. Laura sat down at the dressing table to straighten her hair. She looked at the image of her friend in the glass.

"I hear you're going to California," Alice said.

"We hope to. We'll know tomorrow."

"Is it true that Ralph's uncle saved his life?"

"That's true."

"You're lucky."

"I suppose we are."

"You're lucky, all right." Alice got up from the bed and crossed the room and closed the door, and came back across the room again and sat on the bed. Laura watched her in the glass, but she was not watching Laura. She was stooped. She seemed nervous. "You're lucky," she said. "You're so lucky. Do you know how lucky you are? Let me tell you about this cake of soap," she said. "I have this cake of soap. I mean I had this cake of soap. Somebody gave it to me when I was married, fifteen years ago. I don't know who. Some maid, some music teacher—somebody like that. It was good soap, good English soap, the kind I like, and I decided to save it for the big day when Larry made a killing, when he took me to Bermuda. First, I was going to use it when he got the job in Bound Brook. Then I thought I could use it when we were going to Boston, and then Washington, and then when he got this new job, I thought maybe this is it, maybe *this* is the time when I get to take the boy out of that rotten school and pay the bills and move out of those bum hotels we've been living in. For fifteen years I've been planning to use this cake of soap. Well, last week I was looking through my bureau drawers and I saw this cake of soap. It was all cracked. I threw it out. I threw it out because I knew I was never going to have a chance to use it. Do you realize what that means? Do you know what that feels like? To live for fifteen years on promises and expectations and loans and credits in hotels that aren't fit to live in, never for a single day to be out of debt, and yet to pretend, to feel that every year, every winter, every job, every meeting is going to be the one. To live like this for fifteen years and then to realize that it's never going to end. Do you know what that feels like?" She got up and went over to the dressing table and stood in front of Laura. Tears had risen into her large eyes, and her voice

was harsh and loud. "I'm never going to get to Bermuda," she
said. "I'm never even going to get to Florida. I'm never going
to get out of hock, ever, ever, *ever*. I know that I'm never going
to have a decent home and that everything I own that is worn
and torn and no good is going to stay that way. I know that for
the rest of my life, for the rest of my life, I'm going to wear
ragged slips and torn nightgowns and torn underclothes and
shoes that hurt me. I know that for the rest of my life nobody
is going to come up to me and tell me that I've got on a pretty
dress, because I'm not going to be able to afford that kind of a
dress. I know that for the rest of my life every taxi-driver and
doorman and headwaiter in this town is going to know in a
minute that I haven't got five bucks in that black imitation-
suède purse that I've been brushing and brushing and brushing
and carrying around for ten years. How do you get it? How do
you rate it? What's so wonderful about you that you get a
break like this?" She ran her fingers down Laura's bare arm.
The dress she was wearing smelled of benzine. "Can I rub it
off you? Will that make me lucky? I swear to Jesus I'd murder
somebody if I thought it would bring us in any money. I'd
wring somebody's neck—yours, anybody's—I swear to Jesus I
would—"

Someone began knocking on the door. Alice strode to the
door, opened it, and went out. A woman came in, a stranger
looking for the toilet. Laura lighted a cigarette and waited in
the bedroom for about ten minutes before she went back to
the party. The Holinsheds had gone. She got a drink and sat
down and tried to talk, but she couldn't keep her mind on what
she was saying.

The hunt, the search for money that had seemed to her
natural, amiable, and fair when they first committed themselves to it, now seemed like a hazardous and piratical voyage.
She had thought, earlier in the evening, of the missing. She
thought now of the missing again. Adversity and failure ac-
counted for more than half of them, as if beneath the amenities
in the pretty room a keen race were in progress, in which the

loser's forfeits were extreme. Laura felt cold. She picked the ice out of her drink with her fingers and put it in a flower vase, but the whiskey didn't warm her. She asked Ralph to take her home.

After dinner on Tuesday, Laura washed the dishes and Ralph dried them. He read the paper and she took up some sewing. At a quarter after eight, the telephone, in the bedroom, rang, and he went to it calmly. It was someone with two theatre tickets for a show that was closing. The telephone didn't ring again, and at half past nine he told Laura that he was going to call California. It didn't take long for the connection to be made, and the fresh voice of a young woman spoke to him from Mr. Hadaam's number. "Oh, yes, Mr. Whittemore," she said. "We tried to get you earlier in the evening but your line was busy."

"Could I speak to Mr. Hadaam?"

"No, Mr. Whittemore. This is Mr. Hadaam's secretary. I know he meant to call you, because he had entered this in his engagement book. Mrs. Hadaam has asked me to disappoint as few people as possible, and I've tried to take care of all the calls and appointments in his engagement book. Mr. Hadaam had a stroke on Sunday. We don't expect him to recover. I imagine he made you some kind of promise, but I'm afraid he won't be able to keep it."

"I'm very sorry," Ralph said. He hung up.

Laura had come into the bedroom while the secretary was talking. "Oh, darling!" she said. She put her sewing basket on the bureau and went toward the closet. Then she went back and looked for something in the sewing basket and left the basket on her dressing table. Then she took off her shoes, treed them, slipped her dress over her head and hung it up neatly. Then she went to the bureau, looking for her sewing basket, found it on the dressing table, and took it into the closet, where she put it on a shelf. Then she took her brush and comb into the bathroom and began to run the water for a bath.

The lash of frustration was laid on and the pain stunned Ralph. He sat by the telephone for he did not know how long. He heard Laura come out of the bathroom. He turned when he heard her speak.

"I feel dreadfully about old Mr. Hadaam," she said. "I wish there were something we could do." She was in her nightgown, and she sat down at the dressing table like a skillful and patient woman establishing herself in front of a loom, and she picked up and put down pins and bottles and combs and brushes with the thoughtless dexterity of an experienced weaver, as if the time she spent there were all part of a continuous operation. "It did look like the treasure . . ."

The word surprised him, and for a moment he saw the chimera, the pot of gold, the fleece, the treasure buried in the faint lights of a rainbow, and the primitivism of his hunt struck him. Armed with a sharp spade and a homemade divining rod, he had climbed over hill and dale, through droughts and rain squalls, digging wherever the maps he had drawn himself promised gold. Six paces east of the dead pine, five panels in from the library door, underneath the creaking step, in the roots of the pear tree, beneath the grape arbor lay the bean pot full of doubloons and bullion.

She turned on the stool and held her thin arms toward him, as she had done more than a thousand times. She was no longer young, and more wan, thinner than she might have been if he had found the doubloons to save her anxiety and unremitting work. Her smile, her naked shoulders had begun to trouble the indecipherable shapes and symbols that are the touchstones of desire, and the light from the lamp seemed to brighten and give off heat and shed that unaccountable complacency, that benevolence, that the spring sunlight brings to all kinds of fatigue and despair. Desire for her delighted and confused him. Here it was, here it all was, and the shine of the gold seemed to him then to be all around her arms.

𝒲HEN the train from Chicago left Albany and began to pound down the river valley toward New York, the Malloys, who had already experienced many phases of excitement, felt their breathing quicken, as if there were not enough air in the coach. They straightened their backs and raised their heads, searching for oxygen, like the crew of a doomed submarine. Their daughter, Mildred-Rose, took an enviable way out of the agitation. She fell asleep. Evarts Malloy wanted to get the suitcases down from the rack, but Alice, his wife, studied the timetable and said that it was too soon. She stared out of the window and saw the noble Hudson.

"Why do they call it the rind of America?" she asked her husband.

"The Rhine," Evarts said. "Not the rind."

"Oh."

They had left their home in Wentworth, Indiana, the day before, and in spite of the excitements of travel and their brilliant destination, they both wondered, now and then, if they had remembered to turn off the gas and extinguish the rubbish fire behind the barn. They were dressed, like the people you sometimes see in Times Square on Saturday nights, in clothing that had been saved for their flight. His light shoes had perhaps not been out of the back of the closet since his father's funeral or his brother's wedding. She was wearing her new gloves for the first time—the gloves she had been given for Christmas ten years ago. His tarnished collar pin and his initialled tie clip, with its gilt chain, his fancy socks, the rayon handkerchief in his breast pocket, and the carnation made of feathers in his lapel had all been husbanded in the top drawer of his bureau for years in the firm conviction that life would someday call him from Wentworth.

Alice Malloy had dark, stringy hair, and even her husband, who loved her more than he knew, was sometimes reminded by her lean face of a tenement doorway on a rainy day, for her countenance was long, vacant, and weakly lighted, a passage for the gentle transports and miseries of the poor. Evarts Malloy was very thin. He had worked as a bus driver and he stooped a little. Their child slept with her thumb in her mouth. Her hair was dark and her dirty face was lean, like her mother's. When a violent movement of the train roused her, she drew noisily at her thumb until she lost consciousness again. She had been unable to store up as much finery as her parents, since she was only five years old, but she wore a white fur coat. The matching hat and muff had been lost generations before; the skins of the coat were sere and worn, but as she slept, she stroked them, as if they had remarkable properties that assured her that all was well, all was well.

The conductor who came through the car taking tickets after Albany noticed the Malloys, and something about their appearance worried him. As he came back through the car, he stopped at their seat and talked with them, first about Mildred-Rose and then about their destination.

"You people going to New York for the first time?" he asked.

"Yes," Evarts said.

"Going down to see the sights?"

"Oh, no," Alice said. "We're going on business."

"Looking for a job?" the conductor asked.

"Oh, no," Alice said. "Tell him, Evarts."

"Well, it really isn't a job," Evarts said. "I'm not looking for a job, I mean. I mean I sort of have a job." His manner was friendly and simple and he told his story enthusiastically, for the conductor was the first stranger to ask for it. "I was in the Army, you see, and then, when I got out of the Army, I went back home and began driving the bus again. I'm a night bus driver. But I didn't like it. I kept getting stomach aches, and it hurt my eyes, driving at night, so in my spare time, during the afternoons, I began to write this play. Now, out on Route 7, near Wentworth, where we live, there's this old woman named Mama Finelli, who has a gas station and a snake farm. She's a very salty and haunting old character, and so I decided to write this play about her. She has all these salty and haunting sayings. Well, I wrote this first act—and then Tracy Murchison, the producer, comes out from New York to give a lecture at the Women's Club about the problems of the theatre. Well, Alice went to this lecture, and when he was complaining, when Murchison was complaining about the lack of young playwrights, Alice raises her hand and she tells Murchison that her husband is a young playwright and will he read his play. Didn't you, Alice?"

"Yes," Alice said.

"Well, he hems and haws," Evarts said, "Murchison hems and haws, but Alice pins him down, because all these other people are listening, and when he finishes his lecture, she goes right up on the platform and she gives him the play—she's got it in her pocketbook. Well, then she goes back to his hotel with him and she sits right beside him until he's read the play—the first act, that is. That's all I've written. Well in this play there's a part he wants for his wife, Madge Beatty, right off. I guess you know who Madge Beatty is. So you know what he does then? He sits right down and he writes out a check for thirty-five dollars and he says for me and Alice to come to New York! So we take all our money out of the savings bank and we burn our bridges and here we are."

"Well, I guess there's lots of money in it," the conductor said. Then he wished the Malloys luck and walked away.

Evarts wanted to take the suitcases down at Poughkeepsie and again at Harmon, but Alice checked each place against the timetable and made him wait. Neither of them had seen New York before, and they watched its approaches greedily, for Wentworth was a dismal town and even the slums of Manhattan looked wonderful to them that afternoon. When the train plunged into the darkness beneath Park Avenue, Alice felt that she was surrounded by the inventions of giants, and she roused Mildred-Rose and tied the little girl's bonnet with trembling fingers.

As the Malloys stepped from the train, Alice noticed that the paving, deep in the station, had a frosty glitter, and she wondered if diamonds had been ground into the concrete. She forbade Evarts to ask directions. "If they find out we're green, they'll fleece us," she whispered. They wandered through the marble waiting room, following the noise of traffic and klaxons as if it were the bidding of life. Alice had studied a map of New York, and when they left the station, she knew which direction to take. They walked along Forty-second Street to Fifth Avenue. The faces that passed them seemed purposeful and intent, as if they all belonged to people who were pursuing the destinies of great industries. Evarts had never seen so many beautiful women, so many pleasant, young faces, promising an easy conquest. It was a winter afternoon, and the light in the city was clear and shaded with violet, just like the light on the fields around Wentworth.

Their destination, the Hotel Mentone, was on a side street west of Sixth Avenue. It was a dark place, with malodorous chambers, miserable food, and a lobby ceiling decorated with as much gilt and gesso as the Vatican chapels. It was a popular hotel among the old, it was attractive to the disreputable, and the Malloys had found the way there because the Mentone advertised on railroad-station hoardings all through the West. Many innocents had been there before them, and their sweetness and humility had triumphed over the apparent atmosphere of ruined splendor and petty vice and had left in all the public rooms a humble odor that reminded one of a country feed store on a winter afternoon. A bellboy took them to their room. As soon as he had gone, Alice examined the bath and pulled aside the window curtains. The window looked onto a brick wall, but when she raised it, she could hear the noise of traffic, and it sounded, as it had sounded in the station, like the irresistible and titanic voice of life itself.

The Malloys found their way, that afternoon, to the Broadway Automat. They shouted with pleasure at the magical coffee spigots and the glass doors that sprang open. "Tomorrow, I'm going to have the baked beans," Alice cried, "and the chicken pie the day after that and the fish cakes after that." When they had finished their supper, they went out into the street. Mildred-Rose walked between her parents, holding their calloused hands. It was getting dark, and the lights of Broadway answered all their simple prayers. High in the air were large, brightly lighted pictures of bloody heroes, criminal lovers, monsters, and armed desperadoes. The names of movies and soft drinks, restaurants and cigarettes were written in a jumble of light, and in the distance they could see the pitiless winter afterglow beyond the Hudson River. The tall buildings in the East were lighted and seemed to burn, as if fire had fallen onto their dark shapes. The air was full of music, and the light was brighter than day. They drifted with the crowd for hours.

Mildred-Rose got tired and began to cry, so at last her parents took her back to the Mentone. Alice had begun to undress her when someone knocked softly on the door.

"Come in," Evarts called.

A bellboy stood in the doorway. He had the figure of a boy, but his face was gray and lined. "I just wanted to see if you people were all right," he said. "I just wanted to see if maybe you wanted a little ginger ale or some ice water."

"Oh, no, thank you kindly," Alice said. "It was very nice of you to ask, though."

"You people just come to New York for the first time?" the

[51]

O CITY OF BROKEN DREAMS

bellboy asked. He closed the door behind him and sat on the
arm of a chair.

"Yes," Evarts said. "We left Wentworth—that's in Indiana
—yesterday on the nine-fifteen for South Bend. Then we went
to Chicago. We had dinner in Chicago."

"I had the chicken pie," Alice said. "It was delicious." She
slipped Mildred-Rose's nightgown over her head.

"Then we came to New York," Evarts said.

"What are you doing here?" the bellboy asked. "Anniver-
sary?" He helped himself to a cigarette from a package on the
bureau and slipped down into the chair.

"Oh, no," Evarts said. "We hit the jackpot."

"Our ship's come in," Alice said.

"A contest?" the bellboy asked. "Something like that?"

"Oh, no," Evarts said.

"You tell him, Evarts," Alice said.

"Yes," the bellboy said. "Tell me, Evarts."

"Well, you see," Evarts said, "it began like this." He sat
down on the bed and lighted a cigarette. "I was in the Army,
you see, and then when I got out of the Army, I went back to
Wentworth . . ." He repeated to the bellboy the story he had
told the conductor.

"Oh, you lucky, lucky kids!" the bellboy exclaimed when
Evarts had finished. "Tracey Murchison! Madge Beatty! You
lucky, lucky kids." He looked at the poorly furnished room.
Alice was arranging Mildred-Rose on the sofa, where she would
sleep. Evarts was sitting on the edge of the bed swinging his
legs. "What you need now is a good agent," the bellboy said.
He wrote a name and address on a piece of paper and gave it
to Evarts. "The Hauser Agency is the biggest agency in the
world," he said, "and Charlie Leavitt is the best man in the
Hauser Agency. I want you to feel free to take your problems
to Charlie, and if he asks who sent you, tell him Bitsey sent
you." He went toward the door. "Good night, you lucky, lucky
kids," he said. "Good night. Sweet sleep. Sweet dreams."

The Malloys were the hard working children of an indus-

[52]

trious generation, and they were up at half past six the next
morning. They scrubbed their faces and their ears and brushed
their teeth with soap. At seven o'clock, they started for the
Automat. Evarts had not slept that night. The noise of traffic
had kept him awake, and he had spent the small hours sitting
at the window. His mouth felt scorched with tobacco smoke,
and the loss of sleep had left him nervous. They were all surprised to find New York still sleeping. They were shocked. They
had their breakfast and returned to the Mentone. Evarts called
Tracey Murchison's office, but no one answered. He telephoned
the office several times after that. At ten o'clock, a girl answered
the phone. "Mr. Murchison will see you at three," she said.
She hung up. Since there was nothing to do but wait, Evarts
took his wife and daughter up Fifth Avenue. They stared in the
store windows. At eleven o'clock, when the doors of Radio City
Music Hall opened, they went there.

This was a happy choice. They prowled the lounges and toilets for an hour before they took their seats, and when, during
the stage show, an enormous samovar rose up out of the orchestra pit and debouched forty men in Cossack uniform singing
"Dark Eyes," Alice and Mildred-Rose shouted with joy. The
stage show, beneath its grandeur, seemed to conceal a simple
and familiar intelligence, as if the drafts that stirred the miles
of golden curtain had blown straight from Indiana. The per-
formance left Alice and Mildred-Rose distracted with pleasure,
and on the way back to the Mentone, Evarts had to lead them
along the sidewalk to keep them from walking into hydrants.
It was a quarter of three when they got back to the hotel. Evarts
kissed his wife and child goodbye and started for Murchison's.

He got lost. He was afraid that he would be late. He began
to run. He asked directions of a couple of policemen and finally
reached the office building.

The front room of Murchison's office was dingy—intentionally dingy, Evarts hoped—but it was not inglorious, for there
were many beautiful men and women there, waiting to see Mr.
Murchison. None of them were sitting down, and they chatted

[53]

together as if delighted by the delay that held them there. The receptionist led Evarts into a further office. This office was also crowded, but the atmosphere was of haste and trouble, as if the place were being besieged. Murchison was there and he greeted Evarts strenuously. "I've got your contracts right here," he said, and he handed Evarts a pen and pushed a stack of contracts toward him. "Now I want you to rush over and see Madge," Murchison said as soon as Evarts had signed the contracts. He looked at Evarts, plucked the feather carnation out of his lapel, and tossed it into a wastebasket. "Hurry, hurry, hurry," he said. "She's at 400 Park Avenue. She's crazy to see you. She's waiting now. I'll see you later tonight—I think Madge has something planned—but hurry."

Evarts rushed into the hall and rang impatiently for the elevator. As soon as he had left the building, he got lost and wandered into the fur district. A policeman directed him back to the Mentone. Alice and Mildred-Rose were waiting in the lobby, and he told them what had happened. "I'm on my way to see Madge Beatty now," he said. "I've got to hurry!" Bitsey, the bellboy, overheard this conversation. He dropped some bags he was carrying and joined the group. He told Evarts how to get to Park Avenue. Evarts kissed Alice and Mildred-Rose again. They waved goodbye as he ran out the door.

Evarts had seen so many movies of Park Avenue that he observed its breadth and bleakness with a sense of familiarity. He took an elevator to the Murchisons' apartment and was led by a maid into a pretty living room. A fire was burning, and there were flowers on the mantel. He sprang to his feet when Madge Beatty came in. She was frail, animated, and golden, and her hoarse and accomplished voice made him feel naked. "I read your play, Evarts," she said, "and I loved it, I loved it, I loved it." She moved lightly around the room, talking now directly at him, now over her shoulder. She was not as young as she had first appeared to be, and in the light from the windows she looked almost wizened. "You're going to do more with my part when you write the second act, I hope," she said.

[54]

"You're going to build it up and build it up and build it up."

"I'll do anything you want, Miss Beatty," Evarts said.

She sat down and folded her beautiful hands. Her feet were very big, Evarts noticed. Her shins were thin, and this made her feet seem very big. "Oh, we love your play, Evarts," she said. "We love it, we want it, we need it. Do you know how much we need it? We're in debt, Evarts, we're dreadfully in debt." She laid a hand on her breast and spoke in a whisper. "We owe one million nine hundred and sixty-five thousand dollars." She let the precious light flood her voice again. "But now I'm keeping you from writing your beautiful play," she said. "I'm keeping you from work, and I want you to go back and write and write and write, and I want you and your wife to come here any time after nine tonight and meet a few of our warmest friends."

Evarts asked the doorman how to get back to the Mentone, but he misunderstood the directions and got lost again. He walked around the East Side until he found a policeman, who directed him back to the hotel. It was so late when he returned that Mildred-Rose was crying with hunger. The three of them washed and went to the Automat and walked up and down Broadway until nearly nine. Then they went back to the hotel. Alice put on her evening dress, and she and Evarts kissed Mildred-Rose good night. In the lobby, they met Bitsey and told him where they were going. He promised to keep an eye on Mildred-Rose.

The walk over to the Murchisons' was longer than Evarts remembered. Alice's wrap was light. She was blue with cold when they reached the apartment building. They could hear in the distance, as they left the elevator, someone playing a piano and a woman singing "A kiss is but a kiss, a sigh is but a sigh . . ." A maid took their wraps, and Mr. Murchison greeted them from a farther door. Alice ruffled and arranged the cloth peony that hung from the front of her dress, and they went in.

The room was crowded, the lights were dim, the singer was ending her song. There was a heady smell of animal skins and astringent perfume in the air. Mr. Murchison introduced the Malloys to a couple who stood near the door, and abandoned them. The couple turned their backs on the Malloys. Evarts was shy and quiet, but Alice was excited and began to speculate, in a whisper, about the identities of the people around the piano. She felt sure that they were all movie stars, and she was right.

The singer finished her song, got up from the piano, and walked away. There was a little applause and then a curious silence. Mr. Murchison asked another woman to sing. "I'm not going to go on after *her*," the woman said. The situation, whatever it was, had stopped conversation. Mr. Murchison asked several people to perform, but they all refused. "Perhaps Mrs. Malloy will sing for us," he said bitterly.

"All right," Alice said. She walked to the center of the room. She took a position and, folding her hands and holding them breast-high, began to sing.

Alice's mother had taught her to sing whenever her host asked, and Alice had never violated any of her mother's teachings. As a child, she had taken singing lessons from Mrs. Bachman, an elderly widow who lived in Wentworth. She had sung in grammar-school assemblies and in high-school assemblies. On family holidays, there had always come a time, in the late afternoon, when she would be asked to sing; then she would rise from her place on the hard sofa near the stove or come from the kitchen, where she had been washing dishes, to sing the songs Mrs. Bachman had taught her.

The invitation that night had been so unexpected that Evarts had not had a chance to stop his wife. He had felt the bitterness in Murchison's voice, and he would have stopped her, but as soon as she began to sing, he didn't care. Her voice was well pitched, her figure was stern and touching, and she sang for those people in obedience to her mannerly heart. When he had overcome his own bewilderment, he noticed the respect and

attention the Murchisons' guests were giving her music. Many
of them had come from towns as small as Wentworth; they
were goodhearted people, and the simple air, rendered in Alice's
fearless voice, reminded them of their beginnings. None of them
were whispering or smiling. Many of them had lowered their
heads, and he saw a woman touch her eyes with a handkerchief.
Alice had triumphed, he thought, and then he recognized the
song as "Annie Laurie."

Years ago, when Mrs. Bachman had taught Alice the song,
she had taught her to close it with a piece of business that
brought her success as a child, as a girl, as a high-school senior,
but that, even in the stuffy living room in Wentworth, with its
inexorable smells of poverty and cooking, had begun to tire
and worry her family. She had been taught on the closing line,
"Lay me doun and dee," to fall in a heap on the floor. She fell
less precipitously now that she had got older, but she still fell,
and Evarts could see that night, by her serene face, that a fall
was in her plans. He considered going to her, embracing her,
and whispering to her that the hotel was burning or that Mildred-Rose was sick. Instead, he turned his back.

Alice took a quick breath and attacked the last verse. Evarts
had begun to sweat so freely that the brine got into his eyes.
"I'll lay me doun and dee," he heard her sing; he heard the
loud crash as she hit the floor; he heard the screams of helpless
laughter, the tobacco coughs, and the oaths of a woman who
laughed so hard she broke her pearl bib. The Murchisons' guests
seemed bewitched. They wept, they shook, they stooped, they
slapped one another on the back, and walked, like the demented,
in circles. When Evarts faced the scene, Alice was sitting on
the floor. He helped her to her feet. "Come, darling," he said.
"Come." With his arm around her, he led her into the hall.

"Didn't they like my song?" she asked. She began to cry.

"It doesn't matter, my darling," Evarts said, "it doesn't matter, it doesn't matter." They got their wraps and walked back
through the cold to the Mentone.

Bitsey was waiting for them in the corridor outside their

room. He wanted to hear all about the party. Evarts sent Alice into the room and talked with the bellboy alone. He didn't feel like describing the party. "I don't think I want to have anything more to do with the Murchisons," he said. "I'm going to get a new producer."

"That's the boy, that's the boy," Bitsey said. "Now you're talking. But, first, I want you to go up to the Hauser Agency and see Charlie Leavitt."

"All right," Evarts said. "All right, I'll go and see Charlie Leavitt."

Alice cried herself to sleep that night. Again, Evarts couldn't sleep. He sat in a chair by the window. He fell into a doze, a little before dawn, but not for long. At seven o'clock, he led his family off to the Automat.

Bitsey came up to the Malloys' room after breakfast. He was very excited. A columnist in one of the four-cent newspapers had reported Evarts' arrival in New York. A Cabinet member and a Balkan king were mentioned in the same paragraph. Then the telephone began to ring. First, it was a man who wanted to sell Evarts a second-hand mink coat. Then a lawyer and a dry-cleaner called, a dressmaker, a nursery school, several agencies, and a man who said he could get them a good apartment. Evarts said no to all these importunities, but in each case he had to argue before he could hang up. Bitsey had made a noon appointment for him with Charlie Leavitt, and when it was time, he kissed Alice and Mildred-Rose and went down to the street.

The Hauser Agency was located in one of the buildings in Radio City. Now Evarts' business took him through the building's formidable doors as legitimately, he told himself, as anyone else. The Hauser offices were on the twenty-sixth floor. He didn't call his floor until the elevator had begun its ascent. "It's too late now," the operator said. "You got to tell me the number of the floor when you get in." This branded him as green to all the other people in the car, Evarts knew, and he blushed.

He rode to the sixtieth floor and then back to the twenty-sixth. As he left the car, the elevator operator sneered.

At the end of a long corridor, there was a pair of bronze doors, fastened by a bifurcated eagle. Evarts turned the wings of the imperial bird and stepped into a lofty manor hall. The panelling on its walls was worm-pitted and white with rot. In the distance, behind a small glass window, he saw a woman wearing earphones. He walked over to her, told her his business, and was asked to sit down. He sat on a leather sofa and lighted a cigarette. The richness of the hall impressed him profoundly. Then he noticed that the sofa was covered with dust. So were the table, the magazines on it, the lamp, the bronze cast of Rodin's "Le Baiser"—everything in the vast room was covered with dust. He noticed at the same time the peculiar stillness of the hall. All the usual noises of an office were lacking. Into this stillness, from the distant earth, rose the recorded music from the skating rink, where a carillon played "Joy to the World! The Lord Is Come!" The magazines on the table beside the sofa were all five years old.

After a while, the receptionist pointed to a double door at the end of the hall, and Evarts walked there, timidly. The office on the other side of the door was smaller than the room he had just left but dimmer, richer, and more imposing, and in the distance he could still hear the music of the skating rink. A man was sitting at an antique desk. He stood as soon as he saw Evarts. "Welcome, Evarts, welcome to the Hauser Agency!" he shouted. "I hear you've got a hot property there, and Bitsey tells me you're through with Tracey Murchison. I haven't read your play, of course, but if Tracey wants it, I want it, and so does Sam Farley. I've got a producer for you, I've got a star for you, I've got a theatre for you, and I think I've got a pre-production deal lined up. One hundred thou' on a four-hundred-thou' ceiling. Sit down, sit down."

Mr. Leavitt seemed either to be eating something or to be having trouble with his teeth, for at the end of every sentence he worked his lips noisily and thoughtfully, like a gourmet.

[59]

He might have been eating something, since there were crumbs around his mouth. Or he might have been having trouble with his teeth, because the labial noises continued all through the interview. Mr. Leavitt wore a lot of gold. He had several rings, a gold identification bracelet, and a gold bracelet watch, and he carried a heavy gold cigarette case, set with jewels. The case was empty, and Evarts furnished him with cigarettes as they talked.

"Now, I want you to go back to your hotel, Evarts," Mr. Leavitt shouted, "and I want you to take it easy. Charlie Leavitt is taking care of your property. I want you to promise me you won't worry. Now, I understand that you've signed a contract with Murchison. I'm going to declare that contract null and void, and my lawyer is going to declare that contract null and void, and if Murchison contests it, we'll drag him into court and have the judge declare that contract null and void. Before we go any further, though," he said, softening his voice, "I want you to sign these papers, which will give me authority to represent you." He pressed some papers and a gold fountain pen on Evarts. "Just sign these papers," he said sadly, "and you'll make four hundred thousand dollars. Oh, you authors!" he exclaimed. "You lucky authors!"

As soon as Evarts had signed the papers, Mr. Leavitt's manner changed and he began to shout again. "The producer I've got for you is Sam Farley. The star is Susan Hewitt. Sam Farley is Tom Farley's brother. He's married to Clarissa Douglas and he's George Howland's uncle. Pat Levy's his brother-in-law and Mitch Kababian and Howie Brown are related to him on his mother's side. She was Lottie Mayes. They're a very close family. They're a great little team. When your show opens in Wilmington, Sam Farley, Tom Farley, Clarissa Douglas, George Howland, Pat Levy, Mitch Kababian, and Howie Brown are all right down there in that hotel writing your third act. When your show goes up to Baltimore, Sam Farley, Tom Farley, Clarissa Douglas, George Howland, Pat Levy, Mitch Kababian, and Howie Brown, they go up to Baltimore with it. And when your

[60]

shows opens up on Broadway with a high-class production, who's down there in the front row, rooting for you?" Mr. Leavitt had strained his voice, and he ended in a hoarse whisper, "Sam Farley, Tom Farley, George Howland, Clarissa Douglas, Pat Levy, Mitch Kababian, and Howie Brown.

"Now, I want you to go back to your hotel and have a good time," he shouted after he had cleared his throat. "I'll call you tomorrow and tell you when Sam Farley and Susan Hewitt can see you, and I'll telephone Hollywood now and tell Max Rayburn that he can have it for one hundred thou' on a four-hundred-thou' ceiling, and not one iota less." He patted Evarts on the back and steered him gently toward the door. "Have a good time, Evarts," he said.

As Evarts walked back through the hall, he noticed that the receptionist was eating a sandwich. She beckoned to him.

"You want to take a chance on a new Buick convertible?" she whispered. "Ten cents a chance."

"Oh, no, thank you," Evarts said.

"Fresh eggs?" she asked. "I bring them in from Jersey every morning."

"No, thank you," Evarts said.

Evarts hurried back through the crowds to the Mentone, where Alice, Mildred-Rose, and Bitsey were waiting. He described his interview with Leavitt to them. "When I get that four hundred thou'," he said, "I'm going to send some money to Mama Finelli." Then Alice remembered a lot of other people in Wentworth who needed money. By way of a celebration, they went to a spaghetti house that night instead of the Automat. After dinner, they went to Radio City Music Hall. Again, that night, Evarts was unable to sleep.

In Wentworth, Alice had been known as the practical member of the family. There was a good deal of jocularity on this score. She drew up the budget and managed the egg money, and it was often said that Evarts would have misplaced his head if it hadn't been for Alice. This businesslike strain in her character led her to remind Evarts on the following day that he had not been working on his play. She took the situation in hand. "You just sit in the room," she said, "and write the play, and Mildred-Rose and I will walk up and down Fifth Avenue, so you can be alone."

Evarts tried to work, but the telephone began to ring again and he was interrupted regularly by jewelry salesmen, theatrical lawyers, and laundry services. At about eleven, he picked up the phone and heard a familiar and angry voice. It was Murchison. "I brought you from Wentworth," he shouted, "and I made you what you are today. Now they tell me you breached my contract and double-crossed me with Sam Farley. I'm going to break you, I'm going to ruin you, I'm going to sue you, I'm—" Evarts hung up, and when the phone rang a minute later, he didn't answer it. He left a note for Alice, put on his hat, and walked up Fifth Avenue to the Hauser offices.

When he turned the bifurcated eagle of the double doors and stepped into the manor hall that morning, he found Mr. Leavitt there, in his shirtsleeves, sweeping the carpet. "Oh, good morning," Leavitt said. "Occupational therapy." He hid the broom and dustpan behind a velvet drape. "Come in, come in," he said, slipping into his jacket and leading Evarts toward the inner office. "This afternoon, you're going to meet Sam Farley and Susan Hewitt. You're one of the luckiest men in New York. Some men never see Sam Farley. Not even once in a lifetime— never hear his wit, never feel the force of his unique personality. And as for Susan Hewitt . . ." He was speechless for a moment. He said the appointment was for three. "You're going to meet them in Sam Farley's lovely home," he said, and he gave Evarts the address.

Evarts tried to describe the telephone conversation with Murchison, but Leavitt cut him off. "I asked you one thing," he shouted. "I asked you not to worry. Is that too much? I ask you to talk with Sam Farley and take a look at Susan Hewitt and see if you think she's right for the part. Is that too much? Now, have a good time. Take in a newsreel. Go to the zoo. Go see

Sam Farley at three o'clock." He patted Evarts on the back and pushed him toward the door.

Evarts ate lunch at the Mentone with Alice and Mildred-Rose. He had a headache. After lunch, they walked up and down Fifth Avenue, and when it got close to three, Alice and Mildred-Rose walked with him to Sam Farley's house. It was an impressive building, faced with rough stone, like a Spanish prison. He kissed Mildred-Rose and Alice goodbye and rang the bell. A butler opened the door. Evarts could tell he was a butler because he wore striped pants. The butler led him upstairs to a drawing room.

"I'm here to see Mr. Farley," Evarts said.

"I know," the butler said. "You're Evarts Malloy. You've got an appointment. But he won't keep it. He's stuck in a floating crap game in the Acme Garage, at a Hundred and Sixty-fourth Street and he won't be back until tomorrow. Susan Hewitt's coming, though. You're supposed to see her. Oh, if you only knew what goes on in this place!" He lowered his voice to a whisper and brought his face close to Evarts'. "If these walls could only talk! There hasn't been any heat in this house since we came back from Hollywood and he hasn't paid me since the twenty-first of June. I wouldn't mind so much, but the son of a bitch has never learned to let the water out of his bathtub. He takes a bath and leaves the dirty water standing there. To stagnate. On top of everything else, I cut my finger washing dishes yesterday." There was a dirty bandage on the butler's forefinger, and he began, hurriedly, to unwrap layer after layer of bloody gauze. "Look," he said, holding the wound to Evarts' face. "Cut right through to the bone. Yesterday you could see the bone. Blood. Blood all over everything. Took me half an hour to clean up. It's a miracle I didn't get an infection." He shook his head at this miracle. "When the mouse comes, I'll send her up." He wandered out of the room, trailing the length of bloody bandage after him.

Evarts' eyes were burning with fatigue. He was so tired that if he had rested his head against anything, he would have

[63]

fallen asleep. He heard the doorbell ring and the butler greet Susan Hewitt. She ran up the stairs and into the drawing room.

She was young, and she came into the room as if it were her home and she had just come back from school. She was light, her features were delicate and very small, and her fair hair was brushed simply and had begun to darken, of its own course, and was streaked softly with brown, like the grain in pine wood. "I'm so happy to meet you, Evarts," she said. "I want to tell you that I love your play." How she could have read his play, Evarts did not know, but he was too confused by her beauty to worry or to speak. His mouth was dry. It might have been the antic pace of the last days, it might have been his loss of sleep—he didn't know—but he felt as though he had fallen in love.

"You remind me of a girl I used to know," he said. "She worked in a lunch wagon outside South Bend. Never worked in a lunch wagon outside South Bend, did you?"

"No," she said.

"It isn't only that," he said. "You remind me of all of it. I mean the night drives. I used to be a night bus driver. That's what you remind me of. The stars, I mean, and the grade crossings, and the cattle lined up along the fences. And the girls in the lunch counters. They always looked so pretty. But you never worked in a lunch counter."

"No," she said.

"You can have my play," he said. "I mean I think you're right for the part. Sam Farley can have the play. Everything."

"Thank you, Evarts," she said.

"Will you do me a favor?" he asked.

"What?"

"Oh, I know it's foolish," he said. He got up and walked around the room. "But there's nobody here, nobody will know about it. I hate to ask you."

"What do you want?"

"Will you let me lift you?" he said. "Just let me lift you. Just let me see how light you are."

[64]

"All right," she said. "Do you want me to take off my coat?"

"Yes, yes, yes," he said. "Take off your coat."

She stood. She let her coat fall to the sofa.

"Can I do it now?" he said.

"Yes."

He put his hands under her arms. He raised her off the floor and then put her down gently. "Oh, you're so light!" he shouted. "You're so light, you're so fragile, you don't weigh any more than a suitcase. Why, I could carry you, I could carry you anywhere, I could carry you from one end of New York to the other." He got his hat and coat and ran out of the house.

Evarts felt bewildered and exhausted when he returned to the Mentone. Bitsey was in the room with Mildred-Rose and Alice. He kept asking questions about Mama Finelli. He wanted to know where she lived and what her telephone number was. Evarts lost his temper at the bellboy and told him to go away. He lay down on the bed and fell asleep while Alice and Mildred-Rose were asking him questions. When he woke, an hour later, he felt much better. They went to the Automat and then to Radio City Music Hall, and they got to bed early, so that Evarts could work on his play in the morning. He couldn't sleep.

After breakfast, Alice and Mildred-Rose left Evarts alone in the room and he tried to work. He couldn't work, but it wasn't the telephone that troubled him that day. The difficulty that blocked his play was deep, and as he smoked and stared at the brick wall, he recognized it. He was in love with Susan Hewitt. This might have been an incentive to work, but he had left his creative strength in Indiana. He shut his eyes and tried to recall the strong, dissolute voice of Mama Finelli, but before he could realize a word, it would be lost in the noise from the street.

If there had been anything to set his memory free—a train whistle, a moment of silence, the smells of a barn—he might have been inspired. He paced the room, he smoked, he sniffed the sooty window curtains and stuffed his ears with toilet paper, but there seemed to be no way of recalling Indiana at the Mentone. He stayed near the desk all that day. He went without lunch. When his wife and child returned from Radio City Music Hall, where they had spent the afternoon, he told them he was going to take a walk. Oh, he thought as he left the hotel, if I could only hear the noise of a crow!

He strode up Fifth Avenue, holding his head high, trying to divine in the confusion of sound a voice that might lead him. He walked rapidly until he reached Radio City and could hear, in the distance, the music from the skating rink. Something stopped him. He lighted a cigarette. Then he heard someone calling him. "Behold the lordly moose, Evarts," a woman shouted. It was the hoarse, dissolute voice of Mama Finelli, and he thought that desire had deranged him until he turned and saw her, sitting on one of the benches, by a dry pool. "Behold the lordly moose, Evarts," she called, and she put her hands, spread like antlers, above her head. This was the way she greeted everyone in Wentworth.

"Behold the lordly moose, Mama Finelli," Evarts shouted. He ran to her side and sat down. "Oh, Mama Finelli, I'm so glad to see you," he said. "You won't believe it, but I've been thinking about you all day. I've been wishing all day that I could talk with you." He turned to drink in her vulpine features and her whiskery chin. "How did you ever get to New York, Mama Finelli?"

"Come up on a flying machine," she cried. "Come up on a flying machine today. Have a sandwich." She was eating some sandwiches from a paper bag.

"No, thanks," he said. "What do you think of New York?" he asked. "What do you think of that high building?"

"Well, I don't know," she said, but he could see that she did know and he could see her working her face into shape for a retort. "I guess there's just but the one, for if there hada been two, they'd of pollinated and bore!" She whooped with laughter and struck herself on the legs.

[66]

"What are you doing in New York, Mama Finelli? How did you happen to come here?"

"Well," she said, "man named Tracey Murchison calls me on the telephone long distance and says for me to come up to New York and sue you for libel. Says you wrote a play about me and I can sue you for libel and git a lot of money and split it with him, fairly, he says, and then I don't have to run the gas station no more. So he wires me money for the flying-machine ticket and I come up here and I talk with him and I'm going to sue you for libel and split it with him, sixty-forty. That's what I'm going to do," she said.

Later that night, the Malloys returned to the marble waiting room of Grand Central and Evarts began to search for a Chicago train. He found a Chicago train, bought some tickets, and they boarded a coach. It was a rainy night, and the dark, wet paving, deep in the station, did not glitter, but it was still Alice's belief that diamonds had been ground into it, and that was the way she would tell the story. They had picked up the lessons of travel rapidly, and they arranged themselves adroitly over several seats. After the train started, Alice made friends with a plain-spoken couple across the aisle, who were travelling with a baby to Los Angeles. The woman had a brother there, who had written to her enthusiastically about the climate and the opportunities.

"Let's go to Los Angeles," Alice said to Evarts. "We still have a little money and we can buy tickets in Chicago and you can sell your play in Hollywood, where nobody's ever heard of Mama Finelli or any of the others."

Evarts said that he would make his decision in Chicago. He was weary and he fell asleep. Mildred-Rose put her thumb into her mouth, and soon both she and her mother had lost consciousness, too. Mildred-Rose stroked the sere skins of her coat and they told her that all was well, all was well.

The Malloys may have left the train in Chicago and gone back to Wentworth. It is not hard to imagine their homecoming, for they would be welcomed by their friends and relations, although their stories might not be believed. Or they may have changed, at Chicago, for a train to the West, and this, to tell the truth, is easier to imagine. One can see them playing hearts in the lounge car and eating cheese sandwiches in the railroad stations as they travelled through Kansas and Nebraska—over the mountains and on to the Coast.

THE CHILDREN

MR. HATHERLY had many old-fashioned tastes. He wore high yellow boots, dined at Luchow's in order to hear the music, and slept in a woollen nightshirt. His urge to establish in business a patriarchal liaison with some young man who would serve as his descendant, in the fullest sense of the word, was another of these old-fashioned tastes. Mr. Hatherly picked for his heir a young immigrant named Victor Mackenzie, who had made the crossing from England or Scotland—a winter crossing, I think—when he was sixteen or seventeen. The winter crossing is a guess. He may have worked his way or borrowed passage money or had some relation in this country to help him, but all this was kept in the dark, and his known life began when he went to work for Mr. Hatherly. As an immigrant, Victor may have cherished an obsolete vision of the American businessman. Here and there one saw in Mr. Hatherly a touch of obsolescence. His beginnings were obscure, and, as everyone knows, he got rich enough to be an ambassador. In business, he was known as a harsh and unprincipled trader. He broke wind when he felt like it and relished the ruin of a competitor. He was very short—nearly a dwarf. His legs were spindly and his large belly had pulled his spine out of shape. He decorated his bald skull by combing across it a few threads of gray hair, and he wore an emerald fob on his watch chain. Victor was a tall man, with the kind of handsomeness that is sooner or later disappointing. His square jaw and all his other nicely proportioned features might at first have led you to expect a man of exceptional gifts of character, but you felt in the end that he was merely pleasant, ambitious, and a little ingenuous. For years, this curmudgeon and the young immigrant walked side by side confidently, as if they might have been accepted in the ark.

Of course, it all took a long time; it took years and years. Victor began as an office boy with a hole in his sock. Like the immigrants of an earlier generation, he had released great stores of energy and naïveness through the act of expatriation. He worked cheerfully all day. He stayed cheerfully at night to decorate the showcases in the waiting room. He seemed to have no home to go to. His eagerness reminded Mr. Hatherly, happily, of the apprentices of his own youth. There was little enough in business that did remind him of the past. He kept Victor in his place for a year or two, speaking to him harshly if he spoke to him at all. Then in his crabbed and arbitrary way he began to instruct Victor in the role of an heir. Victor was sent on the road for six months. After this he worked in the Rhode Island mills. He spent a season in the advertising department and another in the sales division. His position in the business was difficult to assess, but his promotions in Mr. Hatherly's esteem were striking. Mr. Hatherly was sensitive about the odd figure he cut, and disliked going anywhere alone. When Victor had worked with him for a few years, he was ordered to get to the old man's apartment, on upper Fifth Avenue, at eight each morning and walk him to work. They never talked much along the way, but then Hatherly was not loquacious. At the close of the business day, Victor either put him into a taxi or walked him home. When the old man went off to Bar Harbor without his eyeglasses, it was Victor who got up in the middle of the night and put the glasses on the early-morning plane. When the old man wanted to send a wedding present, it was Victor who bought it. When the old man was ailing, it was Victor who got him to take his medicine. In the gossip of the trade Victor's position was naturally the target for a lot of jocularity, criticism, and downright jealousy. Much of the criticism was unfair, for he was merely an ambitious young man who expressed his sense of business enterprise by feeding pills to Mr. Hatherly. Running through all his ame-nability was an altogether charming sense of his own identity. When he felt that he had grounds for complaint, he said so. After working for eight years under Mr. Hatherly's thumb, he went to the old man and said that he thought his salary was inadequate. The old man rallied with a masterful blend of in-jury, astonishment, and tenderness. He took Victor to his tailor and let him order four suits. A few months later, Victor again complained—this time about the vagueness of his position in the firm. He was hasty, the old man said, in objecting to his lack of responsibility. He was scheduled to make a presentation, in a week or two, before the board of directors. This was more than Victor had expected, and he was content. Indeed, he was grateful. This was America! He worked hard over his presenta-tion. He read it aloud to the old man, and Mr. Hatherly in-structed him when to raise and when to lower his voice, whose eye to catch and whose to evade, when to strike the table and when to pour himself a glass of water. They discussed the cloth-ing that he would wear. Five minutes before the directors' meeting began, Mr. Hatherly seized the papers, slammed the door in Victor's face, and made the presentation himself.

He called Victor into his office at the end of that trying day. It was past six, and the secretaries had locked up their teacups and gone home. "I'm sorry about the presentation," the old man mumbled. His voice was heavy. Then Victor saw that he had been crying. The old man slipped off the high desk chair that he used to increase his height and walked around the large office. This was, in itself, a demonstration of intimacy and trust. "But that isn't what I want to talk about," he said. "I want to talk about my family. Oh there's no misery worse than bad blood in a family! My wife"—he spoke with disgust—"is a stupid woman. The hours of pleasure I've had from my children I can count on the fingers of one hand. It may be my fault," he said, with manifest insincerity. "What I want you to do now is to help me with my boy, Junior. I've brought Junior up to respect money. I made him earn every nickel he got until he was sixteen, so it isn't my fault that he's a damn fool with money, but he is. I just don't have the time to bother with his bad checks any more. I'm a busy man. You know that. What I want you to do is act as Junior's business adviser. I want you to pay his rent, pay his alimony, pay his maid, pay his household expenses, and give him a cash allowance once a week."

For a moment, anyhow, Victor seemed to breathe the freshness of a considerable skepticism. He had been cheated, that afternoon, out of a vital responsibility and was being burdened now with a foolish one. The tears could be hypocritical. The fact that this request was made to him in a building that had been emptied and was unnaturally quiet and at a time of day when the fading light outside the windows might help to bend his decision were all tricks in the old man's hand. But, even seen skeptically, the hold that Hatherly had on him was complete. "Mr. Hatherly told me to tell you," Victor could always say. "I come from Mr. Hatherly." "Mr. Hatherly . . ." Without this coupling of names his own voice would sound powerless. The comfortable and becoming shirt whose cuffs he shot in indecision had been given to him by Mr. Hatherly. Mr. Hatherly had introduced him into the 7th Regiment. Mr. Hatherly was his only business identity, and to separate himself from this source of power might be mortal. He didn't reply.

"I'm sorry about the presentation," the old man repeated. "I'll see that you make one next year. Promise." He gave his shoulders a hitch to show that he was moving on from this subject to another. "Meet me at the Metropolitan Club tomorrow at two," he said briskly. "I have to buy out Worden at lunch. That won't take long. I hope he brings his lawyer with him. Call his lawyer in the morning and make sure that his papers are in order. Give him hell for me. You know how to do it. You'll help me a great deal by taking care of Junior," he said

with great feeling. "And take care of yourself, Victor. You're
all I have."

After lunch the next day, the old man's lawyer met them at
the Metropolitan Club and went with them to an apartment,
where Junior was waiting. He was a thickset man a good ten
years older than Victor, and he seemed resigned to having his
income taken out of his hands. He called Mr. Hatherly Poppa
and sadly handed over to his father a bundle of unpaid bills.
With Victor and the lawyer, Mr. Hatherly computed Junior's
income and his indebtedness, took into consideration his alimony payments, and arrived at a reasonable estimate for his
household expenses and the size of his allowance, which he was
to get at Victor's office each Monday morning. Junior's goose
was cooked in half an hour.

He came around for his allowance every Monday morning
and submitted his household bills to Victor. He sometimes hung
around the office and talked about his father—uneasily, as if he
might be overheard. All the minutiae of Mr. Hatherly's life—
that he was sometimes shaved three times a day and that he
owned fifty pairs of shoes—interested Victor. It was the old
man who cut these interviews short. "Tell him to come in and
get his money and go," the old man said. "This is a business
office. That's something he's never understood."

Meanwhile, Victor had met Theresa and was thinking of
getting married. Her full name was Theresa Mercereau; her
parents were French but she had been born in the United States.
Her parents had died when she was young, and her guardian
had put her into fourth-string boarding schools. One knows
what these places are like. The headmaster resigns over the
Christmas holidays. He is replaced by the gymnastics instructor. The heating plant breaks down in February and the water
pipes freeze. By this time, most of the parents who are concerned about their children have transferred them to other
schools, and by spring there are only twelve or thirteen board-
ers left. They wander singly or in pairs around the campus,
killing time before supper. It has been apparent to them for

months that Old Palfrey Academy is dying, but in the first long, bleakly lighted days of spring this fact assumes new poignancy and force. The noise of a quarrel comes from the headmaster's quarters, where the Latin instructor is threatening to sue for back wages. The smell from the kitchen windows indicates that there will be cabbage again. A few jonquils are in bloom, and the lingering light and the new ferns enjoin the stranded children to look ahead, ahead, but at the back of their minds there is a suspicion that the jonquils and the robins and the evening star imperfectly conceal the fact that this hour is horror, naked horror. Then a car roars up the driveway. "I am Mrs. Hubert Jones," a woman exclaims, "and I have come to get my daughter . . ." Theresa was always one of the last to be rescued, and these hours seemed to have left some impression on her. It was the quality of an especial sadness, a delicacy that was never forlorn, a charming air of having been wronged, that one remembered about her.

That winter, Victor went to Florida with Mr. Hatherly to hoist his beach umbrella and play rummy with him, and while they were there he said that he wanted to get married. The old man yelled his objections. Victor stood his ground. When they returned to New York, the old man invited Victor to bring Theresa to his apartment one evening. He greeted the young woman with great cordiality and then introduced her to Mrs. Hatherly—a wasted and nervous woman who kept her hands at her mouth. The old man began to prowl around the edges of the room. Then he disappeared. "It's all right," Mrs. Hatherly whispered. "He's going to give you a present." He returned in a few minutes and hung a string of amethysts around Theresa's beautiful neck. Once the old man had accepted her, he seemed happy about the marriage. He made all the arrangements for the wedding, of course, told them where to go for a honeymoon, and rented and furnished an apartment for them one day between a business lunch and a plane to California. Theresa seemed, like her husband, to be able to accommodate his interference. When her first child was born, she named it

Violet—this was her own idea—after Mr. Hatherly's sainted
mother.

When the Mackenzies gave a party, in those years, it was
usually because Mr. Hatherly had told them to give a party.
He would call Victor into his office at the end of the day, tell
him to entertain, and set a date. He would order the liquor and
the food, and overhaul the guest list with the Mackenzies' business and social welfare in mind. He would rudely refuse an
invitation to come to the party himself, but he would appear
before any of the guests, carrying a bunch of flowers that was
nearly as tall as he was. He would make sure that Theresa put
the flowers in the right vase. Then he would go into the
nursery and let Violet listen to his watch. He would go through
the apartment, moving a lamp here or an ashtray there and
giving the curtains a poke. By this time the Mackenzies' guests
would have begun to arrive, but Mr. Hatherly would show no
signs of going. He was a distinguished old man and everyone
liked to talk with him. He would circle the room, making sure
that all the glasses were filled, and if Victor told an anecdote,
the chances were that Mr. Hatherly had drilled him in how to
tell it. When the supper was served, the old man would be
anxious about the food and the way the maids looked.

He was always the last to go. When the other guests had said
good night, he would settle down and all three would have a
glass of milk and talk about the evening. Then the old man
would seem happy—with a kind of merriment that his enemies
would never have believed him capable of. He would laugh
until the tears rolled down his cheeks. He sometimes took off
his boots.The small room seemed to be the only room in which
he was content, but it must always have been at the back of
Mr. Hatherly's mind that these young people were in substance
nothing to him, and that it was because his own flesh and blood
had been such a bitter disappointment that he found himself
in so artificial a position. At last he would get up to go. Theresa
would straighten the knot in his tie, brush the crumbs off his
vest, and bend down to be kissed. Victor would help him into

[75]

THE CHILDREN

his fur coat. All three of them would be deep in the tenderness of a family parting. "Take good care of yourselves," the old man would mumble. "You're all I have."

One night, after a party at the Mackenzies, Mr. Hatherly died in his sleep. The funeral was in Worcester, where he was born. The family seemed inclined to keep the arrangements from Victor, but he found out what they were easily enough, and went, with Theresa, to the church and the cemetery. Old Mrs. Hatherly and her unhappy children gathered at the edge of the grave. They must have watched the old man's burial with such conflicting feelings that it would be impossible to extricate from the emotional confusion anything that could be named. "Goodbye, goodbye," Mrs. Hatherly called, halfheartedly, across the earth, and her hands flew to her lips—a habit that she had never been able to break, although the dead man had often threatened to strike her for it. If the full taste of grief is a privilege, this was now the privilege of the Mackenzies. They were crushed. Theresa had been too young when her parents died for her to have, as a grown person, any clear memories of grieving for them, and Victor's parents—whoever they were—had died a few years back, in England or Scotland, and it seemed at Hatherly's grave that she and Victor were in the throes of an accrual of grief and that they were burying more than the bones of one old man. The real children cut the Mackenzies.

The Mackenzies were indifferent to the fact that they were not mentioned in Mr. Hatherly's will. A week or so after the funeral, the directors elected Junior to the presidency of the firm, and one of the first things he did was to fire Victor. He had been compared with this industrious immigrant for years, and his resentment was understandable and deep. Victor found another job, but his intimate association with Mr. Hatherly was held against him in the trade. The old man had a host of enemies, and Victor inherited them all. He lost his new job after six or eight months, and found another that he regarded as temporary—an arrangement that would enable him to meet

his monthly bills while he looked around for something better.
Nothing better turned up. He and Theresa gave up the apartment that Mr. Hatherly had taken for them, sold all their furniture, and moved around from place to place, but all this—
the ugly rooms they lived in, the succession of jobs that Victor
took—is not worth going into. To put it simply, the Mackenzies
had some hard times; the Mackenzies dropped out of sight.

The scene changes to a fund-raising party for the Girl Scouts
of America, in a suburb of Pittsburgh. It is a black-tie dance in
a large house—Salisbury Hall—that has been picked by the
dance committee with the hope that idle curiosity about this
edifice will induce a lot of people to buy the twenty-five-dollar
tickets. Mrs. Brownlee, the nominal hostess, is the widow of a
pioneer steel magnate. Her house is strung for half a mile along
the spine of one of the Allegheny hills. Salisbury Hall is a
castle, or, rather, a collection of parts of castles and houses.
There is a tower, a battlement, and a dungeon, and the postern
gate is a reproduction of the gate at Château Gaillard. The
stones and timber for the Great Hall and the armory were
brought from abroad. Like most houses of its kind, Salisbury
Hall presents insuperable problems of maintenance. Touch a
suit of chain mail in the armory and your hand comes away
black with rust. The copy of a Mantegna fresco in the ballroom
is horribly stained with water. But the party is a success. A
hundred couples are dancing. The band is playing a rhumba.
The Mackenzies are here.

Theresa is dancing. Her hair is still fair—it may be dyed by
now—and her arms and her shoulders are still beautiful. The
air of sadness, of delicacy, still clings to her. Victor is not on
the dance floor. He is in the orangery, where watery drinks are
being sold. He pays for four drinks, walks around the edge of
the crowded dance floor, and goes through the armory, where
a stranger stops to ask him a question. "Why yes," Victor says
courteously, "I do happen to know about it. It's a suit of mail
that was made for the coronation of Philip II. Mr. Brownlee

had it copied . . ." He continues along another quarter of a mile of halls and parlors, through the Great Hall, to a small parlor, where Mrs. Brownlee is sitting with some friends. "Here's Vic with our drinks!" she cries. Mrs. Brownlee is an old lady, plucked and painted and with her hair dyed an astonishing shade of pink. Her fingers and her forearms are loaded with rings and bracelets. Her diamond necklace is famous. So, indeed, are most of her jewels—most of them have names. There are the Taphir emeralds, the Bertoloti rubies, and the Demidoff pearls, and, feeling that a look at this miscellany should be included in the price of admission, she has loaded herself unsparingly for the benefit of the Girl Scouts. "Everybody's having a good time, aren't they, Vic?" she asks. "Well, they should be having a good time. My house has always been known for its atmosphere of hospitality as well as for its wealth of artistic treasures. Sit down, Vic," she says. "Sit down. Give yourself a little rest. I don't know what I'd do without you and Theresa." But Victor doesn't have time to sit down. He has to run the raffle. He goes back through the Great Hall, the Venetian Salon, and the armory, to the ballroom. He climbs onto a chair. There is a flourish of music. "Ladies and gentlemen!" he calls through a megaphone. "Ladies and gentlemen, can I have your attention for a few minutes . . ." He raffles off a case of Scotch, a case of bourbon, a Waring Mixer, and a power lawn mower. When the raffle is over and the dancing begins again, he goes out onto the terrace for a breath of air, and we follow him and speak to him there.

"Victor?"

"Oh, how nice to see you again," he exclaims. "What in the world are you doing in Pittsburgh?" His hair has grayed along conventionally handsome lines. He must have had some work done on his teeth, because his smile is whiter and more dazzling than ever. The talk is the conversation of acquaintances who have not met for ten or fifteen years—it has been that long— about this and that, then about Theresa, then about Violet. At the mention of Violet, he seems very sad. He sets the mega-

phone on the stone terrace and leans on its metal rim. He bows
his head. "Well, Violet is sixteen now, you know," he says.
"She's given me a lot to worry about. She was suspended from
school about six weeks ago. Now I've got her into a new school
in Connecticut. It took a lot of doing." He sniffs.

"How long have you been in Pittsburgh, Victor?"

"Eight years," he says. He swings the megaphone into the
air and peers through it at a star. "Nine, actually," he says.

"What are you doing, Victor?"

"I'm between jobs now." He lets the megaphone fall.

"Where are you living, Victor?"

"Here," he says.

"I know. But where in Pittsburgh?"

"Here," he says. He laughs. "We live here. At Salisbury Hall.
Here's the head of the dance committee, and if you'll excuse
me, I'll make my report on the raffle. It's been very nice to see
you again."

Anyone—anyone, that is, who did not eat peas off a knife—
might have been invited to Salisbury Hall when the Mackenzies first went there. They had only just arrived in Pittsburgh,
and were living in a hotel. They drove out with some friends
for a weekend. There were fourteen or fifteen guests in the
party, and Prescott Brownlee, the old lady's eldest son. There
was some trouble before dinner. Prescott got drunk at a roadhouse near the estate, and the bartender called Mrs. Brownlee
and told her to have him removed before he called the police.
The old lady was used to this kind of trouble. Her children
were in it most of the time, but that afternoon she did not know
where to turn for help. Nils, the houseman, hated Prescott. The
gardener had gone home. Ernest, the butler, was too old. Then
she remembered Victor's face, although she had only glimpsed
it in the hall when they were introduced. She found him in the
Great Hall and called him aside. He thought he was going to
be asked to mix the cocktails. When she made her request, he
said that he would be glad to help. He drove to the roadhouse,

where he found Prescott sitting at a table. Someone had given him a bloody nose, and his clothing was splattered with blood, but he was still pugnacious, and when Victor told him to come home, he got up swinging. Victor knocked him down. This subdued Prescott, who began to cry and stumbled obediently out to the car. Victor returned to Salisbury Hall by a service driveway. Then, supporting Prescott, who could not walk, he got him into a side door that opened into the armory. No one saw them. The air in the unheated room was harsh and bitter. Victor pushed the sobbing drunk under the rags of royal battle flags and pennants that hung from the rafters and past a statue of a man on horseback that displayed a suit of equestrian armor. He got Prescott up a marble staircase and put him to bed. Then he brushed the sawdust off his own evening clothes and went down to the Great Hall and made the cocktails.

He didn't mention this incident to anyone—not even to Theresa—and on Sunday afternoon Mrs. Brownlee took him aside again, to thank him. "Oh, bless your heart, Mr. Mackenzie!" she said. "You're a good Samaritan. When that man called me up yesterday, I didn't know where to turn." They heard someone approaching across the Great Hall. It was Prescott. He had shaved, dressed his wounds, and soaked his hair down with water, but he was drunk again. "Going to New York," he mumbled to his mother. "Ernest's going to drive me to the plane. *See* you." He turned and wandered back across the library into the Venetian Salon and out of sight, and his mother set her teeth as she watched him go. Then she seized Victor's hand and said, "I want you and your lovely wife to come and live at Salisbury Hall. I know that you're living in a hotel. My house has always been known for its atmosphere of hospitality as well as for its wealth of artistic treasures. You'll be doing me a favor. That's what it amounts to."

The Mackenzies gracefully declined her offer and returned to Pittsburgh on Sunday night. A few days later, the old lady, hearing that Theresa was sick in bed, sent flowers, and a note repeating her invitation. The Mackenzies discussed it that night.

[80]

"We must think of it as a business arrangement, if we think
of it at all," Victor said. "We must think of it as the practical
answer to a practical problem." Theresa had always been frail,
and living in the country would be good for her. This was the
first thing they thought of. Victor had a job in town, but he
could commute from the railroad station nearest Salisbury Hall.
They talked with Mrs. Brownlee again and got her to agree to
accept from them what they would have paid for rent and food,
so that the arrangement would be kept impersonal. Then they
moved into a suite of rooms above the Great Hall.

It worked out very well. Their rooms were large and quiet,
and the relationship with Mrs. Brownlee was easy-going. Any
sense of obligation they may have felt was dispelled by their
knowing that they were useful to their hostess in a hundred
ways. She needed a man around the place, and who else would
want to live in Salisbury Hall? Except for gala occasions, more
than half the rooms were shut, and there were not enough servants to intimidate the rats that lived in the basement. Theresa
undertook the herculean task of repairing Mrs. Brownlee's needle point; there were eighty-six pieces. The tennis court at
Salisbury Hall had been neglected since the war, and Victor,
on his weekends, weeded and rolled it and got it in shape again.
He absorbed a lot of information about Mrs. Brownlee's house
and her scattered family, and when she was too tired to take
interested guests around the place, he was always happy to.
"This hall," he would say, "was removed panel by panel and
stone by stone from a Tudor house near the cathedral in Salisbury. . . . The marble floor is part of the lobby floor of the
old First National Bank. . . . Mr. Brownlee gave Mrs. Brownlee the Venetian Salon as a birthday present, and these four
columns of solid onyx came from the ruins of Herculaneum.
They were floated down Lake Erie from Buffalo to Ashta-
bula. . . ." Victor could also point out the scar on a tree where
Spencer Brownlee had wrecked his car, and the rose garden that
had been planted for Hester Brownlee when she was so sick.

[81]

We have seen how helpful he was on occasions like the dance for the Girl Scout fund.

Violet was away in camps and schools. "Why do you live here?" she asked the first time she came to visit her parents in Salisbury Hall. "What a moldy old wreck! What a regular junk heap!" Mrs. Brownlee may have heard Violet laughing at her house. In any event, she took a violent dislike to the Mackenzies' only child, and Violet's visits were infrequent and brief. The only one of Mrs. Brownlee's children who returned from time to time was Prescott. Then, one evening not long after the Girl Scout dance, Mrs. Brownlee got a wire from her daughter Hester, who had been living in Europe for fifteen years. She had arrived in New York and was coming on to Pittsburgh the following day.

Mrs. Brownlee told the Mackenzies the good news at dinner. She was transported. "Oh, you'll love Hester," she said. "You'll both love her! She was always just like Dresden china. She was sickly when she was a child and I guess that's why she's always been my favorite. Oh, I hope she'll stay! I wish there was time to have her rooms painted! You must urge her to stay, Victor. It would make me so happy. You urge her to stay. I think she'll like you."

Mrs. Brownlee's words echoed through a dining room that had the proportions of a gymnasium; their small table was pushed against a window and separated from the rest of the room by a screen, and the Mackenzies liked to have dinner there. The window looked down the lawns and stairways to the ruin of a formal garden. The iron lace on the roof of the broken greenhouses, the noise of the fountains whose basins were disfigured and cracked, the rattle of the dumbwaiter that brought their tasteless dinner up from the basement kitchens, where the rats lived—the Mackenzies regarded all this foolishness with the deepest respect, as if it had some genuine significance. They may have suffered from an indiscriminate sense of the past or from an inability to understand that the past plays no part in our happiness. A few days earlier, Theresa had stumbled into a third-floor bedroom that was full of old bon-voyage baskets—gilded, and looped with dog-eared ribbons—that had been saved from Mrs. Brownlee's many voyages.

While Mrs. Brownlee talked about Hester that evening, she kept her eye on the garden and saw, in the distance, a man climbing over one of the marble walls. Then a girl handed him down a blanket, a picnic hamper, and a bottle, and jumped into his arms. They were followed by two more couples. They settled themselves in the Temple of Love and, gathering a pile of broken latticework, built a little fire.

"Drive them away, Victor," Mrs. Brownlee said.

Victor left the table and crossed the terrace and went down to the garden and told the party to go.

"I happen to be a very good friend of Mrs. Brownlee's," one of the men said.

"That doesn't matter," Victor said. "You'll have to get out."

"Who says so?"

"I say so."

"Who are you?"

Victor didn't answer. He broke up their fire and stamped out the embers. He was outnumbered and outweighed, and he knew that if it came to a fight, he would probably get hurt, but the smoke from the extinguished fire drove the party out of the temple and gave Victor an advantage. He stood on a flight of steps above them and looked at his watch. "I'll give you five minutes to get over the wall and out," he said.

"But I'm a friend of Mrs. Brownlee's!"

"If you're a friend of Mrs. Brownlee's," Victor said, "come in the front way. I give you five minutes." They started down the path toward the wall, and Victor waited until one of the girls—they were all pretty—had been hoisted over it. Then he went back to the table and finished his dinner while Mrs. Brownlee talked on and on about Little Hester.

The next day was Saturday, but Victor spent most of it in Pittsburgh, looking for work. He didn't get out to Salisbury Hall until about four, and he was hot and dirty. When he stepped into the Great Hall, he saw that the doors onto the terrace were open and the florist's men were unloading a truck full of tubbed orange trees. A maid came up to him excitedly. "Nils is sick and can't drive!" she exclaimed. "Mrs. Brownlee wants you to go down to the station and meet Miss Hester. You'd better hurry. She's coming on the four-fifteen. She doesn't want you to take your car. She wants you to take the Rolls-Royce. She says you have permission to take the Rolls-Royce."

The four-fifteen had come and gone by the time Victor arrived at the station. Hester Brownlee was standing in the waiting room, surrounded by her luggage. She was a middle-aged woman who had persevered with her looks, and might at a distance have seemed pretty. "How do you do, Miss Brownlee?" Victor said. "I'm Victor Mackenzie. I'm—"

"Yes, I know," she said. "I've heard all about you from Prescott." She looked past his shoulder. "You're late."

"I'm sorry," Victor said, "but your mother—"

"These are my bags," she said. She walked out to the Rolls-Royce and got into the back seat.

Victor lighted a cigarette and smoked it halfway down. Then he carried her bags out to the car and started home to Salisbury Hall along a back road.

"You're going the wrong way," Miss Brownlee called. "Don't you *even* know the way?"

"I'm not going the usual way," Victor said patiently, "but a few years ago they built a factory down the road, and the traffic is heavy around closing time. It's quicker this way. But I expect that you'll find a good many changes in the neighborhood. How long has it been, Miss Brownlee, since you've seen Salisbury Hall?" There was no answer to his question, and, thinking that she might not have heard him, he asked again, "How long has it been, Miss Brownlee, since you've seen Salisbury Hall?"

They made the rest of the trip in silence. When they got to the house, Victor unloaded her bags and stood them by the door. Miss Brownlee counted them aloud. Then she opened her

purse and handed Victor a quarter. "Why, thank you!" Victor
said. "Thank you *very* much!" He went down into the garden
to walk off his anger. He decided not to tell Theresa about this
meeting. Finally, he went upstairs. Theresa was at work on one
of the needle-point stools. The room they used for a parlor was
cluttered with half-repaired needle point. She embraced Victor
tenderly, as she always did when they had been separated for
a day. Victor had dressed when a maid knocked on the door.
"Mrs. Brownlee wants to see you, both of you," she said. "She's
in the office. At once."

Theresa clung to Victor's arm as they went downstairs. The
office, a cluttered and dirty room beside the elevator, was
brightly lighted. Mrs. Brownlee, in *grande tenue,* sat at her
husband's desk. "You're the straw that broke the camel's back
—both of you," she said harshly when they came in. "Shut the
door. I don't want everybody to hear me. Little Hester has come
home for the first time in fifteen years, and the first thing she
gets off the train, you have to insult her. For nine years, you've
had the privilege of living in this beautiful house—a wonder of
the world—and how do you repay me? Oh, it's the straw that
breaks the camel's back! Prescott's told me often enough that
you weren't any good, either of you, and Hester feels the same
way, and gradually I'm beginning to see it myself."

The harried and garishly painted old lady wielded over the
Mackenzies the power of angels. Her silver dress glittered like
Saint Michael's raiment, and thunder and lightning, death and
destruction, were in her right hand. "Everybody's been warning me about you for years," she said. "And you may not mean
to do wrong—you may just be unlucky—but one of the first
things Hester noticed is that half the needle point is missing.
You're always repairing the chair that I want to sit down in.
And you, Victor—you told me that you fixed the tennis court,
and, of course, I don't know about that because I can't play
tennis, but when I asked the Beardons over to play tennis last
week, they told me that the court wasn't fit to play on, and you
can imagine how embarrassed I was, and those people you

[85]

drove out of the garden last night turned out to be the children of a very dear friend of the late Mr. Brownlee's. And you're two weeks behind with your rent."

"I'll send you the rent," Victor said. "We will go."

Theresa had not taken her arm out of his during the interview, and they left the office together. It was raining, and Ernest was putting out pails in the Venetian Salon, where the domed ceiling had sprung a leak. "Could you help me with some suitcases?" Victor asked. The old butler must have overheard the interview, because he didn't answer.

There was in the Mackenzies' rooms an accumulation of sentimental possessions—photographs, pieces of silver, and so forth. Theresa hastily began to gather these up. Victor went down to the basement and got their bags. They packed hurriedly—they did not even stop to smoke a cigarette—but it took them most of the evening. When they had finished, Theresa stripped the bed and put the soiled towels into a hamper, and Victor carried the bags down. He wrote a postcard to Violet's school, saying that his address was no longer Salisbury Hall. He waited for Theresa by the front door. "Oh, my darling, where will we go?" she murmured when she met him there. She waited in the rain for him to bring their car around, and they drove away, and God knows where they did go after that.

God knows where they went after that, but for our purposes they next appeared, years later, at a resort on the coast of Maine called Horsetail Beach. Victor had some kind of job in New York, and they had driven to Maine for his vacation. Violet was not with them. She had married and was living in San Francisco. She had a baby. She did not write to her parents, and Victor knew that she thought of him with bitter resentment, although he did not know why. This waywardness of their only child troubled Victor and Theresa, but they could seldom bring themselves to discuss it. Helen Jackson, their hostess at Horsetail Beach, was a spirited young woman with four children. She was divorced. Her house was tracked with sand, and most of the furniture was broken. The Mackenzies arrived there on a stormy evening when the north wind blew straight through the walls of the house. Their hostess was out to dinner, and as soon as they arrived, the cook put on her hat and coat and went off to the movies, leaving them in charge of the children. They carried their bags upstairs, stepping over several wet bathing suits, put the four children to bed, and settled themselves in a cold guest room.

In the morning, their hostess asked them if they minded if she drove into Camden to get her hair washed. She was giving a cocktail party for the Mackenzies that afternoon, although it was the cook's day off. She promised to be back by noon, and when she had not returned by one, Theresa cooked lunch. At three, their hostess telephoned from Camden to say that she had just left the hairdresser's and would Theresa mind getting a head start with the canapés? Theresa made the canapés. Then she swept the sand out of the living room and picked up the wet bathing suits. Helen Jackson finally returned from Camden, and the guests began to arrive at five. It was cold and stormy. Victor shivered in his white silk suit. Most of the guests were young, and they refused cocktails and drank ginger ale, gathered around the piano, and sang. It was not the Mackenzies' idea of a good party. Helen Jackson tried unsuccessfully to draw them into the circle of hearty, if meaningless, smiles, salutations, and handshakes upon which that party, like every other, was rigged. The guests all left at half past six, and the Mackenzies and their hostess made a supper of leftover canapés. "Would you mind dreadfully taking the children to the movies?" Helen Jackson asked Victor. "I promised them they could go to the movies if they were good about the party, and they've been perfect angels, and I hate to disappoint them, and I'm dead myself."

The next morning, it was still raining. Victor could see by his wife's face that the house and the weather were a drain on her strength. Most of us are inured to the inconveniences of a summer house in a cold rain, but Theresa was not. The power that the iron bedsteads and the paper window curtains had on her spirit was out of proportion, as if these were not ugly objects in themselves but threatened to overwhelm her common sense. At breakfast, their hostess suggested that they take a drive in the rain. "I know that it's vile out," she said, "but you could drive to Camden, and it's a way of killing time, isn't it, and you go through a lot of enchanting little villages, and if you did go down to Camden, you could go to the rental library and get *The Silver Chalice*. They've been reserving it for days and days, and I never find the time to get it. The rental library is on Estrella Lane." The Mackenzies drove to Camden and got *The Silver Chalice*. When they returned, there was another chore for Victor. The battery in Helen Jackson's car was dead. He took it to the garage and got a rental battery and installed it. Then, in spite of the weather, he tried to go swimming, but the waves were high and full of gravel, and after diving once he gave up and went back to the house. When he walked into the guest room in his wet bathing trunks, Theresa raised her face and he saw that it was stained with tears. "Oh, my darling," she said, "I'm homesick."

It was, even for Victor, a difficult remark to interpret. Their only home then was a one-room apartment in the city, which, with its kitchenette and studio couch, seemed oddly youthful and transitory for these grandparents. If Theresa was homesick, it could only be for a collection of parts of houses. She must have meant something else.

"Then we'll go," he said. "We'll leave the first thing in the morning." And then, seeing how happy his words had made her, he went on. "We'll get into the car and we'll drive and we'll drive and we'll drive. We'll go to Canada."

When they told Helen Jackson, at dinner, that they were leaving in the morning, she seemed relieved. She got out a road map and marked with a pencil the best route up through the mountains to Ste. Marie and the border. The Mackenzies packed after dinner and left early in the morning. Helen came out to the driveway to say goodbye. She was wearing her wrapper and carrying a silver coffeepot. "It's been perfectly lovely to have you," she said, "even if the weather has been so vile and disagreeable and horrid, and since you've decided to go through Ste. Marie, would you mind terribly stopping for a minute and returning Aunt Marly's silver coffeepot? I borrowed it years ago, and she's been writing me threatening letters and telephoning, and you can just leave it on the doorstep and run. Her name is Mrs. Sauer. The house is near the main road." She gave the Mackenzies some sketchy directions, kissed Theresa, and handed her the coffeepot. "It's been simply wonderful having you," she called as they drove away.

The waves at Horsetail Beach were still high and the wind was cold when the Mackenzies turned their back on the Atlantic Ocean. The noise and the smell of the sea faded. Inland, the sky seemed to be clearing. The wind was westerly and the overcast began to be displaced with light and motion. The Mackenzies came into hilly farmland. It was country they had never seen before, and as the massive clouds broke and the dilated light poured onto it, Theresa felt her spirits rising. She felt as if she were in a house on the Mediterranean, opening doors and windows. It was a house that she had never been in. She had only seen a picture of it, years ago, on a postcard. The saffron walls of the house continued straight down into the blue water, and all the doors and windows were shut. Now she was opening them. It was at the beginning of summer. She was opening doors and windows, and, leaning into the light from one of the highest, she saw a single sail, disappearing in the direction of Africa, carrying the wicked King away. How else could she account for the feeling of perfect contentment that she felt? She sat in the car with her arm and her shoulder against her husband's, as she always did. As they came into the mountains, she noticed that the air seemed cooler and lighter, but the image of opening doors and windows—doors that stuck at the sill, shuttered windows, casement windows, windows with sash weights, and all of them opening onto the water—stayed in her mind until they came down, at dusk, into the little river resort of Ste. Marie.

"God damn that woman," Victor said; Mrs. Sauer's house was not where Helen Jackson had said it would be. If the coffee-pot had not looked valuable, he would have thrown it into a ditch and driven on. They turned up a dirt road that ran parallel to the river, and stopped at a gas station and got out of the car to ask directions. "Sure, sure," the man said. "I know where the Sauers' place is. Their landing's right across the road, and the boatman was in here a minute ago." He threw open the screen door and shouted through his hands. "Perley! There's some people here want to get over to the island."

"I want to leave something," Victor said.

"He'll take you over. It makes a pretty ride this time of day. He don't have nothing to do. He's in here talking my ear off most of the time. Perley! Perley!"

The Mackenzies crossed the road with him to where a crooked landing reached into the water. An old man was polishing the brass on a launch. "I'll take you over and bring you right back," he said.

"I'll wait here," Theresa said.

Trees grew down to the banks on both shores; they touched the water in places. The river at this point was wide, and as it curved between the mountains she could see upstream for miles. The breadth of the view pleased her, and she hardly heard Victor and the boatman talking. "Tell the lady to come," the old man said.

"Theresa?"

She turned, and Victor gave her a hand into the boat. The old man put a dirty yachting cap on his head, and they started upstream. The current was strong, and the boat moved against it slowly, and at first they could not make out any islands, but then they saw water and light separate from the mainland what they had thought was a peninsula. They passed through some narrows and, swinging around abruptly—it was all strange and new to them—came up to a landing in a cove.

Victor followed a path that led from the landing up to an old-fashioned frame camp stained the color of molasses. The arbor that joined the house to the garden was made of cedar posts, from which the bark hung in strips among the roses. Victor rang the bell. An old servant opened the door and led him through the house and out to the porch, where Mrs. Sauer was sitting with some sewing in her lap. She thanked him for bringing the coffeepot and, as he was about to leave, asked him if he was alone.

"Mrs. Mackenzie is with me," Victor said. "We're driving to Quebec."

"Well, as Talbot used to say, the time has come for the drinking to begin," the old lady said. "If you and your wife would stop long enough to have a cocktail with me, you would be doing me a great favor. That's what it amounts to."

Victor got Theresa, who was waiting in the arbor, and brought her out to the porch.

"I know how rushed you children always are," the old lady said. "I know what a kindness it is for you to stop, but Mr. Sauer and I've been quite lonely up here this season. Here I sit, hemming curtains for the cook's room. What a bore!" She held up her sewing and let it fall. "And since you've been kind enough to stay for a cocktail, I'm going to ask another favor. I'm going to ask you to mix the cocktails. Agnes, who let you in, usually makes them, and she waters the gin. You'll find everything in the pantry. Go straight through the dining room."

Navajo rugs covered the floor of the big living room. The fireplace chimney was made of field stone, and fixed to it was, of course, a pair of antlers. At the end of a large and cheerless dining room, Victor found the pantry. The old servant brought him the shaker and the bottles.

"Well, I'm glad you're staying," she said. "I knew she was going to ask you. She's been so lonely this season that I'm worried for her. She's a lovely person—oh, she's a lovely person—but she hasn't been like herself. She begins to drink at about eleven in the morning. Sometimes earlier." The shaker was a sailing trophy. The heavy silver tray had been presented to Mr. Sauer by his business associates.

When Victor returned to the porch, Theresa was hemming the curtains. "How good it is to taste gin again," old Mrs. Sauer exclaimed. "I don't know what Agnes thinks she's accomplishing by watering the cocktails. She's a most devoted and useful servant, and I would be helpless without her, but she's growing old, she's growing old. I sometimes think she's lost her mind. She hides the soap chips in the icebox and sleeps at night with a hatchet under her pillow."

"To what good fortune do we owe this charming visitation?" the old gentleman asked when he joined them. He drew off his gardening gloves and slipped his rose shears into the pocket of his checked coat.

"Isn't it generous of these children to stop and have a drink with us," Mrs. Sauer said, when they had been introduced. The old man did not seem surprised at hearing the Mackenzies described as children. "They've come from Horsetail Beach and they're on their way to Quebec."

"Mrs. Sauer and I have always detested Horsetail Beach," the old gentleman said. "When do you plan to reach Quebec?"

"Tonight," Victor said.

"Tonight?" Mrs. Sauer asked.

"I doubt that you can reach Quebec tonight," the old gentleman said.

"I suppose you can do it," the old lady said, "the way you children drive, but you'll be more dead than alive. Stay for dinner. Stay the night."

"Do stay for dinner," the old man said.

"You will, won't you?" Mrs. Sauer said. "I will not take no for an answer! I am old and privileged, and if you say no, I'll claim to be deaf and pretend not to hear you. And now that you've decided to stay, make another round of these delicious cocktails and tell Agnes that you are to have Talbot's room. Tell her tactfully. She hates guests. Remember that she's very old."

[92]

Victor carried the sailing trophy back into the house, which, in spite of its many large windows, seemed in the early dark like a cave. "Mrs. Mackenzie and I are staying for dinner and the night," he told Agnes. "She said that we were to have Talbot's room."

"Well, that's nice. Maybe it will make her happy. She's had a lot of sorrow in her life. I think it's affected her mind. I knew she was going to ask you, and I'm glad you can stay. It makes me happy. It's more dishes to wash and more beds to make, but it's more— it's more—"

"It's more merrier?"

"Oh, that's it, that's it." The old servant shook with laughter. "You remind me a little of Mr. Talbot. He was always making jokes with me when he came out here to mix the cocktails. God have mercy on his soul. It's hard to realize," she said sadly.

Walking back through the cavelike living room, Victor could hear Theresa and Mrs. Sauer discussing the night air, and he noticed that the cold air had begun to come down from the mountains. He felt it in the room. There were flowers somewhere in the dark, and the night air had heightened their smell and the smell of the boulders in the chimney, so the room smelled like a cave with flowers in it. "Everyone says that the view looks like Salzburg," Mrs. Sauer said, "but I'm patriotic and I can't see that views are improved by such comparisons. They do seem to be improved by good company, however. We used to entertain, but now—"

"Yes, yes," the old gentleman said, and sighed. He uncorked a bottle of citronella and rubbed his wrists and the back of his neck.

"There!" Theresa said. "The cook's curtains are done!"

"Oh, how can I thank you!" Mrs. Sauer said. "Now if someone would be kind enough to get my glasses, I could admire your needlework. They're on the mantelpiece."

Victor found her glasses—not on the mantelpiece but on a nearby table. He gave them to her and then walked up and down the porch a few times. He managed to suggest that he

[93]

was no longer a chance guest but had become a member of the family. He sat down on the steps, and Theresa joined him there. "Look at them," the old lady said to her husband. "Doesn't it do you good to see, for a change, young people who love one another. . . . There goes the sunset gun. My brother George bought that gun for the yacht club. It was his pride and his joy. Isn't it quiet this evening?"

But the tender looks and attitudes that Mrs. Sauer took for pure love were only the attitudes of homeless summer children who had found a respite. Oh, how sweet, how precious the hour seemed to them! Lights burned on another island. Stamped on the twilight was the iron lace of a broken greenhouse roof. What poor magpies. Their ways and airs were innocent; their bones were infirm. Indeed, they impersonated the dead. Come away, come away, sang the wind in the trees and the grass, but it did not sing to the Mackenzies. They turned their heads instead to hear old Mrs. Sauer. "I'm going up to put on my green velvet," she said, "but if you children don't feel like dressing . . ."

Waiting on table that night, Agnes thought that she had not seen such a gay dinner in a long time. She heard them go off after dinner to play billiards on the table that had been bought for poor, dead Talbot. A little rain fell, but, unlike the rain at Horsetail Beach, this was a gentle and excursive mountain shower. Mrs. Sauer yawned at eleven, and the game broke up. They said good night in the upstairs hall, by the pictures of Talbot's crew, Talbot's pony, and Talbot's class. "Good night, good night," Mrs. Sauer exclaimed, and then she set her face, determined to overstep her manners, and declared, "I am delighted that you agreed to stay. I can't tell you how much it means. I'm—" Tears started from her eyes.

"It's lovely to be here," Theresa said.

"Good night, children," Mrs. Sauer said.

"Good night, good night," Mr. Sauer said.

"Good night," Victor said.

"Good night, good night," Theresa said.

"Sleep well," Mrs. Sauer said. "And pleasant dreams."

Ten days later, the Sauers were expecting some other guests
—some young cousins named Wycherly. They had never been
to the house before, and they came up the path late in the afternoon. Victor opened the door to them. "I'm Victor Mackenzie,"
he said cheerfully. He wore tennis shorts and a pullover, but
when he bent down to pick up a suitcase, his knees creaked
loudly. "The Sauers are out driving with my wife," he explained. "They'll be back by six, when the drinking begins."
The cousins followed him across the big living room and up the
stairs. "Mrs. Sauer is giving you Uncle George's room," he said,
"because it has the best view and the most hot water. It's the
only room that's been added to the house since Mr. Sauer's
father built the place in 1903. . . ."

The young cousins did not quite know what to make of him.
Was he a cousin, himself? an uncle, perhaps? a poor relation?
But it was a comfortable house and a brilliant day, and in the
end they would take Victor for what he appeared to be, and he
appeared to be very happy.

TORCH SONG

$\mathscr{A}$FTER Jack Lorey had known Joan Harris in New York for a few years, he began to think of her as The Widow. She always wore black, and he was always given the feeling, by a curious disorder in her apartment, that the undertakers had just left. This impression did not stem from malice on his part, for he was fond of Joan. They came from the same city in Ohio and had reached New York at about the same time in the middle thirties. They were the same age, and during their first summer in the city they used to meet after work and drink Martinis in places like the Brevoort and Charles', and have dinner and play checkers at the Lafayette.

Joan went to a school for models when she settled in the city, but it turned out that she photographed badly, so after spending six weeks learning how to walk with a book on her head she got a job as a hostess in a Longchamps. For the rest of the summer she stood by the hatrack, bathed in an intense pink light and the string music of heartbreak, swinging her mane of dark hair and her black skirt as she moved forward to greet the customers. She was then a big, handsome girl with a wonderful voice, and her face, her whole presence, always seemed infused with a gentle and healthy pleasure at her surroundings, whatever they were. She was innocently and incorrigibly convivial, and would get out of bed and dress at three in the morning if someone called her and asked her to come out for a drink, as

Jack often did. In the fall, she got some kind of freshman executive job in a department store. They saw less and less of each other and then for quite a while stopped seeing each other altogether. Jack was living with a girl he had met at a party, and it never occurred to him to wonder what had become of Joan.

Jack's girl had some friends in Pennsylvania, and in the spring and summer of his second year in town he often went there with her for weekends. All of this—the shared apartment in the Village, the illicit relationship, the Friday-night train to a country house—were what he had imagined life in New York to be, and he was intensely happy. He was returning to New York with his girl one Sunday night on the Lehigh line. It was one of those trains that move slowly across the face of New Jersey, bringing back to the city hundreds of people, like the victims of an immense and strenuous picnic, whose faces are blazing and whose muscles are lame. Jack and his girl, like most of the other passengers, were overburdened with vegetables and flowers. When the train stopped in Pennsylvania Station, they moved with the crowd along the platform, toward the escalator. As they were passing the wide, lighted windows of the diner, Jack turned his head and saw Joan. It was the first time he had seen her since Thanksgiving, or since Christmas. He couldn't remember.

Joan was with a man who had obviously passed out. His head was in his arms on the table, and an overturned highball glass was near one of his elbows. Joan was shaking his shoulders gently and speaking to him. She seemed to be vaguely troubled, vaguely amused. The waiters had cleared off all the other tables and were standing around Joan, waiting for her to resurrect her escort. It troubled Jack to see in these straits a girl who reminded him of the trees and the lawns of his home town, but there was nothing he could do to help. Joan continued to shake the man's shoulders, and the crowd pressed Jack past one after another of the diner's windows, past the malodorous kitchen, and up the escalator.

He saw Joan again, later that summer, when he was having

dinner in a Village restaurant. He was with a new girl, a Southerner. There were many Southern girls in the city that year. Jack and his belle had wandered into the restaurant because it was convenient, but the food was terrible and the place was lighted with candles. Halfway through dinner, Jack noticed Joan on the other side of the room, and when he had finished eating, he crossed the room and spoke to her. She was with a tall man who was wearing a monocle. He stood, bowed stiffly from the waist, and said to Jack, "We are very pleased to meet you." Then he excused himself and headed for the toilet. "He's a count, he's a Swedish count," Joan said. "He's on the radio, Friday afternoons at four-fifteen. Isn't it exciting?" She seemed to be delighted with the count and the terrible restaurant.

Sometime the next winter, Jack moved from the Village to an apartment in the East Thirties. He was crossing Park Avenue one cold morning on his way to the office when he noticed, in the crowd, a woman he had met a few times at Joan's apartment. He spoke to her and asked about his friend. "Haven't you heard?" she said. She pulled a long face. "Perhaps I'd better tell you. Perhaps you can help." She and Jack had breakfast in a drugstore on Madison Avenue and she unburdened herself of the story.

The count had a program called "The Song of the Fiords," or something like that, and he sang Swedish folk songs. Everyone suspected him of being a fake, but that didn't bother Joan. He had met her at a party and, sensing a soft touch, had moved in with her the following night. About a week later, he complained of pains in his back and said he must have some morphine. Then he needed morphine all the time. If he didn't get morphine, he was abusive and violent. Joan began to deal with those doctors and druggists who peddle dope, and when they wouldn't supply her, she went down to the bottom of the city. Her friends were afraid she would be found some morning stuffed in a drain. She got pregnant. She had an abortion. The count left her and moved to a flea bag near Times Square, but she was so impressed by then with his helplessness, so afraid that he would die without her, that she followed him there and shared his room and continued to buy his narcotics. He abandoned her again, and Joan waited a week for him to return before she went back to her place and her friends in the Village.

It shocked Jack to think of the innocent girl from Ohio having lived with a brutal dope addict and traded with criminals, and when he got to his office that morning, he telephoned her and made a date for dinner that night. He met her at Charles'. When she came into the bar, she seemed as wholesome and calm as ever. Her voice was sweet, and reminded him of elms, of lawns, of those glass arrangements that used to be hung from porch ceilings to tinkle in the summer wind. She told him about the count. She spoke of him charitably and with no trace of bitterness, as if her voice, her disposition, were incapable of registering anything beyond simple affection and pleasure. Her walk, when she moved ahead of him toward their table, was light and graceful. She ate a large dinner and talked enthusiastically about her job. They went to a movie and said goodbye in front of her apartment house.

That winter, Jack met a girl he decided to marry. Their engagement was announced in January and they planned to marry in July. In the spring, he received, in his office mail, an invitation to cocktails at Joan's. It was for a Saturday when his fiancée was going to Massachusetts to visit her parents, and when the time came and he had nothing better to do, he took a bus to the Village. Joan had the same apartment. It was a walkup. You rang the bell above the mailbox in the vestibule and were answered with a death rattle in the lock. Joan lived on the third floor. Her calling card was in a slot on the mailbox, and above her name was written the name Hugh Bascomb.

Jack climbed the two flights of carpeted stairs, and when he reached Joan's apartment, she was standing by the open door in a black dress. After she greeted Jack, she took his arm and guided him across the room. "I want you to meet Hugh, Jack," she said.

Hugh was a big man with a red face and pale-blue eyes. His

manner was courtly and his eyes were inflamed with drink. Jack talked with him for a little while and then went over to speak to someone he knew, who was standing by the mantel-piece. He noticed then, for the first time, the indescribable dis-order of Joan's apartment. The books were in their shelves and the furniture was reasonably good, but the place was all wrong, somehow. It was as if things had been put in place without thought or real interest, and for the first time, too, he had the impression that there had been a death there recently.

As Jack moved around the room, he felt that he had met the ten or twelve guests at other parties. There was a woman ex-ecutive with a fancy hat, a man who could imitate Roosevelt, a grim couple whose play was in rehearsal, and a newspaper-man who kept turning on the radio for news of the Spanish Civil War. Jack drank Martinis and talked with the woman in the fancy hat. He looked out of the window at the back yards and the ailanthus trees and heard, in the distance, thunder ex-ploding off the cliffs of the Hudson.

Hugh Bascomb got very drunk. He began to spill liquor, as if drinking, for him, were a kind of jolly slaughter and he en-joyed the bloodshed and the mess. He spilled whiskey from a bottle. He spilled a drink on his shirt and then tipped over someone else's drink. The party was not quiet, but Hugh's hoarse voice began to dominate the others. He attacked a pho-tographer who was sitting in a corner explaining camera tech-niques to a homely woman. "What did you come to the party for if all you wanted to do was to sit there and stare at your shoes?" Hugh shouted. "What did you come for? Why don't you stay at home?"

The photographer didn't know what to say. He was not star-ing at his shoes. Joan moved lightly to Hugh's side. "Please don't get into a fight now, darling," she said. "Not this after-noon."

"Shut up," he said. "Let me alone. Mind your own business." He lost his balance, and in struggling to steady himself he tipped over a lamp.

"Oh, your lovely lamp, Joan," a woman sighed.

"Lamps!" Hugh roared. He threw his arms into the air and worked them around his head as if he were bludgeoning himself. "Lamps. Glasses. Cigarette boxes. Dishes. They're killing me. They're killing me, for Christ's sake. Let's all go up to the mountains, for Christ's sake. Let's all go up to the mountains and hunt and fish and live like men, for Christ's sake."

People were scattering as if a rain had begun to fall in the room. It had, as a matter of fact, begun to rain outside. Someone offered Jack a ride uptown, and he jumped at the chance. Joan stood at the door, saying goodbye to her routed friends. Her voice remained soft, and her manner, unlike that of those Christian women who in the face of disaster can summon new and formidable sources of composure, seemed genuinely simple. She appeared to be oblivious of the raging drunk at her back, who was pacing up and down, grinding glass into the rug, and haranguing one of the survivors of the party with a story of how he, Hugh, had once gone without food for three weeks.

In July, Jack was married in an orchard in Duxbury, and he and his wife went to West Chop for a few weeks. When they returned to town, their apartment was cluttered with presents, including a dozen after-dinner coffee cups from Joan. His wife sent her the required note, but they did nothing else.

Late in the summer, Joan telephoned Jack at his office and asked if he wouldn't bring his wife to see her; she named an evening the following week. He felt guilty about not having called her, and accepted the invitation. This made his wife angry. She was an ambitious girl who liked a social life that offered rewards, and she went unwillingly to Joan's Village apartment with him.

Written above Joan's name on the mailbox was the name Franz Denzel. Jack and his wife climbed the stairs and were met by Joan at the open door. They went into her apartment and found themselves among a group of people for whom Jack, at least, was unable to find any bearings.

[101]

Franz Denzel was a middle-aged German. His face was pinched with bitterness or illness. He greeted Jack and his wife with that elaborate and clever politeness that is intended to make guests feel that they have come too early or too late. He insisted sharply upon Jack's sitting in the chair in which he himself had been sitting, and then went and sat on a radiator. There were five other Germans sitting around the room, drinking coffee. In a corner was another American couple, who looked uncomfortable. Joan passed Jack and his wife small cups of coffee with whipped cream. "These cups belonged to Franz's mother," she said. "Aren't they lovely? They were the only things he took from Germany when he escaped from the Nazis."

Franz turned to Jack and said, "Perhaps you will give us your opinion on the American educational system. That is what we were discussing when you arrived."

Before Jack could speak, one of the German guests opened an attack on the American educational system. The other Germans joined in, and went on from there to describe every vulgarity that had impressed them in American life and to contrast German and American culture generally. Where, they asked one another passionately, could you find in America anything like the Mitropa dining cars, the Black Forest, the pictures in Munich, the music in Bayreuth? Franz and his friends began speaking in German. Neither Jack nor his wife nor Joan could understand German, and the other American couple had not opened their mouths since they were introduced. Joan went happily around the room, filling everyone's cup with coffee, as if the music of a foreign language were enough to make an evening for her.

Jack drank five cups of coffee. He was desperately uncomfortable. Joan went into the kitchen while the Germans were laughing at their German jokes, and he hoped she would return with some drinks, but when she came back, it was with a tray of ice cream and mulberries.

"Isn't this pleasant?" Franz asked, speaking in English again.

Joan collected the coffee cups, and as she was about to take them back to the kitchen, Franz stopped her.

"Isn't one of those cups chipped?"

"No, darling," Joan said. "I never let the maid touch them. I wash them myself."

"What's that?" he asked, pointing at the rim of one of the cups.

"That's the cup that's always been chipped, darling. It was chipped when you unpacked it. You noticed it then."

"These things were perfect when they arrived in this country," he said.

Joan went into the kitchen and he followed her.

Jack tried to make conversation with the Germans. From the kitchen there was the sound of a blow and a cry. Franz returned and began to eat his mulberries greedily. Joan came back with her dish of ice cream. Her voice was gentle. Her tears, if she had been crying, had dried as quickly as the tears of a child. Jack and his wife finished their ice cream and made their escape. The wasted and unnerving evening enraged Jack's wife, and he supposed that he would never see Joan again.

Jack's wife got pregnant early in the fall, and she seized on all the prerogatives of an expectant mother. She took long naps, ate canned peaches in the middle of the night, and talked about the rudimentary kidney. She chose to see only other couples who were expecting children, and the parties that she and Jack gave were temperate. The baby, a boy, was born in May, and Jack was very proud and happy. The first party he and his wife went to after her convalescence was the wedding of a girl whose family Jack had known in Ohio.

The wedding was at St. James', and afterward there was a big reception at the River Club. There was an orchestra dressed like Hungarians, and a lot of champagne and Scotch. Toward the end of the afternoon, Jack was walking down a dim corridor when he heard Joan's voice. "Please don't, darling," she was saying. "You'll break my arm. *Please* don't, darling." She was being pressed against the wall by a man who seemed to be twisting her arm. As soon as they saw Jack, the struggle stopped. All three of them were intensely embarrassed. Joan's face was wet and she made an effort to smile through her tears at Jack. He said hello and went on without stopping. When he returned, she and the man had disappeared.

When Jack's son was less than two years old, his wife flew with the baby to Nevada to get a divorce. Jack gave her the apartment and all its furnishings and took a room in a hotel near Grand Central. His wife got her decree in due course, and the story was in the newspapers. Jack had a telephone call from Joan a few days later.

"I'm awfully sorry to hear about your divorce, Jack," she said. "She seemed like *such* a nice girl. But that wasn't what I called you about. I want your help, and I wondered if you could come down to my place tonight around six. It's something I don't want to talk about over the phone."

He went obediently to the Village that night and climbed the stairs. Her apartment was a mess. The pictures and the curtains were down and the books were in boxes. "You moving, Joan?" he asked.

"That's what I wanted to see you about, Jack. First, I'll give you a drink." She made two Old-Fashioneds. "I'm being evicted, Jack," she said. "I'm being evicted because I'm an immoral woman. The couple who have the apartment downstairs— they're charming people, I've always thought—have told the real-estate agent that I'm a drunk and a prostitute and all kinds of things. Isn't that fantastic? This real-estate agent has always been so nice to me that I didn't think he'd believe them, but he's cancelled my lease, and if I make any trouble, he's threatened to take the matter up with the store, and I don't want to lose my job. This nice real-estate agent won't even talk with me any more. When I go over to the office, the receptionist leers at me as if I were some kind of dreadful woman. Of course, there have been a lot of men here and we sometimes are noisy, but I can't be expected to go to bed at ten every night. Can I?

Well, the agent who manages this building has apparently told
all the other agents in the neighborhood that I'm an immoral
and drunken woman, and none of them will give me an apartment. I went in to talk with one man—he seemed to be such
a nice old gentleman—and he made me an indecent proposal.
Isn't it fantastic? I have to be out of here on Thursday and I'm
literally being turned out into the street."

Joan seemed as serene and innocent as ever while she described this scourge of agents and neighbors. Jack listened carefully for some sign of indignation or bitterness or even urgency
in her recital, but there was none. He was reminded of a torch
song, of one of those forlorn and touching ballads that had been
sung neither for him nor for her but for their older brothers
and sisters by Marion Harris. Joan seemed to be singing her
wrongs.

"They've made my life miserable," she went on quietly. "If
I keep the radio on after ten o'clock, they telephone the agent
in the morning and tell him I had some kind of orgy here. One
night when Phillip—I don't think you've met Phillip; he's in
the Royal Air Force; he's gone back to England—one night
when Phillip and some other people were here, they called the
police. The police came bursting in the door and talked to me
as if I were I don't know what and then looked in the bedroom.
If they think there's a man up here after midnight, they call
me on the telephone and say all kinds of disgusting things. Of
course, I can put my furniture into storage and go to a hotel,
I guess. I guess a hotel will take a woman with my kind of
reputation, but I thought perhaps you might know of an apartment. I thought—"

It angered Jack to think of this big, splendid girl's being per-
secuted by her neighbors, and he said he would do what he
could. He asked her to have dinner with him, but she said she
was busy.

Having nothing better to do, Jack decided to walk uptown
to his hotel. It was a hot night. The sky was overcast. On his
way, he saw a parade in a dark side street off Broadway near

Madison Square. All the buildings in the neighborhood were
dark. It was so dark that he could not see the placards the
marchers carried until he came to a street light. Their signs
urged the entry of the United States into the war, and each
platoon represented a nation that had been subjugated by the
Axis powers. They marched up Broadway, as he watched, to
no music, to no sound but their own steps on the rough cobbles.
It was for the most part an army of elderly men and women
—Poles, Norwegians, Danes, Jews, Chinese. A few idle people
like himself lined the sidewalks, and the marchers passed between them with all the self-consciousness of enemy prisoners.
There were children among them dressed in the costumes in
which they had, for the newsreels, presented the Mayor with
a package of tea, a petition, a protest, a constitution, a check,
or a pair of tickets. They hobbled through the darkness of the
loft neighborhood like a mortified and destroyed people, toward
Greeley Square.

In the morning, Jack put the problem of finding an apartment for Joan up to his secretary. She started phoning real-
estate agents, and by afternoon she had found a couple of avail-
able apartments in the West Twenties. Joan called Jack the
next day to say that she had taken one of the apartments and
to thank him.

Jack didn't see Joan again until the following summer. It
was a Sunday evening; he had left a cocktail party in a Washington Square apartment and had decided to walk a few blocks
up Fifth Avenue before he took a bus. As he was passing the
Brevoort, Joan called to him. She was with a man at one of
the tables on the sidewalk. She looked cool and fresh, and the
man appeared to be respectable. His name, it turned out, was
Pete Bristol. He invited Jack to sit down and join in a celebration. Germany had invaded Russia that weekend, and Joan and
Pete were drinking champagne to celebrate Russia's changed
position in the war. The three of them drank champagne until
it got dark. They had dinner and drank champagne with their
dinner. They drank more champagne afterward and then went

over to the Lafayette and then to two or three other places. Joan had always been tireless in her gentle way. She hated to see the night end, and it was after three o'clock when Jack stumbled into his apartment. The following morning he woke up haggard and sick, and with no recollection of the last hour or so of the previous evening. His suit was soiled and he had lost his hat. He didn't get to his office until eleven. Joan had already called him twice, and she called him again soon after he got in. There was no hoarseness at all in her voice. She said that she had to see him, and he agreed to meet her for lunch in a sea-food restaurant in the Fifties.

He was standing at the bar when she breezed in, looking as though she had taken no part in that calamitous night. The advice she wanted concerned selling her jewelry. Her grandmother had left her some jewelry, and she wanted to raise money on it but didn't know where to go. She took some rings and bracelets out of her purse and showed them to Jack. He said that he didn't know anything about jewelry but that he could lend her some money. "Oh, I couldn't borrow money from you, Jack," she said. "You see, I want to get the money for Pete. I want to help him. He wants to open an advertising agency, and he needs quite a lot to begin with." Jack didn't press her to accept his offer of a loan after that, and the project wasn't mentioned again during lunch.

He next heard about Joan from a young doctor who was a friend of theirs. "Have you seen Joan recently?" the doctor asked Jack one evening when they were having dinner together. He said no. "I gave her a checkup last week," the doctor said, "and while she's been through enough to kill the average mortal—and you'll never know what she's been through—she still has the constitution of a virtuous and healthy woman. Did you hear about the last one? She sold her jewelry to put him into some kind of a business, and as soon as he got the money, he left her for another girl, who had a car—a convertible."

Jack was drafted into the Army in the spring of 1942. He was kept at Fort Dix for nearly a month, and during this time he came to New York in the evening whenever he could get permission. Those nights had for him the intense keenness of a reprieve, a sensation that was heightened by the fact that on the train in from Trenton women would often press upon him dog-eared copies of *Life* and half-eaten boxes of candy, as though the brown clothes he wore were surely cerements. He telephoned Joan from Pennsylvania Station one night. "Come right over, Jack," she said. "Come right over. I want you to meet Ralph."

She was living in that place in the West Twenties that Jack had found for her. The neighborhood was a slum. Ash cans stood in front of her house, and an old woman was there picking out bits of refuse and garbage and stuffing them into a perambulator. The house in which Joan's apartment was located was shabby, but the apartment itself seemed familiar. The furniture was the same. Joan was the same big, easy-going girl. "I'm so glad you called me," she said. "It's so good to see you. I'll make you a drink. I was having one myself. Ralph ought to be here by now. He promised to take me to dinner." Jack offered to take her to Cavanagh's, but she said that Ralph might come while she was out. "If he doesn't come by nine, I'm going to make myself a sandwich. I'm not really hungry."

Jack talked about the Army. She talked about the store. She had been working in the same place for—how long was it? He didn't know. He had never seen her at her desk and he couldn't imagine what she did. "I'm terribly sorry Ralph isn't here," she said. "I'm sure you'd like him. He's not a young man. He's a heart specialist who loves to play the viola." She turned on some lights, for the summer sky had got dark. "He has this dreadful wife on Riverside Drive and four ungrateful children. He—"

The noise of an air-raid siren, lugubrious and seeming to spring from pain, as if all the misery and indecision in the city had been given a voice, cut her off. Other sirens, in distant neighborhoods, sounded, until the dark air was full of their noise. "Let me fix you another drink before I have to turn out the lights," Joan said, and took his glass. She brought the drink back to him and snapped off the lights. They went to the windows, and, as children watch a thunderstorm, they watched the city darken. All the lights nearby went out but one. Air-raid wardens had begun to sound their whistles in the street. From a distant yard came a hoarse shriek of anger. "Put out your lights, you Fascists!" a woman screamed. "Put out your lights, you Nazi Fascist Germans. Turn out your lights. Turn out your lights." The last light went off. They went away from the window and sat in the lightless room.

In the darkness, Joan began to talk about her departed lovers, and from what she said Jack gathered that they had all had a hard time. Nils, the suspect count, was dead. Hugh Bascomb, the drunk, had joined the Merchant Marine and was missing in the North Atlantic. Franz, the German, had taken poison the night the Nazis bombed Warsaw. "We listened to the news on the radio," Joan said, "and then he went back to his hotel and took poison. The maid found him dead in the bathroom the next morning." When Jack asked her about the one who was going to open an advertising agency, she seemed at first to have forgotten him. "Oh, Pete," she said after a pause. "Well, he was always very sick, you know. He was supposed to go to Saranac, but he kept putting it off and putting it off and—" She stopped talking when she heard steps on the stairs, hoping, he supposed, that it was Ralph, but whoever it was turned at the landing and continued to the top of the house. "I wish Ralph would come," she said, with a sigh. "I want you to meet him." Jack asked her again to go out, but she refused, and when the all-clear sounded, he said goodbye.

Jack was shipped from Dix to an infantry training camp in the Carolinas and from there to an infantry division stationed in Georgia. He had been in Georgia three months when he married a girl from the Augusta boarding-house aristocracy. A year or so later, he crossed the continent in a day coach and thought sententiously that the last he might see of the country he loved was the desert towns like Barstow, that the last he might hear of it was the ringing of the trolleys on the Bay Bridge. He was sent into the Pacific and returned to the United States twenty months later, uninjured and apparently unchanged. As soon as he received his furlough, he went to Augusta. He presented his wife with the souvenirs he had brought from the islands, quarrelled violently with her and all her family, and, after making arrangements for her to get an Arkansas divorce, left for New York.

Jack was discharged from the Army at a camp in the East a few months later. He took a vacation and then went back to the job he had left in 1942. He seemed to have picked up his life at approximately the moment when it had been interrupted by the war. In time, everything came to look and feel the same. He saw most of his old friends. Only two of the men he knew had been killed in the war. He didn't call Joan, but he met her one winter afternoon on a crosstown bus.

Her fresh face, her black clothes, and her soft voice instantly destroyed the sense—if he had ever had such a sense—that anything had changed or intervened since their last meeting, three or four years ago. She asked him up for cocktails and he went to her apartment the next Saturday afternoon. Her room and her guests reminded him of the parties she had given when she had first come to New York. There was a woman with a fancy hat, an elderly doctor, and a man who stayed close to the radio, listening for news from the Balkans. Jack wondered which of the men belonged to Joan and decided on an Englishman who kept coughing into a handkerchief that he pulled out of his sleeve. Jack was right. "Isn't Stephen brilliant?" Joan asked him a little later, when they were alone in a corner. "He knows more about the Polynesians than anyone else in the world."

Jack had returned not only to his old job but to his old salary. Since living costs had doubled and since he was paying alimony to two wives, he had to draw on his savings. He took another job, which promised more money, but it didn't last long and he found himself out of work. This didn't bother him at all. He still had money in the bank, and anyhow it was easy to borrow from friends. His indifference was the consequence not of lassitude or despair but rather of an excess of hope. He had the feeling that he had only recently come to New York from Ohio. The sense that he was very young and that the best years of his life still lay before him was an illusion that he could not seem to escape. There was all the time in the world. He was living in hotels then, moving from one to another every five days.

In the spring, Jack moved to a furnished room in the badlands west of Central Park. He was running out of money. Then, when he began to feel that a job was a desperate necessity, he got sick. At first, he seemed to have only a bad cold, but he was unable to shake it and he began to run a fever and to cough blood. The fever kept him drowsy most of the time, but he roused himself occasionally and went out to a cafeteria for a meal. He felt sure that none of his friends knew where he was, and he was glad of this. He hadn't counted on Joan.

Late one morning, he heard her speaking in the hall with his landlady. A few moments later, she knocked on his door. He was lying on the bed in a pair of pants and a soiled pajama top, and he didn't answer. She knocked again and walked in. "I've been looking everywhere for you, Jack," she said. She spoke softly. "When I found out that you were in a place like this I thought you must be broke or sick. I stopped at the bank and got some money, in case you're broke. I've brought you some Scotch. I thought a little drink wouldn't do you any harm. Want a little drink?"

Joan's dress was black. Her voice was low and serene. She sat in a chair beside his bed as if she had been coming there every day to nurse him. Her features had coarsened, he thought, but there were still very few lines in her face. She was heavier. She was nearly fat. She was wearing black cotton gloves. She got two glasses and poured Scotch into them. He drank his whiskey greedily. "I didn't get to bed until three last night," she said. Her voice had once before reminded him of a gentle and despairing song, but now, perhaps because he was sick, her mildness, the mourning she wore, her stealthy grace, made him uneasy. "It was one of those nights," she said. "We went to the theatre. Afterward, someone asked us up to his place. I don't know who he was. It was one of those places. They're so strange. There were some meat-eating plants and a collection of Chinese snuff bottles. Why do people collect Chinese snuff bottles? We all autographed a lampshade, as I remember, but I can't remember much."

Jack tried to sit up in bed, as if there were some need to defend himself, and then fell back again, against the pillows. "How did you find me, Joan?" he asked.

"It was simple," she said. "I called that hotel. The one you were staying in. They gave me this address. My secretary got the telephone number. Have another little drink."

"You know you've never come to a place of mine before— never," he said. "Why did you come now?"

"Why did I come, darling?" she asked. "What a question! I've known you for thirty years. You're the oldest friend I have in New York. Remember that night in the Village when it snowed and we stayed up until morning and drank whiskey sours for breakfast? That doesn't seem like twelve years ago. And that night—"

"I don't like to have you see me in a place like this," he said earnestly. He touched his face and felt his beard.

"And all the people who used to imitate Roosevelt," she said, as if she had not heard him, as if she were deaf. "And that place on Staten Island where we all used to go for dinner when Henry had a car. Poor Henry. He bought a place in Connecticut and went out there by himself, one weekend. He fell asleep with a lighted cigarette and the house, the barn, everything burned. Ethel took the children out to California." She poured more Scotch into his glass and handed it to him. She lighted a cigarette and put it between his lips. The intimacy of this gesture, which made it seem not only as if he were deathly ill but as if he were her lover, troubled him.

[112]

"As soon as I'm better," he said, "I'll take a room at a good hotel. I'll call you then. It was nice of you to come."

"Oh, don't be ashamed of this room, Jack," she said. "Rooms never bother me. It doesn't seem to matter to me where I am. Stanley had a filthy room in Chelsea. At least, other people told me it was filthy. I never noticed it. Rats used to eat the food I brought him. He used to have to hang the food from the ceiling, from the light chain."

"I'll call you as soon as I'm better," Jack said. "I think I can sleep now if I'm left alone. I seem to need a lot of sleep."

"You really *are* sick, darling," she said. "You must have a fever." She sat on the edge of his bed and put a hand on his forehead.

"How is that Englishman, Joan?" he asked. "Do you still see him?"

"What Englishman?" she said.

"You know. I met him at your house. He kept a handkerchief up his sleeve. He coughed all the time. You know the one I mean."

"You must be thinking of someone else," she said. "I haven't had an Englishman at my place since the war. Of course, I can't remember everyone." She turned and, taking one of his hands, linked her fingers in his.

"He's dead, isn't he?" Jack said. "That Englishman's dead." He pushed her off the bed, and got up himself. "Get out," he said.

"You're sick, darling," she said. "I can't leave you alone here."

"Get out," he said again, and when she didn't move, he shouted, "What kind of an obscenity are you that you can smell sickness and death the way you do?"

"You poor darling."

"Does it make you feel young to watch the dying?" he shouted. "Is that the lewdness that keeps you young? Is that why you dress like a crow? Oh, I know there's nothing I can say that will hurt you. I know there's nothing filthy or corrupt or depraved or brutish or base that the others haven't tried, but this time you're wrong. I'm not ready. My life isn't ending. My life's beginning. There are wonderful years ahead of me. There are, there are wonderful, wonderful, wonderful years ahead of me, and when they're over, when it's time, then I'll call you. Then, as an old friend, I'll call you and give you whatever dirty pleasure you take in watching the dying, but until then, you and your ugly and misshapen forms will leave me alone."

She finished her drink and looked at her watch. "I guess I'd better show up at the office," she said. "I'll see you later. I'll come back tonight. You'll feel better then, you poor darling." She closed the door after her, and he heard her light step on the stairs.

Jack emptied the whiskey bottle into the sink. He began to dress. He stuffed his dirty clothes into a bag. He was trembling and crying with sickness and fear. He could see the blue sky from his window, and in his fear it seemed miraculous that the sky should be blue, that the white clouds should remind him of snow, that from the sidewalk he could hear the shrill voices of children shrieking, "I'm the king of the mountain, I'm the king of the mountain, I'm the king of the mountain." He emptied the ashtray containing his nail parings and cigarette butts into the toilet, and swept the floor with a shirt, so that there would be no trace of his life, of his body, when that lewd and searching shape of death came there to find him in the evening.

THE CURE

$\mathcal{T}$HIS happened in the summer. I remember that the weather was very hot, both in New York and in
the suburb where we live. My wife and I had a quarrel, and
Rachel took the children and drove off in the station wagon.
Tom didn't appear—or I wasn't conscious of him—until they
had been gone for about two weeks, but her departure and his
arrival seemed connected. Rachel's departure was meant to be
final. She had left me twice before—the second time, we divorced and then remarried—and I watched her go each time
with a feeling that was far from happy, but also with that re-
newal of self-respect, of nerve, that seems to be the reward for
accepting a painful truth. As I say, it was summer, and I was
glad, in a way, that she had picked this time to quarrel. It
seemed to spare us both the immediate necessity of legalizing
our separation. We had lived together—on and off—for thirteen
years; we had three children and some involved finances. I
guessed that she was content, as I was, to let things ride until
September or October.

I was glad that the separation took place in the summer because my job is most exacting at that time of year and I'm
usually too tired to think of anything else at night, and because
I'd noticed that summer was for me the easiest season of the
year to live through alone. I also expected that Rachel would
get the house when our affairs were settled, and I like our house

and thought of those days as the last I would spend there. There were a few minor symptoms of domestic disorder. First the dog and then the cat ran away. Then I came home one night and found Maureen, the maid, dead drunk. She told me that her husband, when he was with the Army of Occupation in Germany, had fallen in love with another woman. She wept. She got down on her knees. That scene, with the two of us alone in a house unnaturally empty of women and children on a summer evening, was grotesque, and it is this kind of grotesqueness, I know, that can destroy your resolution. I made her some coffee and gave her two weeks' wages and drove her home, and when we said goodbye she seemed composed and sober, and I felt that the grotesqueness could be forgotten. After this, I planned a simple schedule that I hoped to follow until autumn.

You cure yourself of a romantic, carnal, and disastrous marriage, I decided, and, like any addict in the throes of a cure, you must be exaggeratedly careful of every step you take. I decided not to answer the telephone, because I knew that Rachel might repent, and I knew, by then, the size and the nature of the things that could bring us together. If it rained for five days, if one of the children had a passing fever, if she got some sad news in a letter—anything like this might be enough to put her on the telephone, and I did not want to be tempted to resume a relationship that had been so miserable. The first months will be like a cure, I thought, and I scheduled my time with this in mind. I took the eight-ten train into town in the morning and returned on the six-thirty. I knew enough to avoid the empty house in the summer dusk, and I drove directly from the station parking lot to a good restaurant called Orpheo's. There was usually someone there to talk with, and I'd drink a couple of Martinis and eat a steak. Afterward I'd drive over to the Stonybrook Drive-In Theatre and sit through a double feature. All this—the Martinis and the steak and the movie—was intended to induce a kind of anesthesia, and it worked. I didn't want to see anyone outside the people in my office.

But I don't sleep very well in an empty bed, and presently

I had the problem of sleeplessness to cope with. When I got
home from the movies, I would fall asleep, but only for a
couple of hours. I tried to make the best of insomnia. If it was
raining, I listened to the rain and the thunder. If it wasn't
raining, I listened to the distant noise of trucks on the turnpike,
a sound that reminded me of the depression, when I spent some
time on the road. The trucks came gunning down the turnpike
—loaded with chickens or canned goods or soap powder or furniture. The sound meant darkness to me, darkness and head-
lights—and youth, I suppose, since it seemed to be a pleasant
sound. Sometimes the noise of the rain or the traffic or something like that would distract me, and I would be able to go
to sleep again, but one night nothing at all worked, and at three
in the morning I decided to go downstairs and read.

I turned on a light in the living room and looked at Rachel's
books. I chose one by an author named Lin Yutang and sat
down on a sofa under a lamp. Our living room is comfortable.
The book seemed interesting. I was in a neighborhood where
most of the front doors were unlocked, and on a street that is
very quiet on a summer night. All the animals are domesti-
cated, and the only night birds that I've ever heard are some
owls way down by the railroad track. So it was very quiet. I
heard the Barstows' dog bark, briefly, as if he had been waked
by a nightmare, and then the barking stopped. Everything was
quiet again. Then I heard, very close to me, a footstep and a
cough.

I felt my flesh get hard—you know that feeling—but I didn't
look up from my book, although I felt that I was being watched.
Intuition and all that sort of thing may exist, but I am happier
if I discount it, and yet, without lifting my eyes from the book,
I knew not only that I was being watched but that I was being
watched from the picture window at the end of the living room,
by someone whose intent was to watch me and to violate my
privacy. Sitting under a bright lamp, surrounded by the dark,
made me feel defenseless. I turned a page and pretended to go
on reading. Then a fear, much worse than the fear of the fool

outside the window, distracted me. I was afraid that the cough and the step and the feeling that I was being watched had come from my imagination. I looked up.

I saw him, all right, and I think he meant me to; he was grinning. I turned off the light, but it was too dark outside and my eyes were too accustomed to the bright reading light for me to pick out any shape against the glass. I ran into the hall-way and switched on some carriage lamps by the front door (the light they gave was not very bright but it was enough for me to see anyone crossing the lawn), but when I got back to the window, the lawn was empty and I could see that there was no one where he had been standing. There were plenty of places where he could have hidden. There is a big clump of syringa at the foot of the walk that would conceal a man, and there is the lilac and the cut-leaved maple. I wasn't going to get the old samurai sword out and chase him. Not me. I turned out the carriage lights then, and stood in the dark won-dering who it could have been.

I had never had anything to do with night people, but I know that they exist, and I guessed that he was probably some cracked old man from the row of shanties by the railroad tracks, and perhaps because of my determination, my need, to put a pleasant, or at least a calm, face on everything, I even managed to think compassionately of the old man who was driven, in senescence, to leave his home and wander at night in a strange neighborhood, at the mercy of dogs and policemen, only to be rewarded in the end by the sight of a man reading Lin Yutang or a woman feeding pills to a sick child or somebody eating chile con carne out of the icebox. As I climbed the dark stairs, I heard thunder, and a second later a flux of summer rain in-undated the county, and I thought of the poor prowler and his long walk home through the storm.

It was after four then, and I lay in the dark, listening to the rain and to the morning trains coming through. They come from Buffalo and Chicago and the Far West, through Albany and down along the river in the early morning, and at one time or another I've travelled on most of them, and I lay in the dark thinking about the polar air in the Pullman cars and the smell of night clothes and the taste of dining-car water and the way it feels to end a day in Cleveland or Chicago and begin another in New York, particularly after you've been away for a couple of years, and particularly in the summer. I lay in the dark imagining the dark cars in the rain, and the tables set for breakfast, and the smells.

I was very sleepy the next day, but I got my work done and dozed on the train coming home. I might have been able to go to sleep then, but I didn't want to take any chances, and I followed the routine of going to Orpheo's and then to the movies. I saw a terrible double feature. The pictures stupefied me, and I did go to sleep as soon as I got into bed, but then the telephone woke me. It was two o'clock. I lay in bed until the phone stopped ringing. I knew I was too wakeful then for any night sounds—the wind or the traffic—to make me sleepy, and I went downstairs. I didn't expect that the Peeping Tom would return, but my reading light was conspicuous in the dark neighborhood, so I turned on the carriage lamps by the door and sat down again with the book by Lin Yutang. When I heard the Barstows' dog bark, I put down my book and watched the picture window to assure myself that the Peeping Tom was not coming or, if he should come, to see him before he saw me.

I didn't see anything, anything at all, but after a few minutes I experienced that terrible hardening of the flesh, that certainty that I was being watched. I picked up my book again, not because I intended to read but because I wanted to show him that I was indifferent to the fact that he had returned. Of course, there are many other windows in the room, and I wondered for a minute which one he had taken up his stand at this night. Then I knew, and the fact that he was behind me, that he was at my back, frightened and exasperated me, and I jumped up without turning off the lamp and saw his face in the narrow window above the piano. "Get the hell away from here!" I yelled. "She's gone! Rachel's gone! There's noth-

[119]

ing to see! Leave me alone!" I ran to the window, but he had gone. And then, because I had been shouting at the top of my lungs in an empty house, I thought that perhaps I was going crazy. I thought, again, that I might have imagined the face in the window, and I got the flashlight and went outside.

There is a flower bed under the narrow window. I looked at this with the flashlight, and he had been there, all right. There were footprints in the dirt, and he'd stepped on some of the flowers. I followed his tracks out of the flower bed to the edge of the lawn, where I found a man's patent-leather bedroom slipper. It was a little cracked and worn, and I thought it might have belonged to an old man, but I knew it didn't belong to any servant. I guessed that Tom was one of my neighbors. I heaved the slipper over my hedge towards where the Barstows have a compost heap, and went back to the house and turned off the lights and went upstairs.

During the next day, I thought once or twice of calling the police, but I couldn't make up my mind. I thought about it again that night while I was standing at the bar at Orpheo's, waiting for them to cook my steak. The situation, on the surface, was ridiculous, and I could see that, but the dread of seeing his face in the window again was real and cumulative, and I didn't see why I should have to endure it, particularly at a time when I was trying to overhaul my whole way of living. It was getting dark outside. I went to the public telephone then and called the police. Stanley Madison, who sometimes directs traffic at the station, answered. He said "Oh" when I told him that I wanted to report a prowler. He asked me if Rachel was at home. Then he said that the village, since its incorporation in 1916, had never had such a complaint registered. He spoke with that understandable pride that we all take in the neighborhood. I had anticipated putting myself at a disadvantage, but Stanley spoke as if I were deliberately trying to damage real-estate values. He went on to say that a five-man police force was inadequate, that they were underpaid and overworked, and that if I wanted a guard put around my house, I should move to enlarge the police force at the next meeting of the civic-improvement association. He tried not to seem unfriendly and ended the conversation by asking about Rachel and the children, but when I left the telephone booth, I felt that I had made a mistake.

That night, a big thunderstorm broke right in the middle of the movie, and it rained until morning. I guess the storm kept Tom at home, because I didn't see him or hear him. But he was back the next night. I heard him come at about three and leave about an hour later, but I didn't look up from my book. I reasoned that he was probably a harmless nuisance, and that if I only knew who he was—that if I only knew his name— his ability to irritate me would be lost and I could peacefully resume the schedule of my cure. I went upstairs with the question of his identity still on my mind. I was pretty sure that he came from the neighborhood. I wondered if any of my friends or neighbors had a cracked relative staying with them for the summer. I went over the names of everyone I knew, trying to associate with them some eccentric uncle or grandfather. I thought that if I could disengage the stranger from the night, from the dark, everything would be all right.

In the morning, when I went down to the station, I walked through the crowd on the platform looking for some stranger who might be the culprit. Even though I had only seen the face dimly, I thought that I would recognize it. Then I saw my man. It was as simple as that. He was waiting on the platform for the eight-ten with the rest of us, but he wasn't any stranger.

It was Herbert Marston, who lives in the big yellow house on Blenhollow Road. If there had been any question in my mind, it would have been answered by the way he looked when he saw that I recognized him. He looked frightened and guilty. I started across the platform to speak to him. "I don't mind you looking in my windows at night, Mr. Marston," I was going to say, in a voice loud enough to embarrass him, "but I wish that you wouldn't trample on my wife's flowers." Then

I stopped, because I saw that he was not alone. He was with his wife and his daughter. I walked behind them and stood at the corner of the waiting room, looking at this family.

There was nothing irregular in Mr. Marston's features or —when he saw that I was going to leave him alone—in his manner. He's a gray-haired man, a little over medium height, with a bony face that must have been handsome when he was younger. The belief that a crooked heart is betrayed by palsies, tics, and other infirmities dies hard. I felt the loss of it that morning when I searched his face for some mark. He looked solvent, rested, and moral—much more so than Chucky Ewing, who was job-hunting, or Larry Spencer, whose son had polio, or any of a dozen other men on the platform waiting for the train. Then I looked at his daughter, Lydia. Lydia is one of the prettiest girls in our neighborhood. I'd ridden in on the train with her once or twice and I knew that she was doing voluntary secretarial work for the Red Cross. She had on a blue dress that morning, and her arms were bare, and she looked so fresh and pretty and sweet that I wouldn't have embarrassed or hurt her for anything in the world. Then I looked at Mrs. Marston, and if the mark was anywhere, it was on *her* face, although I don't understand why she should be afflicted for her husband's waywardness. It was very hot, but Mrs. Marston had on a brown suit and a worn fur piece. Her face was sallow and plain, but it was wreathed, even while she watched for the morning train, in an impermeable smile. It was a face that must have seemed, long ago, cut out for violent, even malevolent, passion. But years of prayer and abstinence had expunged the inclination to violence, I thought, leaving only a few ugly lines at the mouth and the eyes and rewarding Mrs. Marston with an air of adamant and fetid sweetness. She must pray for him, I thought, while he wanders around the back yards in his bathrobe. I had wanted to know who Tom was, but now that I knew, I didn't feel any better. The graying man and the beautiful girl and the woman, standing together, made me feel worse.

That night, I decided to stay in town and go to a cocktail party. It was in an apartment in one of the tower hotels—way, way, way up. As soon as I got there, I went out onto the terrace, looking around for someone to take to dinner. What I wanted was a pretty girl in new shoes, but it looked as if all the pretty girls had stayed at the shore. There was a gray-haired woman out there, and a woman with a floppy hat, and Grace Harris, this actress I've met a couple of times. Grace Harris is a beauty, a faded one, and we've never had much to say to one another, but that night she gave me a very cordial smile. It was cordial but it was very sad, and the first thing I thought of was that she must have learned that Rachel had left me. I smiled right back at her and went in to the bar, where I found Harry Purcell. I had some drinks and talked with him. I looked around the room a couple of times, and each time I saw Grace Harris giving me this sad, sad look. I wondered about it, and then I thought she had probably mistaken me for somebody else. A lot of those ageless beauties with violet eyes are half blind, I know, and I thought that perhaps she couldn't see across the room. It got late, but there weren't any claims on my time, and I went on drinking. Then Harry went to the bathroom, and I stood alone at the bar for a couple of minutes, but that was too long. Grace Harris, who was with some people at the other end of the room, came over to me. She came right up to me and put her snow-white hand on my arm. "You poor boy," she murmured, "you poor boy."

I'm not a boy, and I'm not poor, and I wished the hell she would get away. She has a clever face, but I felt in it, that night, the force of great sadness and great malice. "I see a rope around your neck," she said sadly. Then she lifted her hand off my coat sleeve and went out of the room, and I guess she must have gone home, because I didn't see her again. Harry came back, and I didn't tell him what had happened, and I tried not to think much about it myself. I stayed at the party too long and got a late train home.

I remember that I took a bath and put on pajamas and lay

down. As soon as I shut my eyes, I saw this rope. It had a hang-
man's noose at the end of it, but I'd known all along what Grace
Harris had been talking about; she'd had a premonition that I
would hang myself. The rope seemed to come down slowly into
my consciousness. I opened my eyes and thought about the
work I had to do in the morning, but when I shut my eyes
again, there was a momentary blankness into which the rope
—as if it had been pushed off a beam—fell, and swung through
space. I opened my eyes and thought some more about the office,
but when I shut them, there was the rope, still swinging. Whenever I closed my eyes that night and tried to go to sleep, it felt
as though sleep had taken on the anguish of blindness. And with
the visible world gone, there was nothing to keep the arbitrary
rope from occupying the dark. I got out of bed and went downstairs and opened the Lin Yutang. I had only been reading for
a few minutes when I heard Mr. Marston in the flower garden.
I thought I knew, at last, what he was waiting to see. This
frightened me. I turned off the light and stood up. It was dark
outside the window and I couldn't see him. I wondered if there
was any rope in the house. Then I remembered the painter on
my son's dinghy in the cellar. I went into the cellar. The dory
was on sawhorses, and there was a long painter on it, long
enough for a man to hang himself by. I went upstairs to the
kitchen and got a knife and hacked the painter off the boat.
Then I got some newspapers and put them into the furnace
and opened the drafts and burned up the rope. Then I went
upstairs and got into bed. I felt saved.

I don't know how long it had been since I had had a good
night's rest. But I felt queer in the morning, and although I
could see from the window that it was a bright day, I didn't
feel up to it. The sky and the light and everything else seemed
dim and remote, as if I saw it all from a great distance. The
thought of seeing the Marston family again revolted me, so I
skipped the eight-ten and took a later train. The image of the
rope was still at the back of my mind, and I saw it once or
twice on the trip. I got through the morning, but when I left

the office at noon, I told my secretary that I wouldn't be back. I had a lunch date with Nathan Shea, at the University Club, and I went there early and drank a Martini at the bar. I stood beside an old gentleman who was describing to a friend the regularity of his habits, and I had a strong impulse to crown him with a bowl of popcorn, but I drank my drink and stared at the bartender's wristwatch, which was hanging on a long-necked bottle of white crème de menthe. When Shea came in, I had two more drinks with him. Anesthetized by gin, I got through the lunch.

We said goodbye on Park Avenue. There my Martinis forsook me and I saw the rope again. It was about two o'clock on a sunny afternoon but it seemed dark to me. I went to the Corn Exchange Bank and cashed a check for five hundred dollars. Then I went to Brooks Brothers and bought some neckties and a box of cigars and went upstairs to look at suits. There were only a few customers in the store, and among them I noticed this girl or young woman who seemed to be alone. I guess she was looking over the stock for her husband. She had fair hair and the kind of white skin that looks like thin paper. It was a very hot day but she looked cool, as if she had been able to preserve, through the train ride in from Rye or Greenwich, the freshness of her bath. Her arms and her legs were beautiful, but the look on her face was sensible, humorous, even house-wifely, and this sensible air seemed to accentuate the beauty of her arms and legs. She walked over and rang for the elevator. I walked over and stood beside her. We rode down together, and I followed her out of the store onto Madison Avenue. The sidewalk was crowded, and I walked beside her. She looked at me once, and she knew that I was following her, but I felt sure she was the kind of woman who would not readily call for help. She waited at the corner for the light to change. I waited beside her. It was all I could do to keep from saying to her, very, very softly, "Madame, will you please let me put my hand around your ankle? That's all I want to do, Madame. It will save my life." She didn't look around again, but I could see that she was

[125]

frightened. She crossed the street and I stayed at her side, and all the time a voice inside my head was pleading, "Please let me put my hand around your ankle. It will save my life. I just want to put my hand around your ankle. I'll be very happy to pay you." I took out my wallet and pulled out some bills. Then I heard someone behind me calling my name. I recognized the hearty voice of an advertising salesman who is in and out of our office. I put the wallet back in my pocket, crossed the street, and tried to lose myself in the crowd.

I walked over to Park Avenue, and then to Lexington, and went into a movie theatre. A stale, cold wind blew down on me from the ventilating machine, like the air in those Pullmans I had listened to coming down the river in the morning from Chicago and the Far West. The lobby was empty, and I felt as if I had stepped into a palace or a basilica. I took a narrow staircase that went up and then turned abruptly, separating itself from the splendor. The landings were dirty and the walls were bare. This stairway brought me into the balcony, and I sat there in the dark, thinking that nothing now was going to save me, that no pretty girl with new shoes was going to cross my path in time.

I took a train home, but I was too tired to go to Orpheo's and then sit through a movie. I drove from the station to the house and put the car in the garage. From there I heard the telephone ringing, and I waited in the garden until the ringing had stopped. As soon as I stepped into the living room, I noticed on the wall some dirty hand prints that had been made by the children before they went away. They were near the baseboard and I had to get down on my knees to kiss them.

Then I sat in the living room for a long time. I fell asleep, and when I woke it was late; all the other houses were dark. I turned on a light. Peeping Tom would be putting on his slippers and his bathrobe, I thought, to begin his prowl through the back yards and gardens. Mrs. Marston would be on her knees, praying. I got down the Lin Yutang and began to read. I heard the Barstows' dog barking. The telephone began to ring.

[126]

"Oh, my darling!" I shouted when I heard Rachel's voice.
"Oh, my darling! Oh, my darling!" She was crying. She was at
Seal Harbor. It had rained for a week, and Tobey had a temperature of a hundred and four. "I'll leave now," I said. "I'll
drive all night. I'll be there tomorrow. I'll get there in the
morning. Oh, my darling!"

That was all. It was all over. I packed a bag and turned off
the icebox and drove all night. We've been happy ever since.
So far as I know, Mr. Marston has never stood outside our
house in the dark, although I've seen him often enough on the
station platform and at the country club. His daughter Lydia
is going to be married next month, and his sallow wife was
recently cited by one of the national charities for her good
works. Everyone here is well.

THE HARTLEYS

$\mathcal{M}$R. AND MRS. HARTLEY and their daughter Anne reached the Pemaquoddy Inn, one winter evening, after dinner and just as the bridge games were getting under way. Mr. Hartley carried the bags across the broad porch and into the lobby, and his wife and daughter followed him. They all three seemed very tired, and they looked around them at the bright, homely room with the gratitude of people who have escaped from tension and danger, for they had been driving in a blinding snowstorm since early morning. They had made the trip from New York, and it had snowed all the way, they said. Mr. Hartley put down the bags and returned to the car to get the skis. Mrs. Hartley sat down in one of the lobby chairs, and her daughter, tired and shy, drew close to her. There was a little snow in the girl's hair, and Mrs. Hartley brushed this away with her fingers. Then Mrs. Butterick, the widow who owned the inn, went out to the porch and called to Mr. Hartley that he needn't put his car up. One of the men would do it, she said. He came back into the lobby and signed the register.

He seemed to be a likeable man with an edge to his voice and an intense, polite manner. His wife was a handsome, dark-haired woman who was dazed with fatigue, and his daughter was a girl of about seven. Mrs. Butterick asked Mr. Hartley if he had ever stayed at the Pemaquoddy before. "When I got the reservation," she said "the name rang a bell."

"Mrs. Hartley and I were here eight years ago February," Mr. Hartley said. "We came on the twenty-third and were here for ten days. I remember the date clearly because we had such a wonderful time." Then they went upstairs. They came down again long enough to make a supper of some leftovers that had been kept warm on the back of the stove. The child was so tired she nearly fell asleep at the table. After supper, they went upstairs again.

In the winter, the life of the Pemaquoddy centered entirely on cold sports. Drinkers and malingerers were not encouraged, and most of the people there were earnest about their skiing. In the morning, they would take a bus across the valley to the mountains, and if the weather was good, they would carry a pack lunch and remain on the slopes until late afternoon. They'd vary this occasionally by skating on a rink near the inn, which had been made by flooding a clothesyard. There was a hill behind the inn that could sometimes be used for skiing when conditions on the mountain were poor. This hill was serviced by a primitive ski tow that had been built by Mrs. Butterick's son. "He bought that motor that pulls the tow when he was a senior at Harvard," Mrs. Butterick always said when she spoke of the tow. "It was in an old Mercer auto, and he drove it up here from Cambridge one night without any license plates!" When she said this, she would put her hand over her heart, as if the dangers of the trip were still vivid.

The Hartleys picked up the Pemaquoddy routine of fresh air and exercise the morning following their arrival.

Mrs. Hartley was an absent-minded woman. She boarded the bus for the mountain that morning, sat down, and was talking to another passenger when she realized that she had forgotten her skis. Her husband went after them while everyone waited. She wore a bright, fur-trimmed parka that had been cut for someone with a younger face, and it made her look tired. Her husband wore some Navy equipment, which was stencilled with his name and rank. Their daughter, Anne, was pretty. Her hair was braided in tight, neat plaits, there was a saddle of freckles across her small nose, and she looked around her with the bleak, rational scrutiny of her age.

Mr. Hartley was a good skier. He was up and down the slope, his skis parallel, his knees bent, his shoulders swinging gracefully in a half circle. His wife was not as clever but she knew what she was doing, and she enjoyed the cold air and the snow. She fell now and then, and when someone offered to help her to her feet, when the cold snow that had been pressed against her face had heightened its color, she looked like a much younger woman.

Anne didn't know how to ski. She stood at the foot of the slope watching her parents. They called to her, but she didn't move, and after a while she began to shiver. Her mother went to her and tried to encourage her, but the child turned away crossly. "I don't want *you* to show me," she said. "I want Daddy to show me." Mrs. Hartley called her husband.

As soon as Mr. Hartley turned his attention to Anne, she lost all of her hesitation. She followed him up and down the hill, and as long as he was with her, she seemed confident and happy. Mr. Hartley stayed with Anne until after lunch, when he turned her over to a professional instructor who was taking a class of beginners out to the slope. Mr. and Mrs. Hartley went with the group to the foot of the slope, where Mr. Hartley took his daughter aside. "Your mother and I are going to ski some trails now," he said, "and I want you to join Mr. Ritter's class and to learn as much from him as you can. If you're ever going to learn to ski, Anne, you'll have to learn without me. We'll be back at around four, and I want you to show me what you've learned when we come back."

"Yes, Daddy," she said.

"Now you go and join the class."

"Yes, Daddy."

Mr. and Mrs. Hartley waited until Anne had climbed the slope and joined the class. Then they went away. Anne watched the instructor for a few miniutes, but as soon as she noticed that her parents had gone, she broke from the group and coasted down the hill toward the hut. "Miss," the instructor called after her. "Miss . . ." She didn't answer. She went into the hut, took off her parka and her mittens, spread them neatly on a table to dry, and sat beside the fire, holding her head down so that her face could not be seen. She sat there all afternoon. A little before dark, when her parents returned to the hut, stamping the snow off their boots, she ran to her father. Her face was swollen from crying. "Oh, Daddy, I thought you weren't coming back," she cried. "I thought you weren't ever coming back!" She threw her arms around him and buried her face in his clothes.

"Now, now, now, Anne," he said, and he patted her back and smiled at the people who happened to notice the scene. Anne sat beside him on the bus ride back, holding his arm.

At the inn that evening, the Hartleys came into the bar before dinner and sat at a wall table. Mrs. Hartley and her daughter drank tomato juice, and Mr. Hartley had three Old-Fashioneds. He gave Anne the orange slices and the sweet cherries from his drinks. Everything her father did interested her. She lighted his cigarettes and blew out the matches. She examined his watch and laughed at all his jokes. She had a sharp, pleasant laugh.

The family talked quietly. Mr. and Mrs. Hartley spoke oftener to Anne than to each other, as if they had come to a point in their marriage where there was nothing to say. They discussed haltingly, between themselves, the snow and the mountain, and in the course of this attempt to make conversation Mr. Hartley, for some reason, spoke sharply to his wife. Mrs. Hartley got up from the table quickly. She might have been crying. She hurried through the lobby and went up the stairs.

Mr. Hartley and Anne stayed in the bar. When the dinner bell rang, he asked the desk clerk to send Mrs. Hartley a tray. He ate dinner with his daughter in the dining room. After dinner, he sat in the parlor reading an old copy of *Fortune* while Anne played with some other children who were staying at the inn. They were all a little younger than she, and she handled them easily and affectionately, imitating an adult. She taught them a simple card game and then read them a story. After the younger children were sent to bed, she read a book. Her father took her upstairs at about nine.

He came down by himself later and went into the bar. He drank alone and talked with the bartender about various brands of bourbon. "Dad used to have his bourbon sent up from Kentucky in kegs," Mr. Hartley said. A slight rasp in his voice, and his intense and polite manner, made what he said seem important. "They were small, as I recall. I don't suppose they held more than a gallon. Dad used to have them sent to him twice a year. When Grandmother asked him what they were, he always told her they were full of sweet cider." After discussing bourbons, they discussed the village and the changes in the inn. "We've only been here once before," Mr. Hartley said. "That was eight years ago, eight years ago February." Then he repeated, word for word, what he had said in the lobby the previous night. "We came on the twenty-third and were here for ten days. I remember the date clearly because we had such a wonderful time."

The Hartleys' subsequent days were nearly all like the first. Mr. Hartley spent the early hours instructing his daughter. The girl learned rapidly, and when she was with her father, she was daring and graceful, but as soon as he left her, she would go to the hut and sit by the fire. Each day, after lunch, they would reach the point where he gave her a lecture on self-reliance. "Your mother and I are going away now," he would say, "and I want you to ski by yourself, Anne." She would nod her head and agree with him, but as soon as he had gone, she would return to the hut and wait there. Once—it was the third day—he lost his temper. "Now, listen, Anne," he shouted, "if you're going to learn to ski, you've got to learn by yourself." His loud voice wounded her, but it did not seem to show her the way to independence. She became a familiar figure in the afternoons, sitting beside the fire.

Sometimes Mr. Hartley would modify his discipline. The three of them would return to the inn on the early bus and he would take his daughter to the skating rink and give her a skating lesson. On these occasions, they stayed out late. Mrs. Hartley watched them sometimes from the parlor window. The rink was at the foot of the primitive ski tow that had been built by Mrs. Butterick's son. The terminal posts of the tow looked like gibbets in the twilight, and Mr. Hartley and his daughter looked like figures of contrition and patience. Again and again they would circle the little rink, earnest and serious, as if he were explaining to her something more mysterious than a sport.

Everyone at the inn liked the Hartleys, although they gave the other guests the feeling that they had recently suffered some loss—the loss of money, perhaps, or perhaps Mr. Hartley had lost his job. Mrs. Hartley remained absent-minded, but the other guests got the feeling that this characteristic was the result of some misfortune that had shaken her self-possession. She seemed anxious to be friendly and she plunged, like a lonely woman, into every conversation. Her father had been a doctor, she said. She spoke of him as if he had been a great power, and she spoke with intense pleasure of her childhood. "Mother's living room in Grafton was forty-five feet long," she said. "There were fireplaces at both ends. It was one of those marvelous old Victorian houses." In the china cabinet in the dining room, there was some china like the china Mrs. Hartley's mother had owned. In the lobby there was a paperweight like a paperweight Mrs. Hartley had been given when she was a girl. Mr. Hartley also spoke of his origins now and then. Mrs. Butterick once asked him to carve a leg of lamb, and as he sharpened the carving knife, he said, "I never do this without thinking of Dad." Among the collection of canes in the hallway, there was a blackthorn embossed with silver. "That's exactly like the blackthorn Mr. Wentworth brought Dad from Ireland," Mr. Hartley said.

[133]

Anne was devoted to her father but she obviously liked her mother, too. In the evenings, when she was tired, she would sit on the sofa beside Mrs. Hartley and rest her head on her mother's shoulder. It seemed to be only on the mountain, where the environment was strange, that her father would become for her the only person in the world. One evening when the Hartleys were playing bridge—it was quite late and Anne had gone to bed—the child began to call her father. "I'll go, darling," Mrs. Hartley said, and she excused herself and went upstairs. "I want my Daddy," those at the bridge table could hear the girl screaming. Mrs. Hartley quieted her and came downstairs again. "Anne had a nightmare," she explained, and went on playing cards.

The next day was windy and warm. In the middle of the afternoon, it began to rain, and all but the most intrepid skiers went back to their hotels. The bar at the Pemaquoddy filled up early. The radio was turned on for weather reports, and one earnest guest picked up the telephone in the lobby and called other resorts. Was it raining in Pico? Was it raining in Stowe? Was it raining in Ste. Agathe? Mr. and Mrs. Hartley were in the bar that afternoon. She was having a drink for the first time since they had been there, but she did not seem to enjoy it. Anne was playing in the parlor with the other children. A little before dinner, Mr. Hartley went into the lobby and asked Mrs. Butterick if they could have their dinner upstairs. Mrs. Butterick said that this could be arranged. When the dinner bell rang, the Hartleys went up, and a maid took them trays. After dinner, Anne went back to the parlor to play with the other children, and after the dining room had been cleared, the maid went up to get the Hartleys' trays.

The transom above the Hartleys' bedroom door was open, and as the maid went down the hall, she could hear Mrs. Hartley's voice, a voice so uncontrolled, so guttural and full of suffering, that she stopped and listened as if the woman's life were in danger. "Why do we have to come back?" Mrs. Hartley was crying. "Why do we have to come back? Why do we have to

make these trips back to the places where we thought we were
happy? What good is it going to do? What good has it ever
done? We go through the telephone book looking for the names
of people we knew ten years ago, and we ask them for dinner,
and what good does it do? What good has it ever done? We go
back to the restaurants, the mountains, we go back to the houses,
even the neighborhoods, we walk in the slums, thinking that
this will make us happy, and it never does. Why in Christ's
name did we ever begin such a wretched thing? Why isn't there
an end to it? Why can't we separate again? It was better that
way. Wasn't it better that way? It was better for Anne—I don't
care what you say, it was better for her than this. I'll take Anne
again and you can live in town. Why can't I do that, why can't
I, why can't I, why can't I . . ." The frightened maid went
back along the corridor. Anne was sitting in the parlor reading
to the younger children when the maid went downstairs.

It cleared up that night and turned cold. Everything froze.
In the morning, Mrs. Butterick announced that all the trails
on the mountain were closed and that the tramway would not
run. Mr. Hartley and some other guests broke the crust on the
hill behind the inn, and one of the hired hands started the
primitive tow. "My son bought the motor that pulls the tow
when he was a senior at Harvard," Mrs. Butterick said when
she heard its humble explosions. "It was in an old Mercer auto,
and he drove it up here from Cambridge one night without any
license plates!" The slope offered the only skiing in the neighborhood, and after lunch a lot of people came there from other
hotels. They wore the snow away under the tow to a surface
of rough stone, and snow had to be shovelled onto the tracks.
The rope was frayed, and Mrs. Butterick's son had planned the
tow so poorly that it gave the skiers a strenuous and uneven
ride. Mrs. Hartley tried to get Anne to use the tow, but she
would not ride it until her father led the way. He showed her
how to stand, how to hold the rope, bend her knees, and drag
her poles. As soon as he was carried up the hill, she gladly fol-

lowed. She followed him up and down the hill all afternoon, delighted that for once he was remaining in her sight. When the crust on the slope was broken and packed, it made good running, and that odd, nearly compulsive rhythm of riding and skiing, riding and skiing, established itself.

It was a fine afternoon. There were snow clouds, but a bright and cheerful light beat through them. The country, seen from the top of the hill, was black and white. Its only colors were the colors of spent fire, and this impressed itself upon one—as if the desolation were something more than winter, as if it were the work of a great conflagration. People talk, of course, while they ski, while they wait for their turn to seize the rope, but they can hardly be heard. There is the exhaust of the tow motor and the creak of the iron wheel upon which the tow rope turns, but the skiers themselves seem stricken dumb, lost in the rhythm of riding and coasting. That afternoon was a continuous cycle of movement. There was a single file to the left of the slope, holding the frayed rope and breaking from it, one by one, at the crown of the hill to choose their way down, going again and again over the same surface, like people who, having lost a ring or a key on the beach, search again and again in the same sand. In the stillness, the child Anne began to shriek. Her arm had got caught in the frayed rope; she had been thrown to the ground and was being dragged brutally up the hill toward the iron wheel. "Stop the tow!" her father roared. "Stop the tow! Stop the tow!" And everyone else on the hill began to shout, "Stop the tow! Stop the tow! Stop the tow!" But there was no one there to stop it. Her screams were hoarse and terrible, and the more she struggled to free herself from the rope, the more violently it threw her to the ground. Space and the cold seemed to reduce the voices—even the anguish in the voices —of the people who were calling to stop the tow, but the girl's cries were piercing until her neck was broken on the iron wheel.

The Hartleys left for New York that night after dark. They

were going to drive all night behind the local hearse. Several
people offered to drive the car down for them, but Mr. Hartley
said that he wanted to drive, and his wife seemed to want him
to. When everything was ready, the stricken couple walked
across the porch, looking around them at the bewildering beauty
of the night, for it was very cold and clear and the constellations
seemed brighter than the lights of the inn or the village. He
helped his wife into the car, and after arranging a blanket over
her legs, they started the long, long drive.

THE SUMMER FARMER

HE Nor'easter is a train the railroad chris-
tened at a moment when its directors were imbued with the
mystery of travel. Memory is often more appealing than fact,
and a passenger who had long ridden the train might overlook
its noise and dirt each time he entered the Grand Central Station
and saw there the name of a northerly three-day rain. This, at
least, was the case with Paul Hollis, who rode the Nor'easter
on nearly every Thursday or Friday night of his summer. He
was a bulky man, who suffered in all Pullmans, but in none so
much as he did on this ride. As a rule, he stayed in the club
car until ten, drinking Scotch. The whiskey ordinarily kept him
asleep until they reached the tumultuous delays of Springfield,
past midnight. North of Springfield, the train fell into the balky
and malingerinig stride of an old local, and Paul lay in his
berth between wakefulness and sleep, like a partially anesthetized patient. The ordeal ended when, after breakfast, he left
the Nor'easter, in Meridian Junction, and was met by his gentle wife. There was this to be said about the journey: It made
one fully conscious of the terrestrial distance that separated the
hot city from the leafy and ingenuous streets of the junction
village.

The conversation between Paul and Virginia Hollis during
the drive from the Junction to their farm, north of Hiems, was
confined to the modest properties and affections they shared;

more than this, it seemed to aim at a deliberate inconsequence, as if to mention the checking balance or the wars might ruin the spell of a mild morning and an open car. The drain in the downstairs shower was leaking, Virginia told Paul one morning in July, his sister Ellen was drinking too much, the Marstons had been over for lunch, and the time had come for the children to have a pet. This was a subject to which she had obviously given some thought. No country dog would last in a New York apartment when they returned in the fall, she said, cats were a nuisance, and she had concluded that rabbits were the best they could do. There was a house on the road with a rabbit cage on its lawn, and they could stop there that morning and buy a pair. They would be a present from Paul to the children, and so much the better for that. The purchase would make that weekend the weekend when they had bought the rabbits, and distinguish it from the weekend when they had transplanted the Christmas fern or the weekend when they had removed the dead juniper. They could put the rabbits into the old duckhouse, Virginia said, and when they went back to the city in the fall, Kasiak could eat them. Kasiak was the hired man.

They were driving upland. From the Junction north, one never quite lost the sense of a gradual climb. Hills blocked off the delicate, the vitiated New Hampshire landscape, with its omnipresence of ruin, but every few miles a tributary of the Merrimack opened a broad valley, with elms, farms, and stone fences. "It's along here," Virginia said. Paul didn't know what she meant until she reminded him of the rabbits. "If you'll slow down here . . . Here, Paul, *here*." He bumped the car over the shoulder of the road and stopped. On the lawn of a white, neat house, darkened by rock maples, there was a rabbit cage. "Hello," Paul shouted, "hello," and a man in overalls came out of a side door, chewing on something, as if had been interrupted at a meal. White rabbits were two dollars, he said. Browns and grays were a dollar and a half. He swallowed, and wiped his mouth with his fist. He spoke uneasily, as if he had wanted to keep the simple transaction from someone, and after Paul had picked a brown and a gray, he ran to the barn for a box. As Paul turned the car back onto the road, they heard behind them a heartbroken shout. A boy ran from the house to the rabbit cage, and they saw the source of the farmer's uneasiness.

The cash market and the antique store, the Civil War cannon and the post office of Hiems fell behind them, and Paul accelerated the car happily when they escaped from the narrow streets of the village and drove into the fresh lake winds. The road brought them, first, along the unfashionable, or gregarious, end of the lake; then the houses thinned and gave way to pine groves and empty fields as they drove north. The sense of home-coming—of returning to a place where he had summered all his life—became for Paul so violent that the difference between the pace of his imagination and the speed of the car annoyed him until they turned off the road onto grass ruts and saw, literally at the road's end, their farm.

The gentle shadow of a cloud was passing the face of the Hollis house. At the edge of the lawn, there was an upside-down piece of porch furniture that had been abandoned in a thunder-shower and that seemed to have been drying there since Paul's youth. The light and heat increased and the shade deepened as the moving shadow of the cloud darkened the barn and the clothesyard and vanished into the woods. "Hello, Brother." It was Paul's sister Ellen calling to him from one of the open windows. His business suit bound at the shoulders when he left the car, as if he had taken on height, for the place told him that he was ten years younger; the maples, the house, the simple mountains all told him this. His two small children stormed around the edge of the barn and collided against his legs. Taller, browner, healthier, more handsome, more intelligent—they seemed to him to be all these things each weekend when he was reunited with them. A sere branch on a maple caught his eye. That would have to be cut. He stooped down to pick up his little boy and girl in a scalding rush of love, for which he was unarmed and, it seemed, unprepared.

The duckhouse, where they put the rabbits that morning,

had been empty for years, but there was a cage and a shelter, and it would do. "Now, these are your pets, these are your rabbits," Paul told the children. His sternness transfixed them, and the little boy began to suck his thumb. "These are your responsibility, and if you take good care of them, perhaps you can have a dog when we get back to New York. You'll have to feed them and clean their house." His love for the children and his desire to draw for them, even faintly, the mysterious shapes of responsibility reduced him to a fatuity that he was conscious of himself. "I don't want you to expect someone else to help you," he said. "You'll have to give them water twice a day. They're supposed to like lettuce and carrots. Now you can put them in the house yourself. Daddy has to get to work."

Paul Hollis was a summer farmer. He mowed, cultivated, and waxed angry about the price of scratch feed, and at that instant when the plangent winds of Labor Day began to sound he hung up his blunted scythe to rust in the back hall, where the kerosene was kept, and happily shifted his interest to the warm apartments of New York. On that day—the day when he bought the rabbits—he went to his bedroom after he had lectured the children, and changed into a pair of coveralls that were still dimly stencilled with his name, rank, and serial number. Virginia sat on the edge of the bed while he dressed, and talked about his sister Ellen, who was spending a month with them. Ellen needed the rest; Ellen drank too much. But there was no suggestion of correction or change in what Virginia said about Ellen, and when Paul glanced at his wife, he thought how forgiving and comely she was. The room was old and pleasant —it had been his parents' room—and what light reached it reached it through the leaves. They lingered there talking about Ellen, the children, tasting the astringency of their contentment and their worthiness, but not so long as to seem idle. Paul was going to help Kasiak scythe the highest field, and Virginia wanted to pick some flowers.

The Hollis property was high, and it was Paul's long-dead

father who had called the highest pasture Elysian, because of its unearthly stillness. This pasture was mowed on alternate years to keep the scrub from taking hold. When Paul reached it that morning, Kasiak was there, and Paul judged that he had been working for about three hours; Kasiak was paid by the hour. The two men spoke briefly—the hired man and the vacationist—and picked up the tacit bond of people who happen to be working together. Paul mowed below and a little to Kasiak's right. He used a scythe well, but there was no confusing, even at a distance, Kasiak's diligent figure with Paul's.

Kasiak was Russian-born. This and everything else Paul knew about him he had been told while they worked. Kasiak had landed in Boston, worked in a shoe factory, studied English at night, rented, and eventually bought, the farm below the Hollis place. They had been neighbors for twenty years. He was doing the Hollises' work that year for the first time. Up until then, he had been merely a persevering and colorful figure on their landscape. He dressed his deaf wife in salt bags and potato sacks. He was miserly. He was bitter. Even on that summer morning, he cut a figure of chagrin and discontent. He kept his woods clear and stored his hay at precisely the right moment, and his fields, his gardens, his compost heap, and the sour smell of milk in his immaculate kitchen conveyed the sense of security that lies in the power of intelligent husbandry. He mowed, he walked, like a prisoner in a prison yard. From the time he went to the barn, an hour before dawn, until his day ended, there was no hesitation in his thought or in his step, and this flawless link of chores was part of a larger chain of responsibilities and aspirations that had begun with his youth in Russia and that would end, he believed, with the birth of a just and peaceable world, delivered in bloodshed and arson.

Virginia had been amused when Paul told her that Kasiak was a Communist. Kasiak had told Paul himself. Two weeks after he had begun to work for them, he had taken to cutting editorials from a Communist newspaper and handing them to Paul or slipping them under the kitchen door. Reasonableness was Paul's watchword with Kasiak, he liked to think. Twice, in the feed store, when Kasiak's politics had been under discussion, Paul had defended Kasiak's right to draw his own conclusions about the future, and in their conversations he always asked Kasiak lightly when he was going to have his revolution.

That day fell at the end of the haying weather. As it got late in the morning, they could hear dull blasts of thunder. A wind rose in the neighborhood, but there was none to speak of in the field. Kasiak trailed after him a rich blend of citronella and vinegar, and both men were plagued with flies. They did not let the chance of a storm change the pace of their scything. It was as if there were some significance, hidden, surely, to them, in completing that field. Then the wet wind climbed the hill behind them, and Paul, taking one hand off the snath, straightened his back. While they had been working, clouds had blackened the sky from the horizon to above his head, so he was given the illusion of a country divided evenly between the lights of catastrophe and repose. The shade of the storm was travelling as rapidly up the field as a man walks, but the hay it had not touched was yellow, and there was no portent of the storm in the delicate sky ahead of him or in the clouds there or in anything he could see except the green wood, whose color the storm had begun to deepen. Then he felt against his skin a coldness that belonged to no part of that day, and heard at his back the rain begin to drop through the trees.

Paul ran for the woods. Kasiak followed slowly, with the storm at his heels. They sat beside each other on stones in the shelter of the dense foliage, watching the moving curtain of rain. Kasiak took off his hat—for the first time that summer to Paul's knowledge. His hair and forehead were gray. Ruddiness began on his high cheekbones and shaded down to a dark brown that spread from his jaw to his neck.

"How much will you charge me for using your horse to cultivate the garden?" Paul asked.

"Four dollars." Kasiak didn't raise his voice, and Paul

couldn't hear him above the noise the rain made crashing into the field.

"How much?"

"Four dollars."

"Let's try it tomorrow morning if it's clear. Shall we?"

"You'll have to do it early. It's too hot for her in the afternoon."

"Six o'clock."

"You want to get up that early?" Kasiak smiled at his gibe at the Hollis family and their disorderly habits. Lightning tipped the woods, so close to them that they could smell the galvanic discharge, and a second later there was an explosion of thunder that sounded as if it had destroyed the county. The front of the storm passed then, the wind died down, and the shower fell around them with the dogged gloom of an autumn rain.

"Have you heard from your family recently, Kasiak?" Paul asked.

"For two years—not for two years."

"Would you like to go back?"

"Yes, yes." There was an intent light in his face. "On my father's farm, there are some big fields. My brothers are still there. I would like to go there in an airplane. I would land the airplane in these big fields, and they would all come running to see who it was and they would see it was me."

"You don't like it here, do you?"

"It's a capitalist country."

"Why did you come, then?"

"I don't know. I think over there they made me work too hard. Over there, we cut the rye at night, when there is some moisture in the air. They put me to work in the fields when I was twelve years old. We get up at three in the morning to cut the rye. My hands are all bleeding, and swollen so I can't sleep. My father beat me like a convict. In Russia, they used to beat convicts. He beat me with a whip for horses until my back was bleeding." Kasiak felt his back, as if the welts still bled. "After that, I decided to go away. I waited six years. That's why I came, I guess—they set me to work in the fields too soon."

"When are you going to have your revolution, Kasiak?"

"When the capitalists make another war."

"What's going to happen to me, Kasiak? What's going to happen to people like me?"

"It depends. If you work on a farm or in a factory, I guess it will be all right. They'll only get rid of useless people."

"All right, Kasiak," Paul said heartily, "I'll work for you," and he slapped the farmer on the back. He frowned at the rain. "I guess I'll go down and get some lunch," he said. "We won't be able to scythe any more today, will we?" He ran down the wet field to the barn. Kasiak followed him a few minutes later, but he did not run. He entered the barn and began to repair a cold frame, as if the thunderstorm fitted precisely into his scheme of things.

Before dinner that night, Paul's sister Ellen drank too much. She was late coming to the table, and when Paul went into the pantry for a spoon, he found her there, drinking out of the silver cocktail shaker. Seated at the table, high in her firmament of gin, she looked critically at her brother and his wife, remembering some real or imagined injustice of her youth, for with any proximity the constellations of some families generate among themselves an asperity that nothing can sweeten. Ellen was a heavy-featured woman who held her strong blue eyes at a squint. She had had her second divorce that spring. She had wrapped a bright scarf around her head for dinner that night and put on an old dress she had found in one of the attic trunks, and, reminded by her faded clothes of a simpler time of life, she talked uninterruptedly about the past and, particularly, about Father—Father this and Father that. The shabby dress and her reminiscent mood made Paul impatient, and it seemed to him that a vast crack had appeared magically in Ellen's heart the night Father died.

[145]

A northwest wind had driven the thundershower out of the county and left in the air a poignant chill, and when they went out on the piazza after dinner to watch the sun go down, there were a hundred clouds in the west—clouds of gold, clouds of silver, clouds like bone and tinder and filth under the bed. "It's so *good* for me to be up here," Ellen said. "It does so much for me." She sat on the rail against the light, and Paul couldn't see her face. "I can't find Father's binoculars," she went on, "and his golf clubs have disappeared." From the open window of the children's room, Paul heard his daughter singing, "How many miles is it to Babylon? Three score miles and ten. Can we get there by candlelight? . . ." Immense tenderness and contentment fell to him with her voice from the open window.

It was so good for them all, as Ellen said; it did so much for them. It was a phrase Paul had heard spoken on that piazza since his memory had become retentive. Ellen was the mote on that perfect evening. There was something wrong, some half-known evil in her worship of the bucolic scene—some measure of her inadequacy and, he supposed, of his.

"Let's have a brandy," Ellen said. They went into the house to drink. In the living room, there was a lot of talk about what they would have—brandy, mint, Cointreau, Scotch. Paul went into the kitchen and put glasses and bottles on a tray. The screen door was shaken by something—the wind, he guessed, until the thumping was repeated and he saw Kasiak standing in the dark. He would offer him a drink. He would settle him in the wing chair and play out that charade of equality between vacationist and hired man that is one of the principal illusions of the leafy months. "Here's something you ought to read," Kasiak said, before Paul could speak, and he passed him a newspaper clipping. Paul recognized the type face of the Communist paper that was mailed to Kasiak from Indiana. LUXURY LIVING WEAKENS U.S. was the headline, and the story described with traitorous joy the hardy and purposeful soldiers of Russia. Paul's face got warm in anger at Kasiak and at the uprush of chauvinism he felt. "Is that all you want?" His voice broke dryly.

Kasiak nodded. "I'll see you tomorrow morning at six," Paul said, master to hired man, and he hooked the screen door and turned his back.

Paul liked to think that his patience with the man was inexhaustible—for, after all, Kasiak not only believed in Bakunin, he believed that stones grow and that thunder curdles milk. In his dealings with Kasiak, he had unconsciously sacrificed some independence, and in order to get to the garden at six the next morning, he got up at five. He made himself some breakfast, and at half past five he heard the rattle of a cart on the road. The puerile race of virtue and industry had begun. Paul was in the garden when Kasiak brought the cart into view. Kasiak was disappointed.

Paul had seen the mare only in pasture, and, aside from the fact that she was costing him four dollars, he was curious about the animal, for, along with a cow and a wife, she made up Kasiak's family. Her coat was dusty, he saw; her belly was swollen; her hoofs were unshod and uncut and had shredded like paper. "What's her name?" he asked, but Kasiak didn't answer. He hitched the mare to the cultivator, and she sighed and labored up the hill. Paul led the mare by the bridle, and Kasiak held down the cultivator.

Halfway along the first row in the garden, a stone stopped them, and when it had been dislodged and rolled away, Kasiak called "Gee-up" to the mare. She didn't move. "Gee-up," he shouted. His voice was harsh, but there was some tenderness hidden in it. "Gee-up, gee-up, gee-up." He slapped her sides lightly with the reins. He looked anxiously at Paul, as if he were ashamed that Paul should notice the mare's extreme decrepitude and reach a mistaken judgment on an animal he loved. When Paul suggested that he might use a whip, Kasiak said no. "Gee-up, gee-up, gee-up," he shouted again, and when she still failed to respond, he struck her rump with the reins. Paul pulled at her bit. They stood for ten minutes in the middle of the row pulling and shouting, and it seemed that the life had gone out of the mare. Then, when they were hoarse and discouraged, she began to stir and gather wind in her lungs. Her carcass worked like a bellows and the wind whistled in her nostrils, and, like the bag Aeolus gave to Ulysses, she seemed to fill with tempests. She shook the flies off her head and pulled the cultivator a few feet forward.

This made for slow work, and by the time they finished, the sun was hot. Paul heard voices from his house as he and Kasiak led the infirm mare back to the cart, and he saw his children, still in their night clothes, feeding their rabbits in the lettuce patch. When Kasiak harnessed the mare to the cart, Paul again asked him her name.

"She has no name," Kasiak said.

"I've never heard of a farm horse without a name."

"To name animals is bourgeois sentimentality," Kasiak said, and he started to drive away.

Paul laughed.

"You never come back!" Kasiak called over his shoulder. It was the only meanness at hand; he knew how deeply Paul loved the hill. His face was dark. "You never come back next year. You wait and see."

There is a moment early on Sunday when the tide of the summer day turns inexorably toward the evening train. You can swim, play tennis, or take a nap or a walk, but it doesn't make much difference. Immediately after lunch, Paul was faced with his unwillingness to leave. This became so strong that he was reminded of the intensity and the apprehensiveness he had felt on furloughs. At six, he put on his tight business suit and had a drink with Virginia in the kitchen. She asked him to buy nail scissors and candy in New York. While they were there, he heard that noise that he lived in dread of above all others—his innocent and gentle children screaming in pain.

He ran out, letting the screen door slam in Virginia's face. Then he turned back and held the door open for her, and she came out and ran up the hill at his side. The children were coming down the road, under the big trees. Lost in their crys-

talline grief, blinded with tears, they stumbled and ran toward
their mother and searched in her dark skirts for a shape to press
their heads against. They were howling. But it was nothing
serious, after all. Their rabbits were dead.

"There, there, there, there . . ." Virginia drew the children
down toward the house. Paul went on up the road and found
the limp rabbits in the hutch. He carried them to the edge of the
garden and dug a hole. Kasiak came by, carrying water for
the chickens, and when he had sized up the situation, he spoke
mournfully. "Why you dig a grave?" he asked. "The skunks
will dig them up tonight. Throw them in Cavis's pasture.
They'll dig them up again. . . ." He went on toward the
chicken house. Paul stamped down the grave. Dirt got into his
low shoes. He went back to the rabbit house to see if he could
find any trace of what had killed them, and in the feeding
trough, below some wilted vegetables that the children had up-
rooted, he saw the crystals of a mortal poison that they used
to kill rats in the winter.

Paul made a serious effort to remember whether he could
have left the poison there himself. The stifling heat in the
hutch raised and sent the sweat rolling down his face. Could
Kasiak have done it? Could Kasiak have been so mean, so per-
verse? Could he, through believing that on some fall evening
fires on the mountain would signal the diligent and the reliable
to seize power from the hands of those who drank Martinis,
have become shrewd enough to put his finger on the only interest in the future Paul had?

Kasiak was in the chicken house. Shadow had begun to cover
the ground, and some of the happy and stupid fowl were roost-
ing. "Did you poison the rabbits, Kasiak?" Paul called. "Did
you? Did you?" His loud voice maddened the fowl. They spread
their heavy wings and cawed. "Did you, Kasiak?" Kasiak didn't
speak. Paul put his hands on the man's shoulders and shook
him. "Don't you know how strong that poison is? Don't you
know that the children might have got into it? Don't you know
that it might have killed them?" The fowl involved themselves

in the fracas. Signals went from the house to the yard; they
pushed one another off the congested gangway and thumped
their wings. As if the life in Kasiak hid slyly from violence
behind cartilage and bone, there was no apparent resistance in
him, and Paul shook him until he creaked. "Did you, Kasiak?"
Paul shouted. "Did you? Oh, Kasiak, if you touch my children,
if you harm them in any way—in any way—I'll cut your head
open." He pushed the man away from him and he sprawled
in the dirt.

When Paul got back to the kitchen, there was no one there,
and he drank two glasses of water. From the living room he
could hear his mourning children, and his sister Ellen, who had
no children of her own, struggling awkwardly to distract them
with a story about a cat she had once owned. Virginia came into
the kitchen and closed the door after her. She asked if the rabbits had been poisoned, and he said yes. She sat in a chair by
the kitchen table. "I put it there," she said. "I put it there last
fall. I never thought we'd use that house again, and I wanted
to keep the rats out of it. I forgot. I never thought we'd use that
house again. I completely forgot."

It is true of even the best of us that if an observer can catch
us boarding a train at a way station; if he will mark our faces,
stripped by anxiety of their self-possession; if he will appraise
our luggage, our clothing, and look out of the window to see
who has driven us to the station; if he will listen to the harsh
or tender things we say if we are with our families, or notice
the way we put our suitcase onto the rack, check the position
of our wallet, our key ring, and wipe the sweat off the back of
our necks; if he can judge sensibly the self-importance, diffi-
dence, or sadness with which we settle ourselves, he will be
given a broader view of our lives than most of us would intend.
Paul barely made the train that Sunday night. When he
pulled himself up the high steps of the coach, he was short-
winded. There was still some straw on his shoes from the violence in the chicken house. The drive had not completely cooled

his temper, and his face was red. No harm had been done, he thought. "No harm," he said under his breath as he swung his suitcase onto the rack—a man of forty with signs of mortality in a tremor of his right hand, signs of obsoleteness in his confused frown, a summer farmer with blistered hands, a sunburn, and lame shoulders, so visibly shaken by some recent loss of principle that it would have been noticed by a stranger across the aisle.

THE SUPERINTENDENT

$\mathcal{T}$HE alarm began ringing at six in the morning. It sounded faintly in the first-floor apartment that Chester Coolidge was given as part wages of an apartment-house superintendent, but it woke him at once, for he slept with the percussive noises of the building machinery on his consciousness, as if they were linked to his own well-being. In the dark, he dressed quickly and ran through the lobby to the back stairs, where his path was obstructed by a peach basket full of dead roses and carnations. He kicked this aside and ran lightly down the iron stairs to the basement and along a hall whose brick walls, encrusted with paint, looked like a passage in some catacomb. The ringing of the bell grew louder as he approached the room where the pump machinery was. The alarm signified that the water tank on the roof was nearly empty and that the mechanism that regulated the water supply wasn't working. In the pump room, Chester turned on the auxiliary pump.

The basement was still. Far up the back elevator shaft he could hear the car moving down, floor by floor, attended by the rattle of milk bottles. It would take an hour for the auxiliary to fill the roof tank, and Chester decided to keep an eye on the gauge himself, and let the handyman sleep. He went upstairs again, and shaved and washed while his wife cooked breakfast. It was a moving day, and before he sat down to breakfast, he saw that the barometer had fallen and, looking out of the window and up eighteen stories, he found the sky as good as black. Chester liked a moving day to be dry and fair, and in the past, when everyone moved on the first of October, the chances for good weather had been favorable; but now all this had been changed for the worse, and they moved in the snow and the rain. The Bestwicks (9-E) were moving out and the Neguses (1-A) were moving up. That was all. While Chester drank his first cup of coffee, his wife talked about the Bestwicks, whose departure excited in her some memories and misgivings. Chester did not answer her questions, nor did she expect him to that early in the day. She talked loosely and, as she put it herself, to hear the sound of her own voice.

Mrs. Coolidge had come with her husband twenty years earlier from Massachusetts. The move had been her idea. Ailing and childless, she had decided that she would be happier in a big city than in New Bedford. Entrenched in a superintendent's apartment in the East Fifties, she was perfectly content. She spent her days in the movies and the stores, and she had seen the Shah of Persia with her own eyes. The only part of city life that troubled her was the inhibitions that it put on her native generosity.

"That poor Mrs. Bestwick," she said. "Oh, that poor woman! You told me they sent the children out to stay with their grandmother, didn't you, until they get settled? I wish there was something I could do to help her. Now, if this was in New Bedford, we could ask her to dinner or give her a basket with a nice dinner in it. You know, I'm reminded by her of those people in New Bedford—the Fenners. The two sisters, they were. They had diamonds as big as filberts, just like Mrs. Bestwick, and no electricity in the house. They used to have to go over to Georgiana Butler's to take a bath."

Chester did not look at his wife, but her mere presence was heartening and wonderful, for he was convinced that she was an extraordinary woman. He felt that there was a touch of genius in her cooking, that her housework was marked with genius, that she had a geniuslike memory, and that her ability to accept the world as she found it was stamped with genius. She had made johnnycake for breakfast, and he ate it with an appreciation that verged on awe. He knew for a fact that no one else in the world could make johnnycake like his wife and that no one else in Manhattan that morning would have tried.

When he had finished breakfast, he lighted a cigar and sat thinking about the Bestwicks. Chester had seen the apartment building through many lives, and it seemed that another was commencing. He had, since 1943, divided the tenants into two groups, the "permanents" and the "ceilings." A rent increase had been granted the management, and he knew that that would weed out a number of the "ceilings." The Bestwicks were the first to go under these conditions, and, like his wife, he was sorry to see them leave. Mr. Bestwick worked downtown. Mrs. Bestwick was a conscientious citizen and she had been building captain for the Red Cross, the March of Dimes, and the Girl Scouts. Whatever Mr. Bestwick made, it was not enough—not for that neighborhood. The liquor store knew. The butcher knew. The doorman and the window washer knew, and it had been known for a year to Retail Credit and the Corn Exchange Bank. The Bestwicks had been the last people in the neighborhood to face the facts. Mr. Bestwick wore a high-crowned felt hat, suit coats that were cut full around the waist, tight pants, and a white raincoat. He duck-footed off to work at eight every morning in a pair of English shoes that seemed to pinch him. The Bestwicks had been used to more money than they now had, and while Mrs. Bestwick's tweed suits were worn, her diamonds, as Mrs. Coolidge had noticed, were as big as filberts. The Bestwicks had two daughters and never gave Chester any trouble.

Mrs. Bestwick had called Chester late one afternoon about a month before and asked him if he would come upstairs. It was not urgent, she explained in her pleasant voice, but if it was not inconvenient, she would like to see him. She let him in graciously, as she did everything. She was a slender woman— a too slender woman with a magnificent bust and a graceful way of moving. He followed her that afternoon into the living room, where an older woman was sitting on a sofa. "This is my mother, Mrs. Doubleday, Chester," Mrs. Bestwick said. "Mother, this is Chester Coolidge, our superintendent." Mrs. Doubleday said she was pleased to meet him, and Chester accepted her invitation to sit down. From one of the bedrooms, Chester heard the older Bestwick girl singing a song. "Up with Chapin, Down with Spence," she sang. "Hang Miss Hewitt To a back-yard fence."

Chester knew every living room in the building, and by his standards the Bestwicks' was as pleasant as any of them. It was his feeling that all the apartments in his building were intrinsically ugly and inconvenient. Watching his self-important tenants walk through the lobby, he sometimes thought that they were a species of the poor. They were poor in space, poor in light, poor in quiet, poor in repose, and poor in the atmosphere of privacy—poor in everything that makes a man's home his castle. He knew the pains they took to overcome these deficiencies: the fans, for instance, to take away the smells of cooking. A six-room apartment is not a house, and if you cook onions in one end of it, you'll likely smell them in the other, but they all installed kitchen exhausts and kept them running, as if ventilating machinery would make an apartment smell like a house in the woods. All the living rooms were, to his mind, too high-ceilinged and too narrow, too noisy and too dark, and he knew how tirelessly the women spent their time and money in the furniture stores, thinking that another kind of carpeting, another set of end tables, another pair of lamps would make the place conform at last to their visions of a secure home. Mrs. Bestwick had done better than most, he thought, or perhaps it was because he liked her that he liked her room.

"Do you know about the new rents, Chester?" Mrs. Bestwick said.

"I never know about rents or leases," Chester said untruthfully. "They handle all of that at the office."

"Our rent's been raised," Mrs. Bestwick said, "and we don't

want to pay that much. I thought you might know if there was a less expensive apartment vacant in the building."

"I'm sorry, Mrs. Bestwick," Chester said. "There isn't a thing."

"I see," Mrs. Bestwick said.

He saw that she had something in mind; probably she hoped that he would offer to speak to the management and persuade them that the Bestwicks, as old and very desirable tenants, should be allowed to stay on at their present rental. But apparently she wasn't going to put herself in the embarrassing position of asking for his help, and he refrained, out of tact, from telling her that there was no way of his bringing pressure to bear on the situation.

"Isn't this building managed by the Marshall Cavises?" Mrs. Doubleday asked.

"Yes," Chester said.

"I went to Farmington with Mrs. Cavis," Mrs. Doubleday said to her daughter. "Do you think it would help if I spoke with her?"

"Mrs. Cavis isn't around here very much," Chester said. "During the fifteen years I worked here, I never laid eyes on either of them."

"But they do manage the building?" Mrs. Doubleday said to him.

"The Marshall Cavis Corporation manages it," Chester said.

"Maude Cavis was engaged to Benton Towler," Mrs. Doubleday said.

"I don't expect they have much to do with it personally," Chester said. "I don't know, but it seems to me I heard they don't even live in New York."

"Thank you very much, Chester," Mrs. Bestwick said. "I just thought there might be a vacancy."

When the alarm began ringing again, this time to signify that the tank on the roof was full, Chester lit out through the lobby and down the iron stairs and turned off the pump. Stan-

ley, the handyman, was awake and moving around in his room
by then, and Chester told him he thought the float switch on
the roof that controlled the pump was broken and to keep an
eye on the gauge. The day in the basement had begun. The milk
and the newspapers had been delivered; Delaney, the porter,
had emptied the waste cans in the back halls; and now the sleep-
out cooks and maids were coming to work. Chester could hear
them greeting Ferarri, the back-elevator man, and their clear
"Good mornings" confirmed his feeling that the level of courtesy was a grade higher in the basement than in the lobby upstairs.

At a little before nine, Chester telephoned the office management. A secretary whose voice he did not recognize took the
message. "The float switch on the water tank is busted," he
told her, "and we're working the auxiliary manually now. You
tell the maintenance crew to get over here this morning."

"The maintenance crew is at one of the other buildings," the
unfamiliar voice said, "and we don't expect them back until
four o'clock."

"This is an emergency, God damn it!" Chester shouted. "I
got over two hundred bathrooms here. This building's just as
important as those buildings over on Park Avenue. If my bathrooms run dry, you can come over here and take the complaints
yourself. It's a moving day, and the handyman and me have
got too much to do to be sitting beside the auxiliary all the
time." His face got red. His voice echoed through the basement.
When he hung up, he felt uncomfortable and his cigar burned
his mouth. Then Ferarri came in with a piece of bad news. The
Bestwicks' move would be delayed. They had arranged for a
small moving company to move them to Pelham, and the truck
had broken down in the night, bringing a load south from
Boston.

Ferarri took Chester up to 9-E in the service car. One of the
cheap, part-time maids that Mrs. Bestwick had been hiring recently had thumbtacked a sign onto the back door. "To Whom
It May Concern," she had printed. "I never play the numbers

and I never will play the numbers and I never played the numbers." Chester put the sign in the waste can and rang the back bell. Mrs. Bestwick opened the door. She was holding a cracked cup full of coffee in one hand, and Chester noticed that her hand was trembling. "I'm terribly sorry about the moving truck, Chester," she said. "I don't quite know what to do. Everything's ready," she said, gesturing toward the china barrels that nearly filled the kitchen. She led Chester across the hall into the living room, where the walls, windows, and floors were bare. "Everything's ready," she repeated. "Mr. Bestwick has gone up to Pelham to wait for me. Mother took the children."

"I wish you'd asked my advice about moving companies," Chester said. "It isn't that I get a cut from them or anything, but I could have put you onto a reliable moving firm that wouldn't cost you any more than the one you got. People try to save money by getting cheap moving companies and in the end they don't save anything. Mrs. Negus—she's in 1-A—she wants to get her things in here this morning."

Mrs. Bestwick didn't answer. "Oh, I'll miss you, Mrs. Bestwick," Chester said, feeling that he might have spoken unkindly. "There's no question about that. I'll miss you and Mr. Bestwick and the girls. You've been good tenants. During the eight years you've been here, I don't believe there's been a complaint from any of you. But things are changing, Mrs. Bestwick. Something's happening. The high cost of living. Oh, I can remember times when most of the tenants in this building wasn't rich nor poor. Now there's none but the rich. And, oh, the things they complain about, Mrs. Bestwick. You wouldn't believe me. The day before yesterday, that grass widow in 7-F called up, and you know what she was complaining about? She said the toilet seats in the apartment wasn't big enough."

Mrs. Bestwick didn't laugh at his joke. She smiled, but her mind seemed to be on something else.

"Well, I'll go down and tell Mrs. Negus that they'll be a delay," Chester said.

Mrs. Negus, who was replacing Mrs. Bestwick, took piano

lessons. Her apartment had an entrance off the lobby, and in
the afternoon she could be heard practicing her scales. The
piano was a difficult instrument for her and she had mastered
only a few jingles. Piano lessons were a new undertaking for
Mrs. Negus. When she first moved into the building, during the
war, her name had been Mary Toms, and she had lived with
Mrs. Lasser and Mrs. Dobree. Chester suspected that Mrs. Lasser and Mrs. Dobree were loose women, and when Mary Toms
joined them, Chester had worried about her, because she was
so young and so pretty. His anxiety was misplaced—the loose
life didn't depress or coarsen her at all. Coming in there as a
poor girl in a cloth coat, she had at the end of the year more
furs than anybody else and she seemed to be as happy as a lark.
It was in the second winter that Mr. Negus began to call. He
went there by chance, Chester guessed, and the visit changed
his whole life. He was a tough-looking middle-aged man, and
Chester remembered him because when he came through the
lobby on his way to 1-A, he used to bury his nose in the collar
of his coat and pull his hat-brim down over his eyes.

As soon as Mr. Negus began to visit Mary Toms regularly,
she eliminated all her other friends. One of them, a French
naval officer, made some trouble, and it took a doorman and a
cop to get him out. After this, Mr. Negus pointed out the door
to Mrs. Lasser and Mrs. Dobree. It was nothing against Mary
Toms, and she tried hard to get her friends another apartment
in the building. Mr. Negus was stubborn, and the two older
women packed their trunks and moved to an apartment on West
Fifty-eighth Street. After they had gone, a decorator came in
and overhauled the place. He was followed by the grand piano,
the poodles, the Book-of-the-Month Club membership, and the
crusty Irish maid. That winter, Mary Toms and Mr. Negus
went down to Miami and got married there, but even after his
marriage Mr. Negus still skulked through the lobby as if he was
acting against his better judgment. Now the Neguses were going
to move the whole caboodle up to 9-E. Chester didn't care one
way or the other, but he didn't think the move was going to be

permanent. Mrs. Negus was on the move. After a year or two in 9-E, he figured she'd ascend to one of the penthouses. From there, she'd probably take off for one of the fancier buildings on upper Fifth.

When Chester rang the bell that morning, Mrs. Negus let him in. She was still as pretty as a picture. "Hi, Chet," she said. "Come on in. I thought you didn't want me to start moving until eleven."

"Well, there may be a delay," Chester said. "The other lady's moving truck hasn't come."

"I got to get this stuff upstairs, Chet."

"Well, if her men don't come by eleven," Chester said, "I'll have Max and Delaney move the stuff down."

"Hi, Chet," Mr. Negus said.

"What's that on the seat of your pants, honey?" Mrs. Negus said.

"There's nothing on my pants," Mr. Negus said.

"Yes, there is, too," Mrs. Negus said. "There's a spot on your pants."

"Look," Mr. Negus said, "these pants just come back from the dry cleaners."

"Well, if you had marmalade for breakfast," Mrs. Negus said, "you could have sat in that. I mean you could have got marmalade on them."

"I didn't have marmalade," he said.

"Well, butter, then," she said. "It's awfully conspicuous."

"I'll telephone you," Chester said.

"You get her stuff out of there, Chet," Mrs. Negus said, "and I'll give you ten dollars. That's been my apartment since midnight. I want to get my things in there." Then she turned to her husband and began to rub his pants with a napkin. Chester let himself out.

In Chester's basement office, the telephone was ringing. He picked up the receiver and a maid spoke to him and said that a bathroom in 5-A was overflowing. The telephone rang repeat-

THE SUPERINTENDENT

edly during the time that he was in the office, and he took down
several complaints of mechanical failures reported by maids or
tenants—a stuck window, a jammed door, a leaky faucet, and
a clogged drain. Chester got the toolbox and made the repairs
himself. Most of the tenants were respectful and pleasant, but
the grass widow in 7-F called him into the dining room and
spoke to him curtly.

"You are the janitor?" she asked.

"I'm the superintendent," Chester said. "The handyman's
busy."

"Well, I want to talk with you about the back halls," she
said. "I don't think this building is as clean as it should be. The
maid thinks that she's seen roaches in the kitchen. We've never
had roaches."

"It's a clean building," Chester said. "It's one of the cleanest
buildings in New York. Delaney washes the back stairs every
second day and we have them painted whenever we get the
chance. Some time when you don't have anything better to do,
you might come down cellar and see my basement. I take just
as much pains with my basement as I do with my lobby."

"I'm not talking about the basement," the woman said. "I'm
talking about the back halls."

Chester left for his office before he lost his temper. Ferarri
told him that the maintenance crew had come and were up on
the roof with Stanley. Chester wished that they had reported
to him, for since he was the superintendent and carried the full
burden of the place on his shoulders, he felt that he should have
been consulted before they went to work on his domain. He
went up to Penthouse F and climbed the stairs from the back
hall to the roof. A north wind was howling in the television
antennas, and there was a little snow left on the roofs and terraces. Tarpaulins covered the porch furniture, and hanging on
the wall of one of the terraces was a large straw hat, covered
with ice. Chester went to the water tank and saw two men in
overalls way up the iron ladder, working on the switch. Stanley
stood a few rungs below them, passing up tools. Chester climbed

the iron ladder and gave them his advice. They took it respectfully, but as he was going down the ladder, he heard one of the maintenance men ask Stanley, "Who's that—the janitor?"

Hurt for the second time that day, Chester went to the edge of the roof and looked out over the city. On his right was the river. He saw a ship coming down it, a freighter pressing forward on the tide, her deck and porthole lights burning in the overcast. She was off to sea, but her lights and her quietness made her look to Chester as warmed and contained as a farmhouse in a meadow. Down the tide she came like a voyaging farmhouse. Compared to his own domain, Chester thought, a ship was nothing. At his feet, there were thousands of arteries hammering with steam; there were hundreds of toilets, miles of drainpipe, and a passenger list of over a hundred people, any one of whom might at that minute be contemplating suicide, theft, arson, or mayhem. It was a huge responsibility, and Chester thought with commiseration of the relatively paltry responsibilities of a ship's captain taking his freighter out to sea.

When he got back to the basement, Mrs. Negus was on the telephone to ask him if Mrs. Bestwick had gone. He said he would call her back, and hung up. Mrs. Negus's ten dollars seemed to commit Chester to building a fire under Mrs. Bestwick, but he didn't want to add to her troubles, and he thought with regret of what a good tenant she had been. The overcast day, the thought of Mrs. Bestwick and the people who had called him janitor convinced Chester that he needed to be cheered up, and he decided to get his shoes shined.

But the shoeshine parlor that morning was still and empty, and Bronco, the shoeshine man, bent mournfully over Chester's shoes. "I'm sixty-two years old, Chester," Bronco said, "and I got a dirty mind. You think it's because I'm around shoes all the time? You think it has something to do with the way the polish smells?" He lathered Chester's shoes and rubbed in the polish with a coarse brush. "That's what my old lady thinks," Bronco said. "She thinks it's got something to do with being around shoes all the time. All I think about," Bronco said sadly, "is love, love, love. It's disgusting. I see in the paper a picture of a young couple eating supper. For all I know, they're nice young clean-minded people, but I've got different thoughts. A lady comes in to have a pair of heels put on her shoes. 'Yes, Madam. No, Madam. They'll be ready for you tomorrow, Madam," I'm saying to her, but what's going through my mind I'd be ashamed to tell you. But if it's from being around shoes all the time, how can I help myself? It's the only way I got to make a living. For a job like yours, you got to be a carpenter, a painter, a politician, a regular nursemaid. Oh, that must be some job you got, Chester! A window gets stuck. A fuse burns out. They tell you to come up and fix it. The lady of the house, she opens the door. She's all alone. She's got on her nightgown. She—" Bronco broke off and applied the shoe rag vigorously.

When Chester returned to the building, Mrs. Bestwick's moving truck still hadn't come, and he went directly to 9-E and rang the back bell. There was no answer. There was no sound. He rang and rang, and then he opened the door with the pass key, just as Mrs. Bestwick came into the kitchen. "I didn't hear the bell," she said. "I'm so upset by this delay that I didn't hear the bell. I was in the other room." She sat down at the kitchen table. She looked pale and troubled.

"Cheer up, Mrs. Bestwick," Chester said. "You'll like it in Pelham. Isn't Pelham where you're moving to? Trees, birds. The children'll put on weight. You'll have a nice house."

"It's a small house, Chester," Mrs. Bestwick said.

"Well, I'm going to tell the porters to take your stuff—your things—out now and put them in the alley," Chester said. "They'll be just as safe there as they will be in here, and if it rains, I'll see that everything's covered and kept dry. Why don't you go up to Pelham now, Mrs. Bestwick?" he asked. "I'll take care of everything. Why don't you just get onto a train and go up to Pelham?"

"I think I'll wait, thank you, Chester," Mrs. Bestwick said.

Somewhere a factory whistle blew twelve o'clock. Chester went downstairs and inspected the lobby. The rugs and the floor were clean, and the glass on the hunting prints was shining. He stood under the canopy long enough to see that the brass stanchions were polished, that the rubber doormat was scrubbed, and that his canopy was a good canopy and, unlike some others, had withstood the winter storms. "Good morning," someone said to him elegantly while he was standing there, and he said, "Good morning, Mrs. Wardsworth," before he realized that it was Katie Shay, Mrs. Wardsworth's elderly maid. It was an understandable mistake, for Katie was wearing a hat and a coat that had been discarded by Mrs. Wardsworth and she wore the dregs of a bottle of Mrs. Wardsworth's perfume. In the eclipsed light, the old woman looked like the spectre of her employer.

Then a moving van, Mrs. Bestwick's moving van, backed up to the curb. This improved Chester's spirits, and he went in to lunch with a good appetite.

Mrs. Coolidge did not sit down at the table with Chester, and because she was wearing her purple dress, Chester guessed that she was going to the movies.

"That woman up in 7-F asked me if I was the janitor today," Chester said.

"Well, don't you let it worry you, Chester," Mrs. Coolidge said. "When I think of all the things you have on your mind, Chester—of all the things you have to do—it seems to me that you have more to do than almost anybody I ever knew. Why, this place might catch fire in the middle of the night, and there's nobody here knows where the hoses are but you and Stanley. There's the elevator machines and the electricity and the gas and the furnace. How much oil did you say that furnace burned last winter, Chester?"

"Over a hundred thousand gallons," Chester said.

"Just think of that," Mrs. Coolidge said.

The moving was proceeding in an orderly way when Chester got downstairs again. The moving men told him that Mrs. Bestwick was still in the apartment. He lighted a cigar, sat down at his desk, and heard someone singing, "Did you ever see a dream walking?" The song, attended with laughing and clapping, came from the far end of the basement, and Chester followed the voice down the dark hall, to the laundry. The laundry was a brightly lighted room that smelled of the gas drier. Banana peels and sandwich papers were spread over the ironing boards, and none of the six laundresses were working. In the center of the room, one of them, dressed in a negligee that someone had sent down to have washed, was waltzing with a second, dressed in a tablecloth. The others were clapping and laughing. Chester was wondering whether or not to interfere with the dance when the telephone in his office rang again. It was Mrs. Negus. "Get that bitch out of there, Chester," she said. "That's been my apartment since midnight. I'm going up there now."

Chester asked Mrs. Negus to wait for him in the lobby. He found her there wearing a short fur coat and dark glasses. They went up to 9-E together and he rang Mrs. Bestwick's front bell. He introduced the two women, but Mrs. Negus overlooked the introduction in her interest in a piece of furniture that the moving men were carrying across the hall.

"That's a lovely piece," she said.

"Thank you," Mrs. Bestwick said.

"You wouldn't want to sell it?" Mrs. Negus said.

"I'm afraid I can't," Mrs. Bestwick said. "I'm sorry that I'm leaving the place in such a mess," she went on. "There wasn't time to have someone come in and clean it up."

"Oh, that doesn't matter," Mrs. Negus said. "I'm going to have the whole thing painted and redecorated anyhow. I just wanted to get my things in here."

"Why don't you go up to Pelham now, Mrs. Bestwick?" Chester said. "Your truck's here, and I'll see that all the stuff is loaded."

"I will in a minute, Chester," Mrs. Bestwick said.

"You've got some lovely stones there," Mrs. Negus said, looking at Mrs. Bestwick's rings.

"Thank you," Mrs. Bestwick said.

"Now, you come down with me, Mrs. Bestwick," Chester

said, "and I'll get you a taxi and I'll see that everything gets into the moving van all right."

Mrs. Bestwick put on her hat and coat. "I suppose there are some things I ought to tell you about the apartment," she said to Mrs. Negus, "but I can't seem to remember any of them. It was very nice to meet you. I hope you'll enjoy the apartment as much as we have." Chester opened the door and she went into the hall ahead of him. "Wait just a minute, Chester," she said. "Wait just a minute, please." Chester was afraid then that she was going to cry, but she opened her purse and went through its contents carefully.

Her unhappiness at that moment, Chester knew, was more than the unhappiness of leaving a place that seemed familiar for one that seemed strange; it was the pain of leaving the place where her accent and her looks, her worn suit and her diamond rings could still command a trace of respect; it was the pain of parting from one class and going into another, and it was doubly painful because it was a parting that would never be completed. Somewhere in Pelham she would find a neighbor who had been to Farmingdale or wherever it was; she would find a friend with diamonds as big as filberts and holes in her gloves.

In the foyer, she said goodbye to the elevator man and the doorman. Chester went outside with her, expecting that she would say goodbye to him under the canopy, and he was prepared again to extoll her as a tenant, but she turned her back on him without speaking and walked quickly to the corner. Her neglect surprised and wounded him, and he was looking after her with indignation when she turned suddenly and came back. "But I forgot to say goodbye to you, Chester, didn't I?" she said. "Goodbye, and thank you, and say goodbye to Mrs. Coolidge for me. Give Mrs. Coolidge my best regards." Then she was gone.

"Well, it looks as though it was trying to clear up, doesn't it," Katie Shay said as she came out the door, a few minutes later. She was carrying a paper bag full of grain. As soon as

Katie crossed the street, the pigeons that roost on the Queens-
boro Bridge recognized her, but she did not raise her head to
see them, a hundred of them, leave their roost and fly loosely
in a circle, as if they were windborne. She heard the roar of
their wings pass overhead and saw their shadows darken the
puddles of water in the street, but she seemed unconscious of
the birds. Her approach was firm and gentle, like that of a
nursemaid with importunate children, and when the pigeons
landed on the sidewalk and crowded up to her feet, she kept
them waiting. Then she began to scatter the yellow grain, first
to the old and the sick, at the edges of the flock, and then to
the others.

A workman getting off a bus at the corner noticed the flock
of birds and the old woman. He opened his lunch pail and
dumped onto the sidewalk the crusts from his meal. Katie was
at his side in a minute. "I'd rather you didn't feed them," she
said sharply. "I'd just as soon you didn't feed them. You see,
I live in that house over there, and I can keep an eye on them,
and I see that they have everything they need. I give them fresh
grain twice a day. Corn in the winter. It costs me nine dollars
a month. I see that they have everything they need and I don't
like to have strangers feed them." As she spoke, she kicked the
stranger's crusts into the gutter. "I change their water twice a
day, and in the winter I always see that the ice is broken on it.
But I'd just as soon that strangers didn't feed them. I know
you'll understand." She turned her back on the workman and
dumped the last of the feed out of her bag. She was queer, Chester thought, she was as queer as the Chinese language. But who
was queerer—she, for feeding the birds, or he, for watching
her?

What Katie had said about the sky was true. The clouds were
passing, and Chester noticed the light in the sky. The days were
getting longer. The light seemed delayed. Chester went out from
under the canopy to see it. He clasped his hands behind his back
and stared outward and upward. He had been taught, as a child,
to think of the clouds as disguising the City of God, and the

low clouds still excited in him the curiosity of a child who thought that he was looking off to where the saints and the prophets lived. But it was more than the liturgical habits of thought that he retained from his pious childhood. The day had failed to have any meaning, and the sky seemed to promise a literal explanation.

Why had it failed? Why was it unrewarding? Why did Bronco and the Bestwicks and the Neguses and the grass widow in 7-F and Katie Shay and the stranger add up to nothing? Was it because the Bestwicks and the Neguses and Chester and Bronco had been unable to help one another; because the old maid had not let the stranger help her feed the birds? Was that it, Chester asked, looking at the blue air as if he expected an answer to be written in vapor. But the sky told him only that it was a long day at the end of winter, that it was late and time to go in.

THE ENORMOUS RADIO

*J*IM and Irene Westcott were the kind of people who seem to strike that satisfactory average of income, endeavor, and respectability that is reached by the statistical reports in college alumni bulletins. They were the parents of two young children, they had been married nine years, they lived on the twelfth floor of an apartment house near Sutton Place, they went to the theatre on an average of 10.3 times a year, and they hoped someday to live in Westchester. Irene Westcott was a pleasant, rather plain girl with soft brown hair and a wide, fine forehead upon which nothing at all had been written, and in the cold weather she wore a coat of fitch skins dyed to resemble mink. You could not say that Jim Westcott looked younger than he was, but you could at least say of him that he seemed to feel younger. He wore his graying hair cut very short, he dressed in the kind of clothes his class had worn at Andover, and his manner was earnest, vehement, and intentionally naïve. The Westcotts differed from their friends, their classmates, and their neighbors only in an interest they shared in serious music. They went to a great many concerts—although they seldom mentioned this to anyone—and they spent a good deal of time listening to music on the radio.

Their radio was an old instrument, sensitive, unpredictable, and beyond repair. Neither of them understood the mechanics of radio—or of any of the other appliances that surrounded them—and when the instrument faltered, Jim would strike the side of the cabinet with his hand. This sometimes helped. One Sunday afternoon, in the middle of a Schubert quartet, the music faded away altogether. Jim struck the cabinet repeatedly, but there was no response; the Schubert was lost to them forever. He promised to buy Irene a new radio, and on Monday when he came home from work he told her that he had got one. He refused to describe it, and said it would be a surprise for her when it came.

The radio was delivered at the kitchen door the following afternoon, and with the assistance of her maid and the handyman Irene uncrated it and brought it into the living room. She was struck at once with the physical ugliness of the large gumwood cabinet. Irene was proud of her living room, she had chosen its furnishings and colors as carefully as she chose her clothes, and now it seemed to her that the new radio stood among her intimate possessions like an aggressive intruder. She was confounded by the number of dials and switches on the instrument panel, and she studied them thoroughly before she put the plug into a wall socket and turned the radio on. The dials flooded with a malevolent green light, and in the distance she heard the music of a piano quintet. The quintet was in the distance for only an instant; it bore down upon her with a speed greater than light and filled the apartment with the noise of music amplified so mightily that it knocked a china ornament from a table to the floor. She rushed to the instrument and reduced the volume. The violent forces that were snared in the ugly gumwood cabinet made her uneasy. Her children came home from school then, and she took them to the Park. It was not until later in the afternoon that she was able to return to the radio.

The maid had given the children their suppers and was supervising their baths when Irene turned on the radio, reduced the volume, and sat down to listen to a Mozart quintet that she knew and enjoyed. The music came through clearly. The new instrument had a much purer tone, she thought, than the old one. She decided that tone was most important and that she could conceal the cabinet behind a sofa. But as soon as she had made her peace with the radio, the interference began. A crackling sound like the noise of a burning powder fuse began to accompany the singing of the strings. Beyond the music, there was a rustling that reminded Irene unpleasantly of the sea, and as the quintet progressed, these noises were joined by many others. She tried all the dials and switches but nothing dimmed the interference, and she sat down, disappointed and bewildered, and tried to trace the flight of the melody. The elevator shaft in her building ran beside the living-room wall, and it was the noise of the elevator that gave her a clue to the character of the static. The rattling of the elevator cables and the opening and closing of the elevator doors were reproduced in her loud-speaker, and, realizing that the radio was sensitive to electrical currents of all sorts, she began to discern through the Mozart the ringing of telephone bells, the dialing of phones, and the lamentation of a vacuum cleaner. By listening more carefully, she was able to distinguish doorbells, elevator bells, electric razors, and Waring mixers, whose sounds had been picked up from the apartments that surrounded hers and transmitted through her loudspeaker. The powerful and ugly instrument, with its mistaken sensitivity to discord, was more than she could hope to master, so she turned the thing off and went into the nursery to see her children.

When Jim Westcott came home that night, he went to the radio confidently and worked the controls. He had the same sort of experience Irene had had. A man was speaking on the station Jim had chosen, and his voice swung instantly from the distance into a force so powerful that it shook the apartment. Jim turned the volume control and reduced the voice. Then, a minute or two later, the interference began. The ringing of telephones and doorbells set in, joined by the rasp of the elevator doors and the whir of cooking appliances. The character of the noise had changed since Irene had tried the radio earlier; the last of the electric razors was being unplugged, the vacuum cleaners had all been returned to their closets, and the static reflected that change in pace that overtakes the city after the sun goes down. He fiddled with the knobs but couldn't get rid of the noises, so he turned the radio off and told Irene that in the morning he'd call the people who had sold it to him and give them hell.

The following afternoon, when Irene returned to the apartment from a luncheon date, the maid told her that a man had come and fixed the radio. Irene went into the living room before she took off her hat or her furs and tried the instrument. From the loudspeaker came a recording of the "Missouri Waltz." It reminded her of the thin, scratchy music from an old-fashioned phonograph that she sometimes heard across the lake where she spent her summers. She waited until the waltz had finished, expecting an explanation of the recording, but there was none. The music was followed by silence, and then the plaintive and scratchy record was repeated. She turned the dial and got a satisfactory burst of Caucasian music—the thump of bare feet in the dust and the rattle of coin jewelry—but in the background she could hear the ringing of bells and a confusion of voices. Her children came home from school then, and she turned off the radio and went to the nursery.

When Jim came home that night, he was tired, and he took a bath and changed his clothes. Then he joined Irene in the living room. He had just turned on the radio when the maid announced dinner, so he left it on, and he and Irene went to the table.

Jim was too tired to make even a pretense of sociability, and there was nothing about the dinner to hold Irene's interest, so her attention wandered from the food to the deposits of silver polish on the candlesticks and from there to the music in the other room. She listened for a few moments to a Chopin prelude and then was surprised to hear a man's voice break in. "For Christ's sake, Kathy," he said, "do you always have to play the piano when I get home?" The music stopped abruptly. "It's the only chance I have," a woman said. "I'm at the office all day."

"So am I," the man said. He added something obscene about an upright piano, and slammed a door. The passionate and melancholy music began again.

"Did you hear that?" Irene asked.

"What?" Jim was eating his dessert.

"The radio. A man said something while the music was still going on—something dirty."

"It's probably a play."

"I don't think it *is* a play," Irene said.

They left the table and took their coffee into the living room. Irene asked Jim to try another station. He turned the knob. "Have you seen my garters?" a man asked. "Button me up," a woman said. "Have you seen my garters?" the man said again. "Just button me up and I'll find your garters," the woman said. Jim shifted to another station. "I wish you wouldn't leave apple cores in the ashtrays," a man said. "I hate the smell."

"This is strange," Jim said.

"Isn't it?" Irene said.

Jim turned the knob again. " 'On the coast of Coromandel where the early pumpkins blow,' " a woman with a pronounced English accent said, " 'in the middle of the woods lived the Yonghy-Bonghy-Bò. Two old chairs, and half a candle, one old jug without a handle . . .' "

"My God!" Irene cried. "That's the Sweeneys' nurse."

" 'These were all his worldly goods,' " the British voice continued.

"Turn that thing off," Irene said. "Maybe they can hear *us*." Jim switched the radio off. "That was Miss Armstrong, the Sweeneys' nurse," Irene said. "She must be reading to the little girl. They live in 17-B. I've talked with Miss Armstrong in the Park. I know her voice very well. We must be getting other people's apartments."

"That's impossible," Jim said.

"Well, that was the Sweeneys' nurse," Irene said hotly. "I know her voice. I know it very well. I'm wondering if they can hear us."

Jim turned the switch. First from a distance and then nearer, nearer, as if borne on the wind, came the pure accents of the Sweeneys' nurse again: " '*Lady Jingly! Lady Jingly!*' " she said, " '*Sitting where the pumpkins blow, will you come and be my wife,* said the Yonghy-Bonghy-Bò . . .' "

Jim went over to the radio and said "Hello" loudly into the speaker.

" '*I am tired of living singly,*' " the nurse went on, " '*on this coast so wild and shingly, I'm a-weary of my life; if you'll come and be my wife, quite serene would be my life . . .*' "

"I guess she can't hear us," Irene said. "Try something else."

Jim turned to another station, and the living room was filled with the uproar of a cocktail party that had overshot its mark. Someone was playing the piano and singing the Whiffenpoof Song, and the voices that surrounded the piano were vehement and happy. "Eat some more sandwiches," a woman shrieked. There were screams of laughter and a dish of some sort crashed to the floor.

"Those must be the Fullers, in 11-E," Irene said. "I knew they were giving a party this afternoon. I saw her in the liquor store. Isn't this too divine? Try something else. See if you can get those people in 18-C."

The Westcotts overheard that evening a monologue on salmon fishing in Canada, a bridge game, running comments on home movies of what had apparently been a fortnight at Sea Island, and a bitter family quarrel about an overdraft at the bank. They turned off their radio at midnight and went to bed, weak with laughter. Sometime in the night, their son began to call for a glass of water and Irene got one and took it to his room. It was very early. All the lights in the neighborhood were extinguished, and from the boy's window she could see the empty street. She went into the living room and tried the radio. There was some faint coughing, a moan, and then a man spoke. "Are you all right, darling?" he asked. "Yes," a woman said wearily. "Yes, I'm all right, I guess," and then she added with great feeling, "but, you know, Charlie, I don't feel like myself any more. Sometimes there are about fifteen or twenty minutes in the week when I feel like myself. I don't like to go to another doctor, because the doctor's bills are so awful already, but I just don't feel like myself, Charlie. I just never feel like myself." They were not young, Irene thought. She guessed from the timbre of their voices that they were middle-aged. The restrained melancholy of the dialogue and the draft from the bedroom window made her shiver, and she went back to bed.

The following morning, Irene cooked breakfast for the family —the maid didn't come up from her room in the basement until ten—braided her daughter's hair, and waited at the door until her children and her husband had been carried away in the elevator. Then she went into the living room and tried the radio. "I don't want to go to school," a child screamed. "I hate school. I won't go to school. I hate school." "You will go to school," an enraged woman said. "We paid eight hundred dollars to get you into that school and you'll go if it kills you." The next number on the dial produced the worn record of the "Missouri Waltz." Irene shifted the control and invaded the privacy of several breakfast tables. She overheard demonstrations of indigestion, carnal love, abysmal vanity, faith, and despair. Irene's life was nearly as simple and sheltered as it appeared to be, and the forthright and sometimes brutal language that came from the loudspeaker that morning astonished and troubled her. She continued to listen until her maid came in. Then she turned off the radio quickly, since this insight, she realized, was a furtive one.

Irene had a luncheon date with a friend that day, and she left her apartment at a little after twelve. There were a number of women in the elevator when it stopped at her floor. She stared at their handsome and impassive faces, their furs, and the cloth flowers in their hats. Which one of them had been to Sea Island, she wondered. Which one had overdrawn her bank account? The elevator stopped at the tenth floor and a woman with a pair of Skye terriers joined them. Her hair was rigged

[175]

high on her head and she wore a mink cape. She was humming the "Missouri Waltz."

Irene had two Martinis at lunch, and she looked searchingly at her friend and wondered what her secrets were. They had intended to go shopping after lunch, but Irene excused herself and went home. She told the maid that she was not to be disturbed; then she went into the living room, closed the doors, and switched on the radio. She heard, in the course of the afternoon, the halting conversation of a woman entertaining her aunt, the hysterical conclusion of a luncheon party, and a hostess briefing her maid about some cocktail guests. "Don't give the best Scotch to anyone who hasn't white hair," the hostess said. "See if you can get rid of that liver paste before you pass those hot things, and could you lend me five dollars? I want to tip the elevator man."

As the afternoon waned, the conversations increased in intensity. From where Irene sat, she could see the open sky above the East River. There were hundreds of clouds in the sky, as though the south wind had broken the winter into pieces and were blowing it north, and on her radio she could hear the arrival of cocktail guests and the return of children and businessmen from their schools and offices. "I found a good-sized diamond on the bathroom floor this morning," a woman said. "It must have fallen out of that bracelet Mrs. Dunston was wearing last night." "We'll sell it," a man said. "Take it down to the jeweller on Madison Avenue and sell it. Mrs. Dunston won't know the difference, and we could use a couple of hundred bucks . . ." " 'Oranges and lemons, say the bells of St. Clement's,'" the Sweeneys' nurse sang. " 'Half-pence and farthings, say the bells of St. Martin's. When will you pay me? say the bells at old Bailey . . .'" "It's not a hat," a woman cried, and at her back roared a cocktail party. "It's not a hat, it's a love affair. That's what Walter Florell said. He said it's not a hat, it's a love affair," and then, in a lower voice, the same woman added, "Talk to somebody, for Christ's sake, honey, talk to somebody. If she catches you standing here not talking to anybody, she'll take us off her invitation list, and I love these parties."

The Westcotts were going out for dinner that night, and when Jim came home, Irene was dressing. She seemed sad and vague, and he brought her a drink. They were dining with friends in the neighborhood, and they walked to where they were going. The sky was broad and filled with light. It was one of those splendid spring evenings that excite memory and desire, and the air that touched their hands and faces felt very soft. A Salvation Army band was on the corner playing "Jesus Is Sweeter." Irene drew on her husband's arm and held him there for a minute, to hear the music. "They're really such nice people, aren't they?" she said. "They have such nice faces. Actually, they're so much nicer than a lot of the people we know." She took a bill from her purse and walked over and dropped it into the tambourine. There was in her face, when she returned to her husband, a look of radiant melancholy that he was not familiar with. And her conduct at the dinner party that night seemed strange to him, too. She interrupted her hostess rudely and stared at the people across the table from her with an intensity for which she would have punished her children.

It was still mild when they walked home from the party, and Irene looked up at the spring stars. " 'How far that little candle throws its beams,' " she exclaimed. " 'So shines a good deed in a naughty world.' " She waited that night until Jim had fallen asleep, and then went into the living room and turned on the radio.

Jim came home at about six the next night. Emma, the maid, let him in, and he had taken off his hat and was taking off his coat when Irene ran into the hall. Her face was shining with tears and her hair was disordered. "Go up to 16-C, Jim!" she screamed. "Don't take off your coat. Go up to 16-C. Mr. Osborn's beating his wife. They've been quarrelling since four o'clock, and now he's hitting her. Go up there and stop him."

From the radio in the living room, Jim heard screams, obscenities, and thuds. "You know you don't have to listen to this sort of thing," he said. He strode into the living room and turned the switch. "It's indecent," he said. "It's like looking in windows. You know you don't have to listen to this sort of thing. You can turn it off."

"Oh, it's so horrible, it's so dreadful," Irene was sobbing. "I've been listening all day, and it's so depressing."

"Well, if it's so depressing, why do you listen to it? I bought this damned radio to give you some pleasure," he said. "I paid a great deal of money for it. I thought it might make you happy. I wanted to make you happy."

"Don't, don't, don't, don't quarrel with me," she moaned, and laid her head on his shoulder. "All the others have been quarrelling all day. Everybody's been quarrelling. They're all worried about money. Mrs. Hutchinson's mother is dying of cancer in Florida and they don't have enough money to send her to the Mayo Clinic. At least, Mr. Hutchinson says they don't have enough money. And some woman in this building is having an affair with the handyman—with that hideous handyman. It's too disgusting. And Mrs. Melville has heart trouble and Mr. Hendricks is going to lose his job in April and Mrs. Hendricks is horrid about the whole thing and that girl who plays the 'Missouri Waltz' is a whore, a common whore, and the elevator man has tuberculosis and Mr. Osborn has been beating Mrs. Osborn." She wailed, she trembled with grief and checked the stream of tears down her face with the heel of her palm.

"Well, why do you have to listen?" Jim asked again. "Why do you have to listen to this stuff if it makes you so miserable?"

"Oh, don't, don't, don't," she cried. "Life is too terrible, too sordid and awful. But we've never been like that, have we, darling? Have we? I mean we've always been good and decent and loving to one another, haven't we? And we have two children, two beautiful children. Our lives aren't sordid, are they, darling? Are they?" She flung her arms around his neck and drew his face down to hers. "We're happy, aren't we, darling? We are happy, aren't we?"

"Of course we're happy," he said tiredly. He began to surrender his resentment. "Of course we're happy. I'll have that damned radio fixed or taken away tomorrow." He stroked her soft hair. "My poor girl," he said.

"You love me, don't you?" she asked. "And we're not hypercritical or worried about money or dishonest, are we?"

"No, darling," he said.

A man came in the morning and fixed the radio. Irene turned it on cautiously and was happy to hear a California-wine commercial and a recording of Beethoven's Ninth Symphony, including Schiller's "Ode to Joy." She kept the radio on all day and nothing untoward came from the speaker.

A Spanish suite was being played when Jim came home. "Is everything all right?" he asked. His face was pale, she thought. They had some cocktails and went in to dinner to the "Anvil Chorus" from "Il Trovatore." This was followed by Debussy's "La Mer."

"I paid the bill for the radio today," Jim said. "It cost four hundred dollars. I hope you'll get some enjoyment out of it."

"Oh, I'm sure I will," Irene said.

"Four hundred dollars is a good deal more than I can afford," he went on. "I wanted to get something that you'd enjoy. It's the last extravagance we'll be able to indulge in this year. I see that you haven't paid your clothing bills yet. I saw them on your dressing table." He looked directly at her. "Why did you tell me you'd paid them? Why did you lie to me?"

"I just didn't want you to worry, Jim," she said. She drank some water. "I'll be able to pay my bills out of this month's allowance. There were the slipcovers last month, and that party."

"You've got to learn to handle the money I give you a little more intelligently, Irene," he said. "You've got to understand that we won't have as much money this year as we had last. I had a very sobering talk with Mitchell today. No one is buying anything. We're spending all our time promoting new issues, and you know how long that takes. I'm not getting any younger, you know. I'm thirty-seven. My hair will be gray next year. I haven't done as well as I'd hoped to do. And I don't suppose things will get any better."

"Yes, dear," she said.

"We've got to start cutting down," Jim said. "We've got to think of the children. To be perfectly frank with you, I worry about money a great deal. I'm not at all sure of the future. No one is. If anything should happen to me, there's the insurance, but that wouldn't go very far today. I've worked awfully hard to give you and the children a comfortable life," he said bitterly. "I don't like to see all of my energies, all of my youth, wasted in fur coats and radios and slipcovers and—"

"Please, Jim," she said. "Please. They'll hear us."

"*Who'll hear us?* Emma can't hear us."

"The radio."

"Oh, I'm sick!" he shouted. "I'm sick to death of your apprehensiveness. The radio can't hear us. Nobody can hear us. And what if they can hear us? Who cares?"

Irene got up from the table and went into the living room. Jim went to the door and shouted at her from there. "Why are you so Christly all of a sudden? What's turned you overnight into a convent girl? You stole your mother's jewelry before they probated her will. You never gave your sister a cent of that money that was intended for her—not even when she needed it. You made Grace Howland's life miserable, and where was all your piety and your virtue when you went to that abortionist? I'll never forget how cool you were. You packed your bag and went off to have that child murdered as if you were going to Nassau. If you'd had any reasons, if you'd had any good reasons—"

Irene stood for a minute before the hideous cabinet, disgraced and sickened, but she held her hand on the switch before she extinguished the music and the voices, hoping that the instru-

ment might speak to her kindly, that she might hear the Sweeneys' nurse. Jim continued to shout at her from the door. The
voice on the radio was suave and noncommittal. "An early-
morning railroad disaster in Tokyo," the loudspeaker said,
"killed twenty-nine people. A fire in a Catholic hospital near
Buffalo for the care of blind children was extinguished early
this morning by nuns. The temperature is forty-seven. The
humidity is eighty-nine."

$\mathcal{M}$Y WIFE has brown hair, dark eyes, and a gentle disposition. Because of her gentle disposition, I sometimes think that she spoils the children. She can't refuse them anything. They always get around her. Ethel and I have been married for ten years. We both come from Morristown, New Jersey, and I can't even remember when I first met her. Our marriage has always seemed happy and resourceful to me. We live in a walkup in the East Fifties. Our son, Carl, who is six, goes to a good private school, and our daughter, who is four, won't go to school until next year. We often find fault with the way we were educated, but we seem to be struggling to raise our children along the same lines, and when the time comes, I suppose they'll go to the same schools and colleges that we went to.

Ethel graduated from a woman's college in the East, and then went for a year to the University of Grenoble. She worked for a year in New York after returning from France, and then we were married. She once hung her diploma above the kitchen sink, but it was a short-lived joke and I don't know where the diploma is now. Ethel is cheerful and adaptable, as well as gentle, and we both come from that enormous stratum of the middle class that is distinguished by its ability to recall better times. Lost money is so much a part of our lives that I am sometimes reminded of expatriates, of a group who have adapted

themselves energetically to some alien soil but who are reminded, now and then, of the escarpments of their native coast.
Because our lives are confined by my modest salary, the surface
of Ethel's life is easy to describe.

She gets up at seven and turns the radio on. After she is
dressed, she rouses the children and cooks the breakfast. Our
son has to be walked to the school bus at eight o'clock. When
Ethel returns from this trip, Carol's hair has to be braided. I
leave the house at eight-thirty, but I know that every move
that Ethel makes for the rest of the day will be determined by
the housework, the cooking, the shopping, and the demands of
the children. I know that on Tuesdays and Thursdays she will
be at the A. & P. between eleven and noon, that on every clear
afternoon she will be on a certain bench in a playground from
three until five, that she cleans the house on Mondays, Wednes-
days, and Fridays, and polishes the silver when it rains. When
I return at six, she is usually cleaning the vegetables or making
some other preparation for dinner. Then when the children
have been fed and bathed, when the dinner is ready, when the
table in the living room is set with food and china, she stands
in the middle of the room as if she has lost or forgotten something, and this moment of reflection is so deep that she will not
hear me if I speak to her, or the children if they call. Then it
is over. She lights the four white candles in their silver sticks,
and we sit down to a supper of corned-beef hash or some other
modest fare.

We go out once or twice a week and entertain about once a
month. Because of practical considerations, most of the people
we see live in our neighborhood. We often go around the corner
to the parties given by a generous couple named Newsome. The
Newsomes' parties are large and confusing, and the arbitrary
impulses of friendship are given a free play.

We became attached at the Newsomes' one evening, for reasons that I've never understood, to a couple named Dr. and
Mrs. Trencher. I think that Mrs. Trencher was the aggressor

in this friendship, and after our first meeting she telephoned
Ethel three or four times. We went to their house for dinner,
and they came to our house, and sometimes in the evening
when Dr. Trencher was walking their old dachshund, he would
come up for a short visit. He seemed like a pleasant man to have
around. I've heard other doctors say that he's a good physician.
The Trenchers are about thirty; at least he is. She is older.

I'd say that Mrs. Trencher is a plain woman, but her plain-
ness is difficult to specify. She is small, she has a good figure
and regular features, and I suppose that the impression of plain-
ness arises from some inner modesty, some needlessly narrow
view of her chances. Dr. Trencher doesn't smoke or drink, and
I don't know whether there's any connection or not, but the
coloring in his slender face is fresh—his cheeks are pink, and
his blue eyes are clear and strong. He has the singular optimism
of a well-adjusted physician—the feeling that death is a chance
misfortune and that the physical world is merely a field for
conquest. In the same way that his wife seems plain, he seems
young.

The Trenchers live in a comfortable and unpretentious private house in our neighborhood. The house is old-fashioned;
its living rooms are large, its halls are gloomy, and the Trenchers don't seem to generate enough human warmth to animate
the place, so that you sometimes take away from them, at the
end of an evening, an impression of many empty rooms. Mrs.
Trencher is noticeably attached to her possessions—her clothes,
her jewels, and the ornaments she's bought for the house—and
to Fräulein, the old dachshund. She feeds Fräulein scraps from
the table, furtively, as if she has been forbidden to do this, and
after dinner Fräulein lies beside her on the sofa. With the play
of green light from a television set on her drawn features and
her thin hands stroking Fräulein, Mrs. Trencher looked to me
one evening like a good-hearted and miserable soul.

Mrs. Trencher began to call Ethel in the mornings for a talk
or to ask her for lunch or a matinée. Ethel can't go out in the
day and she claims to dislike long telephone conversations. She

[184]

complained that Mrs. Trencher was a tireless and aggressive gossip. Then late one afternoon Dr. Trencher appeared at the playground where Ethel takes our two children. He was walking by, and he saw her and sat with her until it was time to take the children home. He came again a few days later, and then his visits with Ethel in the playground, she told me, became a regular thing. Ethel thought that perhaps he didn't have many patients and that with nothing to do he was happy to talk with anyone. Then, when we were washing dishes one night, Ethel said thoughtfully that Trencher's attitude toward her seemed strange. "He stares at me," she said. "He sighs and stares at me." I know what my wife looks like in the playground. She wears an old tweed coat, overshoes, and Army gloves, and a scarf is tied under her chin. The playground is a fenced and paved lot between a slum and the river. The picture of the well-dressed, pink-cheeked doctor losing his heart to Ethel in this environment was hard to take seriously. She didn't mention him then for several days, and I guessed that he had stopped his visits. Ethel's birthday came at the end of the month, and I forgot about it, but when I came home that evening, there were a lot of roses in the living room. They were a birthday present from Trencher, she told me. I was cross at myself for having forgotten her birthday, and Trencher's roses made me angry. I asked her if she'd seen him recently.

"Oh, yes," she said, "he still comes to the playground nearly every afternoon. I haven't told you, have I? He's made his declaration. He loves me. He can't live without me. He'd walk through fire to hear the notes of my voice." She laughed. "That's what he said."

"When did he say this?"

"At the playground. And walking home. Yesterday."

"How long has he known?"

"That's the funny part about it," she said. "He knew before he met me at the Newsomes' that night. He saw me waiting for a crosstown bus about three weeks before that. He just saw me and he said that he knew then, the minute he saw me. Of course, he's crazy."

I was tired that night and worried about taxes and bills, and I could think of Trencher's declaration only as a comical mistake. I felt that he was a captive of financial and sentimental commitments, like every other man I know, and that he was no more free to fall in love with a strange woman he saw on a street corner than he was to take a walking trip through French Guiana or to recommence his life in Chicago under an assumed name. His declaration, the scene in the playground, seemed to me to be like those chance meetings that are a part of the life of any large city. A blind man asks you to help him across the street, and as you are about to leave him, he seizes your arm and regales you with a passionate account of his cruel and ungrateful children; or the elevator man who is taking you up to a party turns to you suddenly and says that his grandson has infantile paralysis. The city is full of accidental revelation, half-heard cries for help, and strangers who will tell you everything at the first suspicion of sympathy, and Trencher seemed to me like the blind man or the elevator operator. His declaration had no more bearing on the business of our lives than these interruptions.

Mrs. Trencher's telephone conversations had stopped, and we had stopped visiting the Trenchers, but sometimes I would see him in the morning on the crosstown bus when I was late going to work. He seemed understandably embarrassed whenever he saw me, but the bus was always crowded at that time of day, and it was no effort to avoid one another. Also, at about this time I made a mistake in business and lost several thousand dollars for the firm I work for. There was not much chance of my losing my job, but the possibility was always at the back of my mind, and under this and under the continuous urgency of making more money the memory of the eccentric Doctor was buried. Three weeks passed without Ethel's mentioning him, and then one evening, when I was reading, I noticed Ethel standing at the window looking down into the street.

"He's really there," she said.

"Who?"

"Trencher. Come here and see."

I went to the window. There were only three people on the sidewalk across the street. It was dark and it would have been difficult to recognize anyone, but because one of them, walking toward the corner, had a dachshund on a leash, it could have been Trencher.

"Well, what about it?" I said. "He's just walking the dog."

"But he wasn't walking the dog when I first looked out of the window. He was just standing there, staring up at this building. That's what he says he does. He says that he comes over here and stares up at our lighted windows."

"When did he say this?"

"At the playground."

"I thought you went to another playground."

"Oh, I do, I do, but he followed me. He's crazy, darling. I know he's crazy, but I feel so sorry for him. He says that he spends night after night looking up at our windows. He says that he sees me everywhere—the back of my head, my eyebrows—that he hears my voice. He says that he's never compromised in his life and that he isn't going to compromise about this. I feel so sorry for him, darling. I can't help but feel sorry for him."

For the first time then, the situation seemed serious to me, for in his helplessness I knew that he might have touched an inestimable and wayward passion that Ethel shares with some other women—an inability to refuse any cry for help, to refuse any voice that sounds pitiable. It is not a reasonable passion, and I would almost rather have had her desire him than pity him. When we were getting ready for bed that night, the telephone rang, and when I picked it up and said hello, no one answered. Fifteen minutes later, the telephone rang again, and when there was no answer this time, I began to shout and swear

[187]

at Trencher, but he didn't reply—there wasn't even the click of a closed circuit—and I felt like a fool. Because I felt like a fool, I accused Ethel of having led him on, of having encouraged him, but these accusations didn't affect her, and when I finished them, I felt worse, because I knew that she was innocent, and that she had to go out on the street to buy groceries and air the children, and that there was no force of law that could keep Trencher from waiting for her there, or from staring up at our lights.

We went to the Newsomes' one night the next week, and while we were taking off our coats, I heard Trencher's voice. He left a few minutes after we arrived, but his manner—the sad glance he gave Ethel, the way he sidestepped me, the sorrowful way that he refused the Newsomes when they asked him to stay longer, and the gallant attentions he showed his miserable wife—made me angry. Then I happened to notice Ethel and saw that her color was high, that her eyes were bright, and that while she was praising Mrs. Newsome's new shoes, her mind was not on what she was saying. When we came home that night, the baby-sitter told us crossly that neither of the children had slept. Ethel took their temperatures. Carol was all right, but the boy had a fever of a hundred and four. Neither of us got much sleep that night, and in the morning Ethel called me at the office to say that Carl had bronchitis. Three days later, his sister came down with it.

For the next two weeks, the sick children took up most of our time. They had to be given medicine at eleven in the evening and again at three in the morning, and we lost a lot of sleep. It was impossible to ventilate or clean the house, and when I came in, after walking through the cold from the bus stop, it stank of cough syrups and tobacco, fruit cores and sickbeds. There were blankets and pillows, ashtrays, and medicine glasses everywhere. We divided the work of sickness reasonably and took turns at getting up in the night, but I often fell asleep at my desk during the day, and after dinner Ethel would fall asleep in a chair in the living room. Fatigue seems to differ for adults and children only in that adults recognize it and so are not overwhelmed by something they can't name; but even with a name for it they are overwhelmed, and when we were tired, we were unreasonable, cross, and the victims of transcendent depressions. One evening after the worst of the sickness was over, I came home and found some roses in the living room. Ethel said that Trencher had brought them. She hadn't let him in. She had closed the door in his face. I took the roses and threw them out. We didn't quarrel. The children went to sleep at nine, and a few minutes after nine I went to bed. Some time later, something woke me.

A light was burning in the hall. I got up. The children's room and the living room were dark. I found Ethel in the kitchen sitting at the table, drinking coffee.

"I've made some fresh coffee," she said. "Carol felt croupy again, so I steamed her. They're both asleep now."

"How long have you been up?"

"Since half past twelve," she said. "What time is it?"

"Two."

I poured myself a cup of coffee and sat down. She got up from the table and rinsed her cup and looked at herself in a mirror that hangs above the sink. It was a windy night. A dog was wailing somewhere in an apartment below ours, and a loose radio antenna was brushing against the kitchen window.

"It sounds like a branch," she said.

In the bare kitchen light, meant for peeling potatoes and washing dishes, she looked very tired.

"Will the children be able to go out tomorrow?"

"Oh, I hope so," she said. "Do you realize that I haven't been out of this apartment in over two weeks?" She spoke bitterly and this startled me.

"It hasn't been quite two weeks."

"It's been over two weeks," she said.

"Well, let's figure it out," I said. "The children were taken sick on a Saturday night. That was the fourth. Today is the——"

"Stop it, stop it," she said. "I know how long it's been. I haven't had my shoes on in two weeks."

"You make it sound pretty bad."

"It is. I haven't had on a decent dress or fixed my hair."

"It could be worse."

"My mother's cooks had a better life."

"I doubt that."

"My mother's cooks had a better life," she said loudly.

"You'll wake the children."

"My mother's cooks had a better life. They had pleasant rooms. No one could come into the kitchen without their permission." She knocked the coffee grounds into the garbage and began to wash the pot.

"How long was Trencher here this afternoon?"

"A minute. I've told you."

"I don't believe it. He was in here."

"He was not. I didn't let him in. I didn't let him in because I looked so badly. I didn't want to discourage him."

"Why not?"

"I don't know. He may be a fool. He may be insane but the things he's told me have made me feel marvellously, he's made me feel marvellously."

"Do you want to go?"

"Go? Where would I go?" She reached for the purse that is kept in the kitchen to pay for groceries and counted out of it two dollars and thirty-five cents. "Ossining? Montclair?"

"I mean with Trencher."

"I don't know, I don't know," she said, "but who can say that I shouldn't? What harm would it do? What good would it do? Who knows. I love the children but that isn't enough, that isn't nearly enough. I wouldn't hurt them, but would I hurt them so much if I left you? Is divorce so dreadful and of all the things that hold a marriage together how many of them are good?" She sat down at the table.

"In Grenoble," she said, "I wrote a long paper on Charles Stuart in French. A professor at the University of Chicago wrote

[190]

me a letter. I couldn't read a French newspaper without a dictionary today, I don't have the time to follow any newspaper, and I am ashamed of my incompetence, ashamed of the way I look. Oh, I guess I love you, I do love the children, but I love myself, I love my life, it has some value and some promise for me and Trencher's roses make me feel that I'm losing this, that I'm losing my self-respect. Do you know what I mean, do you understand what I mean?"

"He's crazy," I said.

"Do you know what I mean? Do you understand what I mean?"

"No," I said. "No."

Carl woke up then and called for his mother. I told Ethel to go to bed. I turned out the kitchen light and went into the children's room.

The children felt better the next day, and since it was Sunday, I took them for a walk. The afternoon sun was clement and pure, and only the colored shadows made me remember that it was midwinter, that the cruise ships were returning, and that in another week jonquils would be twenty-five cents a bunch. Walking down Lexington Avenue, we heard the drone bass of a church organ sound from the sky, and we and the others on the sidewalk looked up in piety and bewilderment, like a devout and stupid congregation, and saw a formation of heavy bombers heading for the sea. As it got late, it got cold and clear and still, and on the stillness the waste from the smokestacks along the East River seemed to articulate, as legibly as the Pepsi-Cola plane, whole words and sentences. Halcyon. Disaster. They were hard to make out. It seemed the ebb of the year—an evil day for gastritis, sinus, and respiratory disease—and remembering other winters, the markings of the light convinced me that it was the season of divorce. It was a long afternoon, and I brought the children in before dark.

I think that the seriousness of the day affected the children, and when they returned to the house, they were quiet. The seriousness of it kept coming to me with the feeling that this change, like a phenomenon of speed, was affecting our watches as well as our hearts. I tried to remember the willingness with which Ethel had followed my regiment during the war, from West Virginia to the Carolinas and Oklahoma, and the day coaches and rooms she had lived in, and the street in San Francisco where I said goodbye to her before I left the country, but I could not put any of this into words, and neither of us found anything to say. Some time after dark, the children were bathed and put to bed, and we sat down to our supper. At about nine o'clock, the doorbell rang, and when I answered it and recognized Trencher's voice on the speaking tube, I asked him to come up.

He seemed distraught and exhilarated when he appeared. He stumbled on the edge of the carpet. "I know that I'm not welcome here," he said in a hard voice, as if I were deaf. "I know that you don't like me here. I respect your feelings. This is your home. I respect a man's feelings about his home. I don't usually go to a man's home unless he asks me. I respect your home. I respect your marriage. I respect your children. I think everything ought to be aboveboard. I've come here to tell you that I love your wife."

"Get out," I said.

"You've got to listen to me," he said. "I love your wife. I can't live without her. I've tried and I can't. I've even thought of going away—of moving to the West Coast—but I know that it wouldn't make any difference. I want to marry her. I'm not romantic. I'm matter-of-fact. I'm very matter-of-fact. I know that you have two children and that you don't have much money. I know that there are problems of custody and property and things like that to be settled. I'm not romantic. I'm hardheaded. I've talked this all over with Mrs. Trencher, and she's agreed to give me a divorce. I'm not underhanded. Your wife can tell you that. I realize all the practical aspects that have to be considered—custody, property, and so forth. I have plenty of money. I can give Ethel everything she needs, but there are

[192]

the children. You'll have to decide about them between yourselves. I have a check here. It's made out to Ethel. I want her
to take it and go to Nevada. I'm a practical man and I realize
that nothing can be decided until she gets her divorce."

"Get out of here!" I said. "Get the hell out of here!"

He started for the door. There was a potted geranium on the
mantelpiece, and I threw this across the room at him. It got
him in the small of the back and nearly knocked him down.
The pot broke on the floor. Ethel screamed. Trencher was still
on his way out. Following him, I picked up a candlestick and
aimed it at his head, but it missed and bounced off the wall.
"Get the hell out of here!" I yelled, and he slammed the door.
I went back into the living room. Ethel was pale but she wasn't
crying. There was a loud rapping on the radiator, a signal from
the people upstairs for decorum and silence—urgent and ex-
pressive, like the communications that prisoners send to one
another through the plumbing in a penitentiary. Then everything was still.

We went to bed, and I woke sometime during the night. I
couldn't see the clock on the dresser, so I don't know what time
it was. There was no sound from the children's room. The
neighborhood was perfectly still. There were no lighted windows anywhere. Then I knew that Ethel had wakened me. She
was lying on her side of the bed. She was crying.

"Why are you crying?" I asked.

"Why am I crying?" she said. "Why am I crying?" And to
hear my voice and to speak set her off again, and she began to
sob cruelly. She sat up and slipped her arms into the sleeves
of a wrapper and felt along the table for a package of cigarettes.
I saw her wet face when she lighted a cigarette. I heard her
moving around in the dark.

"Why do you cry?"

"Why do I cry? Why do I cry?" she asked impatiently. "I
cry because I saw an old woman cuffing a little boy on Third
Avenue. She was drunk. I can't get it out of my mind." She
pulled the quilt off the foot of our bed and wandered with it

[193]

toward the door. "I cry because my father died when I was twelve and because my mother married a man I detested or thought that I detested. I cry because I had to wear an ugly dress—a hand-me-down dress—to a party twenty years ago, and I didn't have a good time. I cry because of some unkindness that I can't remember. I cry because I'm tired—because I'm tired and I can't sleep." I heard her arrange herself on the sofa and then everything was quiet.

I like to think that the Trenchers have gone away, but I still see Trencher now and then on a crosstown bus when I'm late going to work. I've also seen his wife, going into the neighborhood lending library with Fräulein. She looks old. I'm not good at judging ages, but I wouldn't be surprised to find that Mrs. Trencher is fifteen years older than her husband. Now when I come home in the evenings, Ethel is still sitting on the stool by the sink cleaning vegetables. I go with her into the children's room. The light there is bright. The children have built something out of an orange crate, something preposterous and ascendant, and their sweetness, their compulsion to build, the brightness of the light are reflected perfectly and increased in Ethel's face. Then she feeds them, bathes them, and sets the table, and stands for a moment in the middle of the room, trying to make some connection between the evening and the day. Then it is over. She lights the four candles, and we sit down to our supper.

CHRISTMAS IS A SAD
SEASON FOR THE POOR

CHRISTMAS is a sad season. The phrase came to Charlie an instant after the alarm clock had waked him, and named for him an amorphous depression that had troubled him all the previous evening. The sky outside his window was black. He sat up in bed and pulled the light chain that hung in front of his nose. Christmas is a very sad day of the year, he thought. Of all the millions of people in New York, I am practically the only one who has to get up in the cold black of 6 A.M. on Christmas Day in the morning; I am practically the only one.

He dressed, and when he went downstairs from the top floor of the rooming house in which he lived, the only sounds he heard were the coarse sounds of sleep; the only lights burning were lights that had been forgotten. Charlie ate some breakfast in an all-night lunchwagon and took an Elevated train uptown. From Third Avenue, he walked over to Sutton Place. The neighborhood was dark. House after house put into the shine of the street lights a wall of black windows. Millions and millions were sleeping, and this general loss of consciousness generated an impression of abandonment, as if this were the fall of the city, the end of time. He opened the iron-and-glass doors of the apartment building where he had been working for six months as an elevator operator, and went through the elegant lobby to a locker room at the back. He put on a striped vest with brass buttons, a false ascot, a pair of pants with a light-blue stripe on the seam, and a coat. The night elevator man was dozing on the little bench in the car. Charlie woke him. The night elevator man told him thickly that the day doorman had been taken sick and wouldn't be in that day. With the doorman sick, Charlie wouldn't have any relief for lunch, and a lot of people would expect him to whistle for cabs.

Charlie had been on duty a few minutes when 14 rang—a Mrs. Hewing, who, he happened to know, was kind of immoral. Mrs. Hewing hadn't been to bed yet, and she got into the elevator wearing a long dress under her fur coat. She was followed by her two funny-looking dogs. He took her down and watched her go out into the dark and take her dogs to the curb. She was outside for only a few minutes. Then she came in and he took her up to 14 again. When she got off the elevator, she said, "Merry Christmas, Charlie."

"Well, it isn't much of a holiday for me, Mrs. Hewing," he said. "I think Christmas is a very sad season of the year. It isn't that people around here ain't generous—I mean I got plenty of tips—but, you see, I live alone in a furnished room and I don't have any family or anything, and Christmas isn't much of a holiday for me."

"I'm sorry, Charlie," Mrs. Hewing said. "I don't have any family myself. It is kind of sad when you're alone, isn't it?" She called her dogs and followed them into her apartment. He went down.

It was quiet then, and Charlie lighted a cigarette. The heating plant in the basement encompassed the building at that hour in a regular and profound vibration, and the sullen noises of arriving steam heat began to resound, first in the lobby and then to reverberate up through all the sixteen stories, but this was a mechanical awakening, and it didn't lighten his loneliness or his petulance. The black air outside the glass doors had begun to turn blue, but the blue light seemed to have no source: it

[196]

appeared in the middle of the air. It was a tearful light, and as it picked out the empty street he wanted to cry. Then a cab drove up, and the Walsers got out, drunk and dressed in evening clothes, and he took them up to their penthouse. The Walsers got him to brooding about the difference between his life in a furnished room and the lives of the people overhead. It was terrible.

Then the early church goers began to ring, but there were only three of these that morning. A few more went off to church at eight o'clock, but the majority of the building remained unconscious, although the smell of bacon and coffee had begun to drift into the elevator shaft.

At a little after nine, a nursemaid came down with a child. Both the nursemaid and the child had a deep tan and had just returned, he knew, from Bermuda. He had never been to Bermuda. He, Charlie, was a prisoner, confined eight hours a day to a six-by-eight elevator cage, which was confined, in turn, to a sixteen-story shaft. In one building or another, he had made his living as an elevator operator for ten years. He estimated the average trip at about an eighth of a mile, and when he thought of the thousands of miles he had travelled, when he thought that he might have driven the car through the mists above the Caribbean and set it down on some coral beach in Bermuda, he held the narrowness of his travels against his passengers, as if it were not the nature of the elevator but the pressure of their lives that confined him, as if they had clipped his wings.

He was thinking about this when the DePauls, on 9, rang. They wished him a merry Christmas.

"Well, it's nice of you to think of me," he said as they descended, "but it isn't much of a holiday for me. Christmas is a sad season when you're poor. I live alone in a furnished room. I don't have any family."

"Who do you have dinner with, Charlie?" Mrs. DePaul asked.

"I don't have any Christmas dinner," Charlie said. "I just get a sandwich."

"Oh, Charlie!" Mrs. DePaul was a stout woman with an impulsive heart, and Charlie's plaint struck at her holiday mood

[197]

as if she had been caught in a cloudburst. "I do wish we could share our Christmas dinner with you, you know," she said. "I come from Vermont, you know, and when I was a child, you know, we always used to have a great many people at our table. The mailman, you know, and the schoolteacher, and just anybody who didn't have any family of their own, you know, and I wish we could share our dinner with you the way we used to, you know, and I don't see any reason why we can't. We can't have you at the table, you know, because you couldn't leave the elevator—could you?—but just as soon as Mr. DePaul has carved the goose, I'll give you a ring, and I'll arrange a tray for you, you know, and I want you to come up and at least share our Christmas dinner."

Charlie thanked them, and their generosity surprised him, but he wondered if, with the arrival of friends and relatives, they wouldn't forget their offer.

Then old Mrs. Gadshill rang, and when she wished him a merry Christmas, he hung his head.

"It isn't much of a holiday for me, Mrs. Gadshill," he said. "Christmas is a sad season if you're poor. You see, I don't have any family. I live alone in a furnished room."

"I don't have any family either, Charlie," Mrs. Gadshill said. She spoke with a pointed lack of petulance, but her grace was forced. "That is, I don't have any children with me today. I have three children and seven grandchildren, but none of them can see their way to coming East for Christmas with me. Of course, I understand their problems. I know that it's difficult to travel with children during the holidays, although I always seemed to manage it when I was their age, but people feel differently, and we mustn't condemn them for the things we can't understand. But I know how you feel, Charlie. I haven't any family either. I'm just as lonely as you."

Mrs. Gadshill's speech didn't move him. Maybe she was lonely, but she had a ten-room apartment and three servants and bucks and bucks and diamonds and diamonds, and there were plenty of poor kids in the slums who would be happy at a chance at the food her cook threw away. Then he thought about poor kids. He sat down on a chair in the lobby and thought about them.

They got the worst of it. Beginning in the fall, there was all this excitement about Christmas and how it was a day for them. After Thanksgiving, they couldn't miss it. It was fixed so they couldn't miss it. The wreaths and decorations everywhere, and bells ringing, and trees in the park, and Santa Clauses on every corner, and pictures in the magazines and newspapers and on every wall and window in the city told them that if they were good, they would get what they wanted. Even if they couldn't read, they couldn't miss it. They couldn't miss it even if they were blind. It got into the air the poor kids inhaled. Every time they took a walk, they'd see all the expensive toys in the store windows, and they'd write letters to Santa Claus, and their mothers and fathers would promise to mail them, and after the kids had gone to sleep, they'd burn the letters in the stove. And when it came Christmas morning, how could you explain it, how could you tell them that Santa Claus only visited the rich, that he didn't know about the good? How could you face them when all you had to give them was a balloon or a lollipop?

On the way home from work a few nights earlier, Charlie had seen a woman and a little girl going down Fifty-ninth Street. The little girl was crying. He guessed she was crying, he knew she was crying, because she'd seen all the things in the toy-store windows and couldn't understand why none of them were for her. Her mother did housework, he guessed, or maybe was a waitress, and he saw them going back to a room like his, with green walls and no heat, on Christmas Eve, to eat a can of soup. And he saw the little girl hang up her ragged stocking and fall asleep, and he saw the mother looking through her purse for something to put into the stocking— This reverie was interrupted by a bell on 11. He went up, and Mr. and Mrs. Fuller were waiting. When they wished him a merry Christmas, he said, "Well, it isn't much of a holiday for me, Mrs. Fuller. Christmas is a sad season when you're poor."

[199]

"Do you have any children, Charlie?" Mrs. Fuller asked. "Four living," he said. "Two in the grave." The majesty of his lie overwhelmed him. "Mrs. Leary's a cripple," he added.

"How sad, Charlie," Mrs. Fuller said. She started out of the elevator when it reached the lobby, and then she turned. "I want to give your children some presents, Charlie," she said. "Mr. Fuller and I are going to pay a call now, but when we come back, I want to give you some things for your children."

He thanked her. Then the bell rang on 4, and he went up to get the Westons.

"It isn't much of a holiday for me," he told them when they wished him a merry Christmas. "Christmas is a sad season when you're poor. You see, I live alone in a furnished room."

"Poor Charlie," Mrs. Weston said. "I know just how you feel. During the war, when Mr. Weston was away, I was all alone at Christmas. I didn't have any Christmas dinner or a tree or anything. I just scrambled myself some eggs and sat there and cried." Mr. Weston, who had gone into the lobby, called impatiently to his wife. "I know just how you feel, Charlie," Mrs. Weston said.

By noon, the climate in the elevator shaft had changed from bacon and coffee to poultry and game, and the house, like an enormous and complex homestead, was absorbed in the preparations for a domestic feast. The children and their nursemaids had all returned from the Park. Grandmothers and aunts were arriving in limousines. Most of the people who came through the lobby were carrying packages wrapped in colored paper, and were wearing their best furs and new clothes. Charlie continued to complain to most of the tenants when they wished him a merry Christmas, changing his story from the lonely bachelor to the poor father, and back again, as his mood changed, but this outpouring of melancholy, and the sympathy it aroused, didn't make him feel any better.

At half past one, 9 rang, and when he went up, Mr. DePaul was standing in the door of their apartment holding a cocktail shaker and a glass. "Here's a little Christmas cheer, Charlie," he said, and he poured Charlie a drink. Then a maid appeared with a tray of covered dishes, and Mrs. DePaul came out of the living room. "Merry Christmas, Charlie," she said. "I had Mr. DePaul carve the goose early, so that you could have some, you know. I didn't want to put the dessert on the tray, because I was afraid it would melt, you know, so when we have our dessert, we'll call you."

"And what is Christmas without presents?" Mr. DePaul said, and he brought a large, flat box from the hall and laid it on top of the covered dishes.

"You people make it seem like a real Christmas to me," Charlie said. Tears started into his eyes. "Thank you, thank you."

"Merry Christmas! Merry Christmas!" they called, and they watched him carry his dinner and his present into the elevator. He took the tray and the box into the locker room when he got down. On the tray, there was a soup, some kind of creamed fish, and a serving of goose. The bell rang again, but before he answered it, he tore open the DePauls' box and saw that it held a dressing gown. Their generosity and their cocktail had begun to work on his brain, and he went jubilantly up to 12. Mrs. Gadshill's maid was standing in the door with a tray, and Mrs. Gadshill stood behind her. "Merry Christmas, Charlie!" she said. He thanked her, and tears came into his eyes again. On the way down, he drank off the glass of sherry on Mrs. Gadshill's tray. Mrs. Gadshill's contribution was a mixed grill. He ate the lamb chop with his fingers. The bell was ringing again, and he wiped his face with a paper towel and went up to 11. "Merry Christmas, Charlie," Mrs. Fuller said, and she was standing in the door with her arms full of packages wrapped in silver paper, just like a picture in an advertisement, and Mr. Fuller was beside her with an arm around her, and they both looked as if they were going to cry. "Here are some things I want you to take home to your children," Mrs. Fuller said. "And here's something for Mrs. Leary and here's something for you. And if you want to take these things out to the elevator, we'll have your dinner ready for you in a minute." He carried the things into the elevator and came back for the tray. "Merry Christmas, Charlie!" both of the Fullers called after him as he closed the door. He took their dinner and their presents into the locker room and tore open the box that was marked for him. There was an alligator wallet in it, with Mr. Fuller's initials in the corner. Their dinner was also goose, and he ate a piece of the meat with his fingers and was washing it down with a cocktail when the bell rang. He went up again. This time it was the Westons. "Merry Christmas, Charlie!" they said, and they gave him a cup of eggnog, a turkey dinner, and a present. Their gift was also a dressing gown. Then 7 rang, and when he went up, there was another dinner and some more toys. Then 14 rang, and when he went up, Mrs. Hewing was standing in the hall, in a kind of negligee, holding a pair of riding boots in one hand and some neckties in the other. She had been crying and drinking. "Merry Christmas, Charlie," she said tenderly. "I wanted to give you something, and I've been thinking about you all morning, and I've been all over the apartment, and these are the only things I could find that a man might want. These are the only things that Mr. Brewer left. I don't suppose you'd have any use for the riding boots, but wouldn't you like the neckties?" Charlie took the neckties and thanked her and hurried back to the car, for the elevator bell had rung three times.

By three o'clock, Charlie had fourteen dinners spread on the table and the floor of the locker room, and the bell kept ringing. Just as he started to eat one, he would have to go up and get another, and he was in the middle of the Parsons' roast beef when he had to go up and get the DePauls' dessert. He kept the door of the locker room closed, for he sensed that the quality of charity is exclusive and that his friends would have been disappointed to find that they were not the only ones to try to lessen his loneliness. There were goose, turkey, chicken, pheas-

[202]

CHRISTMAS IS A SAD SEASON FOR THE POOR

ant, grouse, and pigeon. There were trout and salmon, creamed scallops and oysters, lobster, crabmeat, whitebait, and clams. There were plum puddings, mince pies, mousses, puddles of melted ice cream, layer cakes, *Torten*, éclairs, and two slices of Bavarian cream. He had dressing gowns, neckties, cuff links, socks, and handkerchiefs, and one of the tenants had asked for his neck size and then given him three green shirts. There were a glass teapot filled, the label said, with jasmine honey, four bottles of after-shave lotion, some alabaster bookends, and a dozen steak knives. The avalanche of charity he had precipitated filled the locker room and made him hesitant, now and then, as if he had touched some well-spring in the female heart that would bury him alive in food and dressing gowns. He had made almost no headway on the food, for all the servings were preternaturally large, as if loneliness had been counted on to generate in him a brutish appetite. Nor had he opened any of the presents that had been given to him for his imaginary children, but he had drunk everything they sent down, and around him were the dregs of Martinis, Manhattans, Old-Fashioneds, champagne-and-raspberry-shrub cocktails, eggnogs, Bronxes, and Side Cars.

His face was blazing. He loved the world, and the world loved him. When he thought back over his life, it appeared to him in a rich and wonderful light, full of astonishing experiences and unusual friends. He thought that his job as an elevator operator—cruising up and down through hundreds of feet of perilous space—demanded the nerve and the intellect of a birdman. All the constraints of his life—the green walls of his room and the months of unemployment—dissolved. No one was ringing, but he got into the elevator and shot it at full speed up to the penthouse and down again, up and down, to test his wonderful mastery of space.

A bell rang on 12 while he was cruising, and he stopped in his flight long enough to pick up Mrs. Gadshill. As the car started to fall, he took his hands off the controls in a paroxysm of joy and shouted, "Strap on your safety belt, Mrs. Gadshill!

We're going to make a loop-the-loop!" Mrs. Gadshill shrieked. Then, for some reason, she sat down on the floor of the elevator. Why was her face so pale, he wondered; why was she sitting on the floor? She shrieked again. He grounded the car gently, and cleverly, he thought, and opened the door. "I'm sorry if I scared you, Mrs. Gadshill," he said meekly. "I was only fooling." She shrieked again. Then she ran out into the lobby, screaming for the superintendent.

The superintendent fired Charlie and took over the elevator himself. The news that he was out of work stung Charlie for a minute. It was his first contact with human meanness that day. He sat down in the locker room and gnawed on a drumstick. His drinks were beginning to let him down, and while it had not reached him yet, he felt a miserable soberness in the offing. The excess of food and presents around him began to make him feel guilty and unworthy. He regretted bitterly the lie he had told about his children. He was a single man with simple needs. He had abused the goodness of the people upstairs. He was unworthy.

Then up through this drunken train of thought surged the sharp figure of his landlady and her three skinny children. He thought of them sitting in their basement room. The cheer of Christmas had passed them by. This image got him to his feet. The realization that he was in a position to give, that he could bring happiness easily to someone else, sobered him. He took a big burlap sack, which was used for collecting waste, and began to stuff it, first with his presents and then with the presents for his imaginary children. He worked with the haste of a man whose train is approaching the station, for he could hardly wait to see those long faces light up when he came in the door. He changed his clothes, and, fired by a wonderful and unfamiliar sense of power, he slung his bag over his shoulder like a regular Santa Claus, went out the back way, and took a taxi to the lower East Side.

The landlady and her children had just finished off a turkey, which had been sent to them by the local Democratic Club, and they were stuffed and uncomfortable when Charlie began pounding on the door, shouting "Merry Christmas!" He dragged the bag in after him and dumped the presents for the children onto the floor. There were dolls and musical toys, blocks, sewing kits, an Indian suit, and a loom, and it appeared to him that, as he had hoped, his arrival in the basement dispelled its gloom. When half the presents had been opened, he gave the landlady a bathrobe and went upstairs to look over the things he had been given for himself.

Now, the landlady's children had already received so many presents by the time Charlie arrived that they were confused with receiving, and it was only the landlady's intuitive grasp of the nature of charity that made her allow the children to open some of the presents while Charlie was still in the room, but as soon as he had gone, she stood between the children and the presents that were still unopened. "Now, you kids have had enough already," she said. "You kids have got your share. Just look at the things you got there. Why, you ain't even played with the half of them. Mary Anne, you ain't even looked at that doll the Fire Department give you. Now, a nice thing to do would be to take all this stuff that's left over to those poor people on Hudson Street—them Deckkers. They ain't got nothing." A beatific light came into her face when she realized that she could give, that she could bring cheer, that she could put a healing finger on a case needier than hers, and—like Mrs. DePaul and Mrs. Weston, like Charlie himself and like Mrs. Deckker, when Mrs. Deckker was to think, subsequently, of the poor Shannons—first love, then charity, and then a sense of power drove her. "Now, you kids help me get all this stuff together. Hurry, hurry, hurry," she said, for it was dark then, and she knew that we are bound, one to another, in licentious benevolence for only a single day, and that day was nearly over. She was tired, but she couldn't rest, she couldn't rest.

THE SUTTON PLACE STORY

$\mathcal{D}$EBORAH TENNYSON waited in her nursery on Sunday morning for a signal from her father that would mean she could enter her parents' bedroom. The signal came late, for her parents had been up the night before with a business friend from Minneapolis and they both had had a good deal to drink, but when Deborah was given the signal she ran clumsily down the dark hall, screaming with pleasure. Her father took her in his arms and kissed her good morning, and then she went to where her mother lay in bed. "Hello, my sweet, my love," her mother said. "Did Ruby give you your breakfast? Did you have a good breakfast?"

"The weather is lovely out," Deborah said. "Weather is divine."

"Be kind to poor Mummy," Robert said. "Mummy has a terrible hangover."

"Mummy has a terrible hangover," Deborah repeated, and she patted her mother's face lightly.

Deborah was not quite three years old. She was a beautiful girl with wonderful, heavy hair that had lights of silver and gold. She was a city child and she knew about cocktails and hangovers. Both her parents worked and she most often saw them in the early evening, when she was brought in to say good night. Katherine and Robert Tennyson would be drinking with friends, and Deborah would be allowed to pass the smoked salmon, and she had naturally come to assume that cocktails were the axis of the adult world. She made Martinis in the sand pile and thought all the illustrations of cups, goblets, and glasses in her nursery books were filled with Old-Fashioneds.

While the Tennysons waited for breakfast that morning, they read the *Times*. Deborah spread the second news section on the floor and began an elaborate fantasy that her parents had seen performed so often they hardly noticed it. She pretended to pick clothing and jewelry from the advertisements in the paper and to dress herself with these things. Her taste, Katherine thought, was avaricious and vulgar, but there was such clarity and innocence in her monologue that it seemed like a wonderful part of the bright summer morning. "Put on the shoes," she said, and pretended to put on shoes. "Put on the mink coat," she said.

"It's too hot for a mink coat, dear," Katherine told her. "Why don't you wear a mink scarf?"

"Put on the mink scarf," Deborah said. Then the cook came into the bedroom with the coffee and orange juice, and said that Mrs. Harley was there. Robert and Katherine kissed Deborah goodbye and told her to enjoy herself in the park.

The Tennysons had no room for a sleep-in nurse, so Mrs. Harley came to the house every morning and took care of Deborah during the day. Mrs. Harley was a widow. She had lived a hearty and comfortable life until her husband's death, but he had left her with no money and she had been reduced to working as a nursemaid. She said that she loved children and had always wanted children herself, but this was not true. Children bored and irritated her. She was a kind and ignorant woman, and this, more than any bitterness, showed in her face when she took Deborah downstairs. She was full of old-country blessings for the elevator man and the doorman. She said that it was a lovely morning, wasn't it, a morning for the gods.

Mrs. Harley and Deborah walked to a little park at the edge of the river. The child's beauty was bright, and the old woman was dressed in black, and they walked hand in hand, like some amiable representation of winter and spring. Many people

wished them good morning. "Where did you get that enchanting child?" someone asked. Mrs. Harley enjoyed these compli-
ments. She was sometimes proud of Deborah, but she had been
taking care of her for four months, and the little girl and the
old woman had established a relationship that was not as simple
as it appeared.

They quarrelled a good deal when they were alone, and they
quarrelled like adults, with a cunning knowledge of each other's
frailties. The child had never complained about Mrs. Harley;
it was as though she already understood the evil importance of
appearances. Deborah was taciturn about the way in which she
spent her days. She would tell no one where she had been or
what she had done. Mrs. Harley had found that she could count
on this trait, and so the child and the old woman had come to
share a number of secrets.

On several late-winter afternoons when the weather had been
bitter and dark and Mrs. Harley had been ordered to keep Deborah out until five, she had taken the child to the movies.
Deborah had sat beside her in the dark theatre and never complained or cried. Now and then she craned her neck to look at
the screen, but most of the time she just sat quiet, listening to
the voices and the music. A second secret—and one much less
sinful, in Mrs. Harley's opinion—was that on Sunday mornings, sometimes, and sometimes on weekday afternoons, Mrs.
Harley had left the little girl with a friend of the Tennysons.
This was a woman named Renée Hall, and there was no harm
in it, Mrs. Harley thought. She had never told the Tennysons,
but what they didn't know wouldn't hurt them. When Renée
took Deborah on Sundays, Mrs. Harley went to the eleven-
o'clock Mass, and there was nothing wrong, surely, with an
old woman's going into the house of God to pray for her dead.

Mrs. Harley sat down on one of the benches in the park
that morning. The sun was hot and it felt good on her old legs.
The air was so clear that the perspective of the river seemed to
have changed. You could throw a stone onto Welfare Island,
it seemed, and a trick of the light made the downtown bridges

look much closer to the center of the city. Boats were going up and down the river, and as they cut the water they left in the air a damp and succinct odor, like the smell of fresh earth that follows a plow. Another nurse and child were the only other people in the park. Mrs. Harley told Deborah to go play in the sand. Then Deborah saw the dead pigeon. "The pigeon is sleeping," Deborah said. She stooped down to touch its wings.

"That dirty bird is dead, and don't you dare touch it!" Mrs. Harley shouted.

"The pretty pigeon is sleeping," Deborah said. Her face clouded suddenly and tears came into her eyes. She stood with her hands folded in front of her and her head bowed, an attitude that was a comical imitation of Mrs. Harley's reaction to sorrow, but the grief in her voice and her face came straight from her heart.

"Get away from that dirty bird!" Mrs. Harley shouted, and she got up and kicked the dead bird aside. "Go play in the sand," she told Deborah. "I don't know what's the matter with you. They must have given twenty-five dollars for that doll carriage you have up in your room, but you'd rather play with a dead bird. Go look at the river. Go look at the boats! And don't climb up on that railing, either, for you'll drop in, and with that terrible current that will be the end of you." Deborah walked obediently over to the river. "Here I am," Mrs. Harley said to the other nurse, "here I am, a woman going on sixty who lived forty years in a house of her own, sitting on a park bench like any old bum on a Sunday morning while the baby's parents are up there on the tenth floor sleeping off last night's liquor." The other nurse was a well-bred Scotch woman who was not interested in Mrs. Harley. Mrs. Harley turned her attention to the steps leading down to the park from Sutton Place, to watch for Renée Hall. The arrangement between them had been established for about a month.

Renée Hall had met Mrs. Harley and the child at the Tennysons', where she had frequently been a guest for cocktails that winter. She had been brought there by a business friend of

Katherine's. She was pleasant and entertaining, and Katherine
had been impressed with her clothes. She lived around the corner and didn't object to late invitations and most men liked her.
The Tennysons knew nothing about her other than that she
was an attractive guest and did some radio acting.

On the evening when Renée first went to the Tennysons',
Deborah had been brought in to say good night, and the actress
and the neglected child had sat together on a sofa. There was
an odd sympathy between the two, and Renée let the child
play with her jewelry and her furs. Renée was kind to Deborah,
for she was at a time in her life when she appreciated kindness
herself.

She was about thirty-five years old, dissipated and gentle.
She liked to think of the life she was living as an overture to
something wonderful, final, and even conventional, that would
begin with the next season or the season after that, but she was
finding this hope more and more difficult to sustain. She had
begun to notice that she always felt tired unless she was drinking. It was just that she didn't have the strength. When she
was not drinking she was depressed, and when she was depressed she quarrelled with headwaiters and hairdressers, accused people in restaurants of staring at her, and quarrelled
with some of the men who paid her debts. She knew this in-
stability in her temperament well, and was clever at concealing
it—among other things—from casual friends like the Tennysons.

Renée had come to the house again a week later, and when
Deborah heard her voice, she escaped from Mrs. Harley and
flew down the hall. The child's adoration excited Renée. They
sat together again. Renée wore a string of furs and a hat piled
with cloth roses, and Deborah thought her the most beautiful
lady in the world.

After that, Renée went to the Tennysons' often. It was a
standing joke that she came there to see the child and not the
Tennysons or their guests. Renée had always wanted children
of her own, and now all her regrets seemed centered in Deb-

orah's bright face. She began to feel possessive toward the child. She sent her expensive clothes and toys. "Has she ever been to the dentist?" she asked Katherine. "Are you sure of your doctor? Have you entered her in nursery school?" She made the mistake one night of suggesting that Deborah saw too little of her parents and lacked the sense of security they should give her. "She has eight thousand dollars in the bank in her own name," Katherine said. She was angry. Renée continued to send Deborah elaborate presents. Deborah named all her dolls and her pleasures after Renée, and on several nights she cried for Renée after she had been put to bed. Robert and Katherine thought it would be better if they didn't see Renée any more. They stopped asking her to the house. "After all," Katherine said, "I've always felt that there was something unsavory about that girl." Renée called them twice and asked them for cocktails, and Katherine said no, no thanks, they were all suffering with colds.

Renée knew that Katherine was lying and she determined to forget the Tennysons. She missed the little girl, but she might never have seen her again if it hadn't been for something that happened later that week. One night she left a dull party early in the evening and went home by herself. She was afraid of missing telephone calls and she used a telephone-answering service. They told her that night that a Mrs. Walton had called and left a number.

Walton, Walton, Walton, Renée thought, and then she remembered that she had once had a lover named Walton. That would have been eight or ten years ago. She had once been taken to dinner with his mother, who was visiting from Cleveland. She remembered the evening clearly then. Walton drank too much and his mother had taken Renée aside and told her what a good influence she thought she was, and couldn't she make him stop drinking and go to church oftener? Walton and she had quarrelled over his drinking, in the end, Renée remembered, and she had never seen him after that. He might be sick, or drunk, or getting married. She had no idea how old he was, because the thirties were all jumbled in her memory and she could not tell the beginning of the decade from its end. She dialled the number. It was a hotel on the West Side. Mrs. Walton's voice, when she answered, was the small, cracked voice of an old woman. "Billy's dead, Renée," she said. She began to sob. "I'm so glad you called. He's going to be buried tomorrow. I wish you'd come to the funeral. I feel so alone."

Renée put on a black dress the next day and took a cab to the funeral parlor. As soon as she opened the door, she was in the hands of a gloved and obsequious usher, ready to sympathize with a grief more profound and sedate than any grief of hers would ever be. An elevator took her up to the chapel. When she heard the electric organ playing "Oh, What a Beautiful Morning!," she thought she would have to sit down before she had the strength to see Mrs. Walton, and then she saw Mrs. Walton standing by the open door of the chapel. The two women embraced, and Renée was introduced to Mrs. Walton's sister, a Mrs. Henlein. They were the only people there. At the far end of the room, under a meagre show of gladioli, lay her dead lover. "He was so alone, Renée dear," Mrs. Walton said. "He was so terribly alone. He died alone, you know, in that furnished room." Mrs. Walton began to cry. Mrs. Henlein cried. A minister came in and the service began. Renée knelt and tried to remember the Lord's Prayer, but she got no further than ". . . on earth as it is in Heaven." She began to cry, but not because she remembered the man tenderly; she had not remembered him for years and it was only by forcing her memory that she could recall that he sometimes brought her breakfast in bed, and that he sewed the buttons on his own shirts. She cried for herself, she cried because she was afraid that she herself might die in the night, because she was alone in the world, because her desperate and empty life was not an overture but an ending, and through it all she could see the rough, brutal shape of a coffin.

The three women left the chapel, helped by the obsequious usher, and rode down in the elevator. Renée said she couldn't go to the cemetery, that she had an appointment. Her hands were shaking with fright. She kissed Mrs. Walton goodbye and took a taxi to Sutton Place. She walked down to the little park where Deborah and Mrs. Harley would be.

Deborah saw Renée first. She called Renée's name and ran toward her, struggling up the steps one at a time. Renée picked her up. "Pretty Renée," the little girl said. "Pretty, pretty Renée." Renée and the child sat down beside Mrs. Harley. "If you want to go shopping," she said, "I'll take Deborah for a few hours."

"Now, I don't know whether I ought to or not," Mrs. Harley said.

"She'll be perfectly safe with me," Renée said. "I'll take her up to my apartment and you can call for her there at five. Mr. and Mrs. Tennyson needn't know."

"Well, maybe I'll do that, now," Mrs. Harley said. In this way, Mrs. Harley had begun an arrangement that gave her a few free hours each week.

When Renée hadn't come by half past ten that Sunday, Mrs. Harley knew that she wasn't coming, and she was disappointed because she had counted on going to church that morning. She thought of the Latin and the bells, and the exhilarating sense of having been sanctified and cleansed that she always felt when she got up from her knees. It angered her to think that Renée was lying in bed and that only Renée's laziness was keeping her from prayer. As the morning passed, a lot of children had come to the park, and now she looked for Deborah's yellow coat in the crowd.

The warm sun excited the little girl. She was running with a few children of her age. They were skipping and singing and circling the sand pile with no more purpose than swallows. Deborah tagged a little behind the others, because her coördination was still impulsive and she sometimes threw herself to the ground with her own exertions. Mrs. Harley called to her, and she ran obediently to the old woman and leaned on her knees and began to talk about some lions and little boys. Mrs. Harley asked if she would like to go and see Renée. "I want to go and stay with Renée," the little girl said. Mrs. Harley took her hand and they climbed the steps out of the playground and walked to the apartment house where Renée lived. Mrs. Harley called upstairs on the house phone, and Renée answered after a little delay. She sounded sleepy. She said she would be glad to watch the child for an hour if Mrs. Harley would bring her upstairs. Mrs. Harley took Deborah up to the fifteenth floor and said goodbye to her there. Renée was wearing a negligee trimmed with feathers, and her apartment was dark.

Renée closed the door and picked the little girl up in her arms. Deborah's skin and hair were soft and fragrant, and Renée kissed her, tickled her, and blew down her neck until the child nearly suffocated with laughter. Then Renée pulled up the blinds and let some light into the room. The place was dirty and the air was sour. There were whiskey glasses and spilled ashtrays, and some dead roses in a tarnished silver bowl.

Renée had a lunch date, and she explained this to Deborah. "I'm going to the Plaza for lunch," she said. "I'm going to take a bath and dress, and you'll have to be a good girl." She gave Deborah her jewel box and turned on the water in the bathtub. Deborah sat quietly at the dressing table and loaded herself with necklaces and clips. While Renée was drying herself, the doorbell rang, and she put on a wrapper and went out to the living room. Deborah followed her. A man was there.

"I'm driving up to Albany," he told Renée. "Why don't you put some things in a bag and come on up with me? I'll drive you back on Wednesday."

"I'd love to, darling," Renée said, "but I can't. I'm having lunch with Helen Foss. She thinks she might be able to get me some work."

"Call off the lunch," the man said. "Come on."

"I can't, darling," Renée said. "I'll see you on Wednesday."

"Who's the kid?" the man asked.

"It's the Tennysons' little girl. I take care of her while the

nurse goes to church." The man embraced Renée vigorously
and kissed her and left after they had arranged to meet Wednesday night.

"That was your rich Uncle Loathsome," Renée told the child.

"I have a friend. Her name is Martha," the little girl said.

"Yes, I'm sure you have a friend named Martha," Renée
said. She noticed that the child was scowling and that her eyes
were full of tears. "What's the matter, darling?" she asked.
"What is the matter? Here, here, you sit on the sofa and listen
to the radio. I've got to fix my face." She went into the bedroom
to arrange her face and brush her hair.

A few minutes later the doorbell rang again. This time it
was Mrs. Harley. "Did you enjoy the service?" Renée asked.
"I'll put on Deborah's coat." She looked for the hat and coat.
They were not where she had left them, and the child was not
in the living room. Her heart began to beat fiercely. She went
into her bedroom. "It does my soul so much good to go to
church," she heard Mrs. Harley say. Renée thought in terror
of the open windows. The window in her bedroom was open.
She looked out, and fifteen stories below she could see the sidewalk and the canopy and the doorman at the corner whistling
for a cab and a blonde walking a poodle. Renée ran back to the
living room.

"Where's Deborah?" Mrs. Harley asked.

"I was dressing," Renée said. "She was in here a minute ago.
She must have slipped out. She could have opened the door
herself."

"You mean you've *lost* the little girl!" Mrs. Harley shouted.

"Please don't get excited," Renée said. "She can't have gone
very far. The only way she could get downstairs would be the
elevators." She went out the kitchen door and rang for the
service elevator. She noticed the perilous service stairs. They
were made of iron and concrete, painted a dirty gray, and they
fell fifteen stories to the ground. She listened down the stair
well, but all she could hear was the hiss of cooking and someone, way below, singing,

I'm a soldier, in the army of the Lord,
I'm a soldier,
In the army . . .

The service elevator was full of stinking garbage. "There was a little girl in my apartment," Renée said to the man who had brought the elevator up. "She's disappeared. Would you look for her?" Then she ran into the front hall and rang for the passenger elevator. "Why, yes," the man said. "I took a little girl down, about ten minutes ago. She had on a yellow coat." Renée smelled whiskey on his breath. She called to Mrs. Harley. Then she went back into the apartment to get some cigarettes. "I'm not going to stay here by myself," Mrs. Harley said. Renée pushed her into a chair. She closed the door and rode down in the elevator. "I thought it was strange, her going down by herself," the elevator man said. "I thought maybe she was going to meet somebody in the lobby." As he spoke, Renée smelled the whiskey on his breath again. "You've been drinking," she said. "If you hadn't been drinking, this wouldn't have happened. You ought to know that a child of that age can't be left alone. You ought not to drink while you're working."

When he reached the ground floor, he brought the elevator to a sudden stop and slammed the door open. Renée ran into the lobby. The mirrors, the electric candles, and the doorman's soiled ascot sickened her. "Yes," the doorman said. "It seems to me that I saw a little girl go out. I didn't pay much attention to it. I was out there, trying to get a cab." Renée ran into the street. The child was not there. She ran down to where she could see the river. She felt helpless and feeble, as though she had lost her place in the city in which she had lived for fifteen years. The traffic on the street was heavy. She stood at the corner with her hands cupped to her mouth and screamed, "Deborah! Deborah!"

The Tennysons were going out that afternoon, and they had begun to dress when the telephone rang. Robert answered.

Katherine could hear Renée's voice. ". . . I know it's a terrible thing, Bob, I know I should never have done it."

"You mean Mrs. Harley left her with you?"

"Yes, yes. I know it's a terrible thing. I've looked everywhere. Mrs. Harley is here now. Do you want her to come over?"

"No."

"Shall I call the police?"

"No," Robert said. "I'll call the police. Tell me what she was wearing." When Robert had finished talking with Renée, he called the police. "I'll wait here until you come up," he said. "Please come as quickly as you can."

Katherine was standing in the bathroom doorway. She walked over to Robert, and he took her in his arms. He held her firmly, and she began to cry. Then she left his arms and sat on the bed. He went to the open window. Down in the street he could see a truck with COMFORT CARPET COMPANY painted on its roof. There were some tennis courts in the next block, and people were playing tennis. There was a hedge of privet around the tennis courts, and an old woman was cutting some privet with a knife. She wore a round hat and a heavy winter coat that reached to her ankles. He realized that she was stealing the privet. She worked quickly and furtively, and she kept looking over her shoulder to make sure that no one saw her. When she had cut a good bunch of the green branches, she stuffed them into a bag and hurried down the street.

The doorbell rang. A police sergeant and a plainclothesman were there. They took off their hats. "This kind of thing is hard on the ladies," the sergeant said. "Now, if you'd give me the facts again, Mr. Tennyson. We already have men looking for her. You say she went down in the elevator herself. That was about an hour ago." He checked all the facts with Robert. "Now, I don't want to alarm either of you," he said, "but would anyone have any reason to kidnap the child? We have to consider every possibility."

"Yes," Katherine said suddenly and in a strong voice. She

got up and began to walk back and forth in the room. "It may be unreasonable, but it's at least worth considering. She may have been kidnapped. I've seen that woman in the neighborhood twice this week and I had a feeling that she was following me. I didn't think anything about it then. And she did write me that letter. I'm not making myself clear. You see, before we had Mrs. Harley to take care of Deborah, we had a woman named Mrs. Emerson. I quarrelled with her about Deborah, and she told me, while we were quarrelling—I never told you any of this, darling, because I didn't want to worry you and I didn't think any of it was important —but when we quarrelled, she said the child would be taken away from me. I tried to forget about it, because I thought she was eccentric. The city is full of strange women like that. Then I saw her on the street twice this week, and I had a sense that she was following me. She lives at the Hotel Princess. It's on the West Side. At least, she used to live there."

"I'll go over," Robert said. "I'll get the car."

"I'll drive you over, Mr. Tennyson," the sergeant said.

"Do you want to come?" Robert asked Katherine.

"No, darling," Katherine said. "I'll be all right."

Robert put on his hat, and he and the sergeant left. The elevator man spoke to Robert. "I'm very sorry, Mr. Tennyson," he said. "We all loved her in this house. I telephoned my wife and she went right over to St. John's and lit a vigil light for the little girl."

There was a police car in front of the house, and Robert and the sergeant got into it and drove west. Robert kept turning his head from side to side, and he did this to avert his eyes from the image of the child's death. He imagined the accident in the clichés of "Drive Safely" posters, badly drawn and in crude colors. He saw a stranger carrying the limp body away from the fenders of a taxi; he saw the look of surprise and horror on a lovely face that had never known any horror; he heard the noise of horns, the shrieking of brakes; he saw a car coming

[218]

over the rise of a hill. He made a physical effort to force his eyes to look beyond these images into the bright street.

The day had got hot. A few low, swift clouds touched the city with shadow, and he could see the fast darkness travelling from block to block. The streets were crowded. He saw the city only in terms of mortal danger. Each manhole cover, excavation, and flight of stairs dominated the brilliance of the day like the reverse emphasis of a film negative, and he thought the crowds and the green trees in Central Park looked profane. The Hotel Princess was on a dingy street in the West Seventies. The air in the lobby was fetid. The desk clerk became uneasy when he saw the policeman. He looked for Mrs. Emerson's key and said that she was in. There was no telephone in her room. They could go up.

They went up in an elevator cage of gilded iron, driven by an old man. They knocked on the door, and Mrs. Emerson told them to come in. Robert had never known the woman. He had only seen her when she stood in the doorway of the nursery and sent Deborah in to say good night. She was English, he remembered. Her voice had always sounded troubled and re-fined. "Oh, Mr. Tennyson," she said when she recognized him. The sergeant asked her suddenly where she had been that morning.

"It's all right, Mrs. Emerson," Robert said. He was afraid she would become hysterical and tell them nothing. "Deborah ran away this morning. We thought you might know something about it. Mrs. Tennyson said you wrote her a letter."

"Oh, I'm terribly sorry to hear about Deborah," she said. It was the fine, small voice of someone who knew her place as a lady. "Yes, yes. Of course I wrote that letter to Mrs. Tennyson. It came to me in a dream that you would lose the little girl unless you were very careful. I have a profession, you know. I interpret dreams. I told Mrs. Tennyson when I left her that she should take very good care of the little girl. She was born, after all, under that dreadful new planet, Pluto. I was on the

[219]

Riviera when they discovered it, in 1938. We knew something dreadful was going to happen then.

"I loved the little girl dearly and I regretted my disagreement with Mrs. Tennyson," she went on. "The little girl was one of the fire people—banked fire. I gave her palm a good deal of study. We were left alone a great deal, of course. She had a long life line and a good sense of balance and a good head. There were signs of imprudence there, but a great deal of that would depend upon you. I saw deep water there and some great danger, some great hazard. That's why I wrote the letter to Mrs. Tennyson. I never charged Mrs. Tennyson for any of my professional services."

"What did you and Mrs. Tennyson fight about?" the sergeant asked.

"We're wasting time," Robert said. "We're wasting so much time. Let's go back." He got up and went out of the room, and the sergeant followed him. It took them a long time to drive back. The Sunday crowds crossing the streets stopped them at every intersection. The plainclothesman was waiting in front of the house. "You'd better go up and see your wife," he told Robert. Neither the doorman nor the elevator man spoke to him. He stepped into his apartment and called to Katherine. She was in their bedroom, sitting by the window. She had a black book in her lap. He saw that it was the Bible. It was a Gideon copy that a drunken friend of theirs had stolen from a hotel. They had used it once or twice as a reference. Beyond the open window, he could see the river, a wide, bright field of light. The room was very still.

"What about Mrs. Emerson?" Katherine asked.

"It was a mistake. It was a mistake to think that she would hurt the child."

"Renée called again. She took Mrs. Harley home. She wants us to telephone her when we find Deborah. I never want to see Renée again."

"I know."

"If anything happens to Deborah," Katherine said, "I can

never forgive myself. I can never forgive myself. I'll feel as though we had sacrificed her. I've been reading about Abraham." She opened the Bible and began to read. " 'And he said, Take now thy son, thine only son Isaac, whom thou lovest and get thee into the land of Moriah; and offer him there for a burnt offering upon one of the mountains which I will tell thee of. And Abraham rose up early in the morning, and saddled his ass, and took two of his young men with him, and Isaac his son, and clave the wood for the burnt offering, and rose up, and went unto the place of which God had told him.' " She closed the book. "The thing I'm afraid of is that I'll go out of my mind. I keep repeating our address and telephone number to myself. That doesn't make any sense, does it?"

Robert put his hand on her forehead and ran it over her hair. Her dark hair was parted at the side and brushed simply, like a child's.

"I'm afraid I'm going out of my mind," Katherine said. "You know what my first impulse was when you left me alone? I wanted to take a knife, a sharp knife, and go into my closet and destroy my clothes. I wanted to cut them to pieces. That's because they're so expensive. That's not a sensible thing to want to do, is it? But I'm not insane, of course. I'm perfectly rational.

"I had a little brother who died. His name was Charles—Charles, junior. He was named after my father and he died of some kind of sickness when he was two and a half years old, about Deborah's age. Of course it was very hard on Mother and Dad, but it wasn't anything as bad as this. You see, I think children mean much more to us than they did to our parents. That's what I've been thinking. I suppose it's because we're not as religious and because the way we live makes us much more vulnerable. I feel filthy with guilt. I feel as though I'd been a rotten mother and a rotten wife and as though this were punishment. I've broken every vow and every promise that I've ever made. I've broken all the good promises. When I was a little girl, I used to make promises on the new moon and the first snow. I've broken everything good. But I'm talking as

[221]

though we'd lost her, and we haven't lost her, have we? They'll find her, the policeman said they'd find her."

"They'll find her," Robert said.

The room darkened. The low clouds had touched the city. They could hear the rain as it fell against the building and the windows.

"She's lying somewhere in the rain!" Katherine cried. She wrenched her body around in the chair and covered her face. "She's lying in the rain."

"They'll find her," Robert said. "Other children get lost. I've read stories about it in the *Times*. This sort of thing happens to everyone who has children. My sister's little girl fell downstairs. She fractured her skull. They didn't think she was going to live."

"It does happen to other people, doesn't it?" Katherine asked. She turned and looked at her husband. The rain had stopped suddenly. It left in the air a smell as powerful as though ammonia had been spilled in the streets. Robert saw the rain clouds darken the bright river. "I mean there are all the sicknesses and the accidents," Katherine said, "and we've been so lucky. You know, Deborah hasn't had any lunch. She'll be terribly hungry. She hasn't had anything to eat since breakfast."

"I know."

"Darling, you go out," Katherine said. "It will be easier for you than staying here."

"What will you do?"

"I'm going to clean the living room. We left the windows open last night and everything's covered with soot. You go out. I'll be all right." She smiled. Her face was swollen from crying. "You go out. It will be easier for you, and I'll clean the room."

Robert went down again. The police car was still parked in front of the house. A policeman came up to Robert, and they talked for a while. "I'm going to look around the neighborhood again," the policeman said, "if you want to come with me."

Robert said that he would go. He noticed that the policeman carried a flashlight.

Near the apartment house was the ruin of a brewery that had been abandoned during prohibition. The sidewalk had been inherited by the dogs of the neighborhood and was littered with their filth. The basement windows of a nearby garage were broken, and the policeman flashed his light through a window frame. Robert started when he saw some dirty straw and a piece of yellow paper. It was the color of Deborah's coat. He said nothing and they walked along. In the distance he could hear the vast afternoon noise of the city.

There were some tenements near the brewery. They were squalid, and over the door to one hung a crude sign: "Welcome Home Jerry." The iron gate that led to the steep cellar stairs was open. The policeman flashed his light down the stairs. They were broken. There was nothing there.

An old woman sat on the stoop of the next house, and she watched them suspiciously when they looked down the cellar stairs. "You'll not find my Jimmy there," she screamed, "you —you—" Someone threw open a window and told her to shut up. Robert saw that she was drunk. The policeman paid no attention to her. He looked methodically into the cellar of each house, and then they went around a corner. There were stores, here, along the front of an apartment house. There were no stairs or areaways.

Robert heard a siren. He stopped, and stopped the policeman with him. A police car came around the corner and drew up to the curb where they stood. "Hop in, Mr. Tennyson," the driver said. "We found her. She's down at the station." He started the siren, and they drove east, dodging through the traffic. "We found her down on Third Avenue," the policeman said. "She was sitting out in front of an antique store, eating a piece of bread. Somebody must have given her the bread. She isn't hungry."

She was waiting for him at the station house. He put his hands on her and knelt in front of her and began to laugh. His eyes were burning. "Where have you been, Deborah? Who gave you the bread? Where have you been? Where have you been?"

"The lady gave the bread," she said. "I had to find Martha."

"What lady gave you the bread, Deborah? Where have you been? Who is Martha? Where have you been?" He knew that she would never tell him and that as long as he lived he would never know, and against his palm he could feel the strong beating of her heart, but he went on asking, "Where have you been? Who gave you the bread? Who is Martha?"

CLANCY IN THE
TOWER OF BABEL

---

*J*AMES and Nora Clancy came from farms near the little town of Newcastle. Newcastle is near Limerick. They had been poor in Ireland and they were not much better off in the new country, but they were cleanly and decent people. Their home farms had been orderly places, long inhabited by the same families, and the Clancys enjoyed the grace of a tradition. Their simple country ways were so deeply ingrained that twenty years in the New World had had little effect on them. Nora went to market with a straw basket under her arm, like a woman going out to a kitchen garden, and Clancy's pleasant face reflected a simple life. They had only one child, a son named John, and they had been able to pass on to him their peaceable and contented views. They were people who centered their lives in half a city block, got down on their knees on the floor to say "Hail Mary, full of grace," and took turns in the bathtub in the kitchen on Saturday night.

When Clancy was still a strong man in his forties, he fell down some stairs in the factory and broke his hip. He was out of work for nearly a year, and while he got compensation for this time, it was not as much as his wages had been and he and his family suffered the pain of indebtedness and need. When Clancy recovered, he was left with a limp and it took him a long time to find another job. He went to church every day, and in the end it was the intercession of a priest that got work for him, running an elevator in one of the big apartment houses on the East Side. Clancy's good manners and his clean and pleasant face pleased the tenants, and with his salary and the tips they gave him he made enough to pay his debts and support his wife and son.

The apartment house was not far from the slum tenement where James and Nora had lived since their marriage, but financially and morally it was another creation, and Clancy at first looked at the tenants as if they were made out of sugar. The ladies wore coats and jewels that cost more than Clancy would make in a lifetime of hard work, and when he came home in the evenings, he would, like a returned traveller, tell Nora what he had seen. The poodles, the cocktail parties, the children and their nursemaids interested him, and he told Nora that it was like the Tower of Babel.

It took Clancy a while to memorize the floor numbers to which his tenants belonged, to pair the husbands and wives, to join the children to their parents, and the servants (who rode on the back elevators) to these families, but he managed at last and was pleased to have everything straight. Among his traits was a passionate sense of loyalty, and he often spoke of The Building as if it were a school or a guild, the product of a community of sentiment and aspiration. "Oh, I wouldn't do anything to harm The Building," he often said. His manner was respectful but he was not humorless, and when 11-A sent his tailcoat out to the dry cleaner's, Clancy put it on and paraded up and down the back hall. Most of the tenants were regarded by Clancy with an indiscriminate benevolence, but there were a few exceptions. There was a drunken wife-beater. He was a bulky, duck-footed lunkhead, in Clancy's eyes, and he did not belong in The Building. Then, there was a pretty girl in 11-B who went out in the evenings with a man who was a weak character—Clancy could tell because he had a cleft chin. Clancy warned the girl, but she did not act on his advice. But the tenant about whom he felt most concerned was Mr. Rowantree.

Mr. Rowantree, who was a bachelor, lived in 4-A. He had been in Europe when Clancy first went to work, and he had not returned to New York until winter. When Mr. Rowantree appeared, he seemed to Clancy to be a well-favored man with graying hair who was tired from his long voyage. Clancy waited for him to reëstablish himself in the city, for friends and relatives to start telephoning and writing, and for Mr. Rowantree to begin the give and take of parties in which most of the tenants were involved.

Clancy had discovered by then that his passengers were not made of sugar. All of them were secured to the world intricately by friends and lovers, dogs and songbirds, debts, inheritances, trusts, and jobs, and he waited for Mr. Rowantree to put out his lines. Nothing happened. Mr. Rowantree went to work at ten in the morning and returned home at six; no visitors appeared. A month passed in which he did not have a single guest. He sometimes went out in the evening, but he always returned alone, and for all Clancy knew he might have continued his friendless state in the movies around the corner. The man's lack of friends amazed and then began to aggravate and trouble Clancy. One night when he was on the evening shift and Mr. Rowantree came down alone, Clancy stopped the car between floors.

"Are you going out for dinner, Mr. Rowantree?" he asked.

"Yes," the man said.

"Well, when you're eating in this neighborhood, Mr. Rowantree," Clancy said, "you'll find that Bill's Clam Bar is the only restaurant worth speaking of. I've been living around here for twenty years and I've seen them come and go. The others have fancy lighting and fancy prices, but you won't get anything to eat that's worth sticking to your ribs excepting at Bill's Clam Bar."

"Thank you, Clancy," Mr. Rowantree said. "I'll keep that in mind."

"Now, Mr. Rowantree," Clancy said, "I don't want to sound

inquisitive, but would you mind telling me what kind of a business you're in?"

"I have a store on Third Avenue," Mr. Rowantree said. "Come over and see it someday."

"I'd like to do that," Clancy said. "But now, Mr. Rowantree, I should think you'd want to have dinner with your friends and not be alone all the time." Clancy knew that he was interfering with the man's privacy, but he was led on by the thought that this soul might need help. "A good-looking man like you must have friends," he said, "and I'd think you'd have your supper with them."

"I'm going to have supper with a friend, Clancy," Mr. Rowantree said.

This reply made Clancy feel easier, and he put the man out of his mind for a while. The Building gave him the day off on Saint Patrick's, so that he could march in the parade, and when the parade had disbanded and he was walking home, he decided to look for the store. Mr. Rowantree had told him which block it was in. It was easy to find. Clancy was pleased to see that it was a big store. There were two doors to go in by, separated by a large glass window. Clancy looked through the window to see if Mr. Rowantree was busy with a customer, but there was no one there. Before he went in, he looked at the things in the window. He was disappointed to see that it was not a clothing store or a delicatessen. It looked more like a museum. There were glasses and candlesticks, chairs and tables, all of them old. He opened the door. A bell attached to the door rang and Clancy looked up to see the old-fashioned bell on its string. Mr. Rowantree came out from behind a screen and greeted him cordially.

Clancy did not like the place. He felt that Mr. Rowantree was wasting his time. It troubled him to think of the energy in a man's day being spent in this place. A narrow trail, past tables and desks, urns and statues, led into the store and then branched off in several directions. Clancy had never seen so much junk. Since he couldn't imagine it all being manufactured in any one country, he guessed that it had been brought there from the four corners of the world. It seemed to Clancy a misuse of time to have gathered all these things into a dark store on Third Avenue. But it was more than the confusion and the waste that troubled him; it was the feeling that he was surrounded by the symbols of frustration and that all the china youths and maidens in their attitudes of love were the company of bitterness. It may have been because he had spent his happy life in bare rooms that he associated goodness with ugliness.

He was careful not to say anything that would offend Mr. Rowantree. "Do you have any clerks to help you?" he asked.

"Oh, yes," Mr. Rowantree said. "Miss James is here most of the time. We're partners."

That was it, Clancy thought. Miss James. That was where he went in the evenings. But why, then, wouldn't Miss James marry him? Was it because he was already married? Perhaps he had suffered some terrible human misfortune, like having his wife go crazy or having his children taken away from him.

"Have you a snapshot of Miss James?" Clancy asked.

"No," Mr. Rowantree said.

"Well, I'm glad to have seen your store and thank you very much," Clancy said. The trip had been worth his while, because he took away from the dark store a clear image of Miss James. It was a good name, an Irish name, and now in the evenings when Mr. Rowantree went out, Clancy would ask him how Miss James was.

Clancy's son, John, was a senior in high school. He was captain of the basketball team and a figure in school government, and that spring he entered an essay he had written on democracy in a contest sponsored by a manufacturer in Chicago. There were millions of entries, but John won honorable mention, which entitled him to a trip to Chicago in an airplane and a week's visit there with all expenses paid. The boy was naturally excited by this bonanza and so was his mother, but Clancy was the one who seemed to have won the prize. He told all the tenants in the building about it and asked them what kind of city Chicago was and if travelling in airplanes was safe. He would get up in the middle of the night and go into John's room to look at the wonderful boy while he slept. The boy's head was crammed with knowledge, Clancy thought. His heart was kind and strong. It was sinful, Clancy knew, to confuse the immortality of the Holy Spirit with earthly love, but when he realized that John was his flesh and blood, that the young man's face was *his* face improved with mobility and thought, and that when he, Clancy, was dead, some habit or taste of his would live on in the young man, he felt that there was no pain in death.

John's plane left for Chicago late one Saturday afternoon. He went to confession and then walked over to The Building to say goodbye to his father. Clancy kept the boy in the lobby as long as he could and introduced him to the tenants who came through. Then it was time for the boy to go. The doorman took the elevator, and Clancy walked John up to the corner. It was a clear, sunny afternoon in Lent. There wasn't a cloud in the sky. The boy had on his best suit and he looked like a million dollars. They shook hands at the corner, and Clancy limped back to The Building. Traffic was slow on the elevator, and he stood at the front door, watching the people on the sidewalk. Most of them were dressed in their best clothes and they were off to enjoy themselves. Clancy's best wishes followed them all. At the far end of the street he saw Mr. Rowantree's head and shoulders and saw that he was with a young man. Clancy waited and opened the door for them.

"Hello, Clancy," Mr. Rowantree said. "I'd like to have you meet my friend Bobbie. He's going to live here now."

Clancy grunted. The young man was not a young man. His hair was cut short and he wore a canary-yellow sweater and a padded coat but he was as old as Mr. Rowantree, he was nearly as old as Clancy. All the qualities and airs of youth, which a good man puts aside gladly when the time comes, had been preserved obscenely in him. He had dope in his eyes to make

them shine and he smelled of perfume, and Mr. Rowantree took
his arm to help him through the door, as if he were a pretty
girl. As soon as Clancy saw what he had to deal with, he took
a stand. He stayed at the door. Mr. Rowantree and his friend
went through the lobby and got into the elevator. They reached
out and rang the bell.

"I'm not taking you up in my car!" Clancy shouted down
the lobby.

"Come here, Clancy," Mr. Rowantree said.

"I'm not taking that up in my car," Clancy said.

"I'll have you fired for this," Mr. Rowantree said.

"That's no skin off my nose," Clancy said. "I'm not taking
you up in my car."

"Come here, Clancy," Mr. Rowantree said. Clancy didn't answer. Mr. Rowantree put his finger on the bell and held it there.
Clancy didn't move. He heard Mr. Rowantree and his friend
talking. A moment later, he heard them climb the stairs. All
the solicitude he had felt for Mr. Rowantree, the times he had
imagined him walking in the Park with Miss James, seemed
like money lost in a terrible fraud. He was hurt and bitter. The
idea of Bobbie's being in The Building was a painful one for
him to take, and he felt as if it contested his own simple view
of life. He was curt with everyone for the rest of the day. He
even spoke sharply to the children. When he went to the basement to take off his uniform, Mr. Coolidge, the superintendent,
called him into his office.

"Rowantree's been trying to get you fired for the last hour,
Jim," he said. "He said you wouldn't take him up in your car.
I'm not going to fire you, because you're a good, steady man,
but I'm warning you now. He knows a lot of rich and influen-
tial people, and if you don't mind your own business, it won't
be hard for him to get you kicked out." Mr. Coolidge was surrounded by all the treasures he had extricated from the rubbish
baskets in the back halls—broken lamps, broken vases, a perambulator with three wheels.

"But he—" Clancy began.

"It's none of your business, Jim," Mr. Coolidge said. "He's been very quiet since he come back from Europe. You're a good, steady man, Clancy, and I don't want to fire you, but you got to remember that you aren't the boss around here."

The next day was Palm Sunday, and, by the grace of God, Clancy did not see Mr. Rowantree. On Monday, Clancy joined his bitterness at having to live in Sodom to the deep and general grief he always felt at the commencement of those events that would end on Golgotha. It was a gloomy day. Clouds and darkness were over the city. Now and then it rained. Clancy took Mr. Rowantree down at ten. He didn't say anything, but he gave the man a scornful look. The ladies began going off for lunch around noon. Mr. Rowantree's friend Bobbie went out then.

About half past two, one of the ladies came back from lunch, smelling of gin. She did a funny thing. When she got into the elevator, she stood with her face to the wall of the car, so that Clancy couldn't see it. He was not a man to look into somebody's face if they wanted to hide it, and this made him angry. He stopped the car. "Turn around," he said. "Turn around. I'm ashamed of you, a woman with three grown children, standing with your face to the wall like a crybaby." She turned around. She was crying about something. Clancy put the car into motion again. "You ought to fast," he mumbled. "You ought to go without cigarettes or meat during Lent. It would give you something to think about." She left the car, and he answered a ring from the first floor. It was Mr. Rowantree. He took him up. Then he took Mrs. DePaul up to 9. She was a nice woman, and he told her about John's trip to Chicago. On the way down, he smelled gas.

For a man who has lived his life in a tenement, gas is the odor of winter, sickness, need, and death. Clancy went up to Mr. Rowantree's floor. That was it. He had the master key and he opened the door and stepped into that hellish breath. It was dark. He could hear the petcocks hissing in the kitchen. He put a rug against the door to keep it open and threw up a window

in the hall. He stuck his head out for some air. Then, in terror
of being blown into hell himself, and swearing and praying
and half closing his eyes as if the poisonous air might blind
him, he started for the kitchen and gave himself a cruel bang
against the doorframe that made him cold all over with pain.
He stumbled into the kitchen and turned off the gas and opened
the doors and windows. Mr. Rowantree was on his knees with
his head in the oven. He sat up. He was crying. "Bobbie's gone,
Clancy," he said. "Bobbie's gone."

Clancy's stomach turned over, his gorge opened and filled
up with bitter spit. "Dear Jesus!" he shouted. "Dear Jesus!"
He stumbled out of the apartment. He was shaking all over.
He took the car down and shouted for the doorman and told
him what had happened.

The doorman took the elevator, and Clancy went into the
locker room and sat down. He didn't know how long he had
been there when the doorman came in and said that he smelled
more gas. Clancy went up to Mr. Rowantree's apartment again.
The door was shut. He opened it and stood in the hall and heard
the petcocks. "Take your God-damned fool head out of that
oven, Mr. Rowantree!" he shouted. He went into the kitchen
and turned off the gas. Mr. Rowantree was sitting on the floor.
"I won't do it again, Clancy," he said. "I promise, I promise."

Clancy went down and got Mr. Coolidge, and they went into
the basement together and turned off Mr. Rowantree's gas. He
went up again. The door was shut. When he opened it, he heard
the hissing of the gas. He yanked the man's head out of the
oven. "You're wasting your time, Mr. Rowantree!" he shouted.
"We've turned off your gas! You're wasting your time!" Mr.
Rowantree scrambled to his feet and ran out of the kitchen.
Clancy heard him running through the apartment, slamming
doors. He followed him and found him in the bathroom, shaking pills out of a bottle into his mouth. Clancy knocked the pill
bottle out of his hand and knocked the man down. Then he
called the precinct station on Mr. Rowantree's phone. He waited
there until a policeman, a doctor, and a priest came.

Clancy walked home at five. The sky was black. It was raining soot and ashes. Sodom, he thought, the city undeserving of clemency, the unredeemable place, and, raising his eyes to watch the rain and the ashes fall through the air, he felt a great despair for his kind. They had lost the warrants for mercy, there was no movement in the city around him but toward self-destruction and sin. He longed for the simple life of Ireland and the City of God, but he felt that he had been contaminated by the stink of gas.

He told Nora what had happened, and she tried to comfort him. There was no letter or card from John. In the evening, Mr. Coolidge telephoned. He said it was about Mr. Rowantree.

"Is he in the insane asylum?" Clancy asked.

"No," Mr. Coolidge said. "His friend came back and they went out together. But he's been threatening to get you fired again. As soon as he felt all right again, he said he was going to get you fired. I don't want to fire you, but you got to be careful, you got to be careful." This was the twist that Clancy couldn't follow, and he felt sick. He asked Mr. Coolidge to get a man from the union to take his place for a day or so, and he went to bed.

Clancy stayed in bed the next morning. He got worse. He was cold. Nora lighted a fire in the range, but he shivered as if his heart and his bones were frozen. He doubled his knees up to his chest and snagged the blankets around him, but he couldn't keep warm. Nora finally called the doctor, a man from Limerick. It was after ten before he got there. He said that Clancy should go to the hospital. The doctor left to make the arrangements, and Nora got Clancy's best clothes together and helped him into them. There was still a price tag on his long underwear and there were pins in his shirt. In the end, nobody saw the new underwear and the clean shirt. At the hospital, they drew a curtain around his bed and he handed the finery out to Nora. Then he stretched out in bed, and Nora gave him a kiss and went away.

He groaned, he moaned for a while, but he had a fever and this put him to sleep. He did not know or care where he was for the next few days. He slept most of the time. When John came back from Chicago, the boy's company and his story of the trip picked Clancy's spirits up a little. Nora visited him every day, and one day, a couple of weeks after Clancy entered the hospital, she brought Frank Quinn, the doorman, with her. Frank gave Clancy a narrow manila envelope, and when Clancy opened it, asking crossly what it was, he saw that it was full of currency.

"That's from the tenants, Clancy," Frank said.

"Now, why did they do this?" Clancy said. He was smitten. His eyes watered and he couldn't count the money. "Why did they do this?" he asked weakly. "Why did they go to this trouble? I'm nothing but an elevator man."

"It's nearly two hundred dollars," Frank said.

"Who took up the collection?" Clancy said. "Was it you, Frank?"

"It was one of the tenants," Frank said.

"It was Mrs. DePaul," Clancy said. "I'll bet it was that Mrs. DePaul."

"One of the tenants," Frank said.

"It was you, Frank," Clancy said warmly. "You was the one who took up the collection."

"It was Mr. Rowantree," Frank said sadly. He bent his head. "You're not going to give the money back, Jim?" Nora asked.

"I'm not a God-damned fool!" Clancy shouted. "When I pick up a dollar off the street, I'm not the man to go running down to the lost-and-found department with it!"

"Nobody else could have gotten so much, Jim," Frank said. "He went from floor to floor. They say he was crying."

Clancy had a vision. He saw the church from the open lid of his coffin, before the altar. The sacristan had lighted only a few of the vaseline-colored lamps, for the only mourners were those few people, all of them poor and old, who had come from Limerick with Clancy on the boat. He heard the priest's youthful voice mingling with the thin music of the bells. Then in the back of the church he saw Mr. Rowantree and Bobbie. They were crying and crying. They were crying harder than Nora. He could see their shoulders rise and fall, and hear their sighs.

"Does he think I'm dying, Frank?" Clancy asked.

"Yes, Jim. He does."

"He thinks I'm dying," Clancy said angrily. "He's got one of them soft heads. Well, I ain't dying. I'm not taking any of his grief. I'm getting out of here." He climbed out of bed. Nora and Frank tried unsuccessfully to push him back. Frank ran out to get a nurse. The nurse pointed a finger at Clancy and commanded him to get back into bed, but he had put on his pants and was tying his shoelaces. She went out and got another nurse, and the two young women tried to hold him down, but he shook them off easily. The first nurse went to get a doctor. The doctor who returned with her was a young man, much smaller than Clancy. He said that Clancy could go home. Frank and Nora took him back in a taxi, and as soon as he got into the tenement, he telephoned Mr. Coolidge and said that he was coming back to work in the morning. He felt a lot better, surrounded by the smells and lights of his own place. Nora cooked him a nice supper and he ate it in the kitchen.

After supper, he sat by the window in his shirtsleeves. He thought about going back to work, about the man with the cleft chin, the wife-beater, Mr. Rowantree and Bobbie. Why should a man fall in love with a monster? Why should a man try to kill himself? Why should a man try to get a man fired and then collect money for him with tears in his eyes, and then perhaps, a week later, try to get him fired again? He would not return the money, he would not thank Mr. Rowantree, but he wondered what kind of judgment he should pass on the pervert. He began to pick the words he would say to Mr. Rowantree when they met. "It's my suggestion, Mr. Rowantree," he would say, "that the next time you want to kill yourself, you get a rope or a gun. It's my suggestion, Mr. Rowantree," he would say, "that you go to a good doctor and get your head examined."

The spring wind, the south wind that in the city smells of drains, was blowing. Clancy's window looked onto an expanse of clotheslines and ailanthus trees, yards that were used as dumps, and the naked backs of tenements, with their lighted and unlighted windows. The symmetry, the reality of the scene heartened Clancy, as if it conformed to something good in himself. Men with common minds like his had built these houses. Nora brought him a glass of beer and sat near the window. He put an arm around her waist. She was in her slip, because of the heat. Her hair was held down with pins. She appeared to Clancy to be one of the glorious beauties of his day, but a stranger, he guessed, might notice the tear in her slip and that her body was bent and heavy. A picture of John hung on the wall. Clancy was struck with the strength and intelligence of his son's face, but he guessed that a stranger might notice the boy's glasses and his bad complexion. And then, thinking of Nora and John and that this half blindness was all that he knew himself of mortal love, he decided not to say anything to Mr. Rowantree. They would pass in silence.

ABOUT THE AUTHOR

John Cheever was born in Quincy, Massachusetts, in 1912, the son of Frederick and Mary Cheever. His schooling was at Thayer Academy in South Braintree, Massachusetts. During World War II he spent four years in the army. Since then he has divided his time between New York, New Hampshire, and Westchester, all of which serve as locales for the stories in this collection. He is married and the father of two children, a boy and a girl.

In 1951 Mr. Cheever received a Guggenheim Fellowship for creative writing. Recently he has been writing for the Columbia Broadcasting System. His stories have appeared in magazines, anthologies, and collections, and many of them have been reprinted in England and France. An earlier group of his stories, titled Why Some People Live, *was published in the United States in 1943. The fourteen stories of* The Enormous Radio *were originally printed in* The New Yorker *over the last six years. At the present time Mr. Cheever is at work on a novel.*

DATE DUE

GAYLORD | | | PRINTED IN U.S A.